Lord of the Ralphs

Also by the Author

Lord
of the
Ralphs

John McNally

LACEWING BOOKS
INDIANAPOLIS

Lacewing Books
an imprint of Engine Books
PO Box 44167
Indianapolis, IN 46244
lacewingbooks.org

Printed in the United States of America

10   9   8   7   6   5   4   3   2   1

ISBN: 978-1938126314

Library of Congress Control Number: 2014944274

This book is for those grade school and high school teachers who encouraged my creativity. If I hadn't been asked to write a play in the fourth grade, you wouldn't be holding this book today.

1

At the end of seventh grade, Ralph hired a sixth grader to spray-paint "We're outta here!" across the sidewalk in front of our school, but Ralph hadn't had time to check it out for himself until today, just a few weeks before the start of eighth grade. There had been reports that the kid had screwed it up, so Ralph and I walked over to Jacqueline Bouvier Kennedy Grade School to inspect the work ourselves.

"We're outta *hair?*" Ralph said to me as the two of us stood there looking down at what the sixth grader had spray-painted. "What is this? A campaign slogan for bald people?" He sighed and said, "If you want a job done right, you got to do it yourself."

Ralph had failed both the third and fifth grades, making him the tallest and oldest student in our class. He was a foot taller than the rest of us, and what I had begun to think of as his dirty upper lip was actually the early stages of a mustache.

Ralph pulled a spray-paint can from his back pocket, shook it a few dozen times, and then started correcting the error. I stood watch, making sure no one was coming. I was a good kid and couldn't afford the kind of punishment that Ralph regularly received.

So this is it, I thought. Eighth grade!

Every school year was a chance to start all over again, and so while the first seven months of 1978 had sucked, I had high hopes that August would be the beginning of the year not sucking. And because it would be my last year of grade school, I had secretly hoped that eighth grade would be different somehow, that a cute girl from another state would transfer to my school and fall insanely in love with me, maybe even start stalking me all over Chicago's South Side, or that I would crack a joke on the playground, my best joke ever, and win over a whole new batch of friends, or that my clothes would fit better, that my teachers would take me under their wings, and that, for reasons I couldn't imagine yet, the principal, Mr. Santoro, would commission a bronze bust likeness of me to be placed in the school's entryway so that all the new kids, from here on out, could walk respectfully past it and think, *So THAT'S what Hank Boyd looked like!* I bought a shirt with a "Class of 1979" iron-on decal, and I planned on wearing it every day leading up to the first day of school. I would chew gum and lean against walls, and with a toothpick stuck in the corner of my mouth, I would say things like, "So you're class of 1981? Is that right? Well, good luck, kiddo." I would wink, or maybe I would point my finger like a gun at the kid and then make a popping sound with my tongue. And all of this would make me happy. Very happy.

"There," Ralph said.

I waited until the mist of paint disappeared before stepping forward and examining Ralph's work. Instead of changing the word "hair" to "here," Ralph had drawn a man behind the counter of a wig store. It was a simple drawing, really: three lines for the counter, a man's head hovering above it, and a sign that said "wigs" next to the man's head. Ralph had turned the words into a dialog balloon, which was attached to the man's mouth. "We're outta hair," the man was saying.

"Nice," I said. "But what does this have to do with anything?"

Ralph stuffed the spray-paint can into his back pocket and said, "One day we'll both be old and bald, and walking some old dog that nobody wants, and who knows…maybe we'll be working in a wig store. It's a statement about where we're heading. It has everything to do with everything, Hank. I should find the kid who screwed up and thank him."

Before we left the scene of the crime, I took one last long look at what Ralph had painted. The guy, whose round head was decorated with little more than two eyes, a nose, and a mouth, looked a bit like me. I shivered at the sight of it.

"Come on," Ralph said, "before the police come."

"Where next?" I asked.

"Nowhere," Ralph said. "Anywhere." He shrugged. "It's all the same to me."

2

One week before school started, my father insisted that he would take me to Kmart so that I could buy all the back-to-school crap I needed, but I knew the truth: my father couldn't resist a blue-light special. As soon as the raspy voice came over the intercom, my father would start peering over the aisles to find the swirling blue light.

"I see it over in auto repair," he might say. Or: "Is that the blue light over by the flip-flops?" Or, when I was younger, he'd hoist me up onto his shoulders and say, "Where is it, kiddo? Where's the blue devil today?"

My dad didn't care what was on sale. Cans of Pledge, socket sets, Rice-A-Roni. He used his shopping cart as a barrier, blocking old women from the display, keeping everyone away from all the things he didn't realize he wanted until they had become blue-light specials.

But my father's obsession really kicked into high gear this past summer. He made at least one stop at Kmart each day, sometimes two. And I went with him nearly every time. I was twelve years old; I didn't have much say in what I did. My father and my mother spent most of that summer arguing, usually about money, and one morning my mother caught my father actually poking through her pocket book, searching for loose bills and change. "Just what the hell do you think you're doing?" she yelled. I expected her to end the sentence with "MISTER," which is how she addressed me when I'd done something wrong. Instead of being grounded, which is what would have happened to me if I were in his shoes, my father was the opposite of grounded: he was banned from entering the bedroom. It seemed to me that he should have been happy about this—I would have been—but he wasn't. He slept on the couch and moaned in the mornings about how bad the couch was for his back.

My father kept away from Kmart during his couch phase, but we ended up going back there the morning after he was finally allowed back into his own bedroom. The blue-light special that day was L'eggs pantyhose, and he was holding one of the eggs up into the air, toward the bank of fluorescent lights, staring at it as though he had found something prehistoric.

He placed the egg up against his ear, shook it a few times, and asked, "You think your mom would like these?" but before I could answer him, another customer—a woman as old as my grandmother—tried reaching for one, and my father began tossing them two at a time into his cart.

I knew my mother was going to be mad when she saw what he'd bought. I'd never seen her wear pantyhose. Ever. For the life of me I couldn't figure out why my father didn't realize that she was going to be mad, but I didn't tell him what I was thinking. I almost never told him what I was thinking because I knew that what I was thinking wasn't what he wanted to hear.

"Can I go get an Icee?" I asked instead.

Dad stared hard at me, trying to remember what an Icee was, then pulled a dollar bill from his pocket and handed it to me.

"Meet me outside," he said. "I'm not done here yet."

The only reason I didn't mind being dragged to Kmart by my father was because he gave me money when I asked for it. My mother, on the other hand, denied all requests for cash. She was especially opposed to giving me money so that I could buy, according to her, "sugar-flavored crushed ice."

"That's the *last* thing you need, Hank," my mom said to me the few times I had asked.

I never asked my father for money until he had found the blue-light special. Something about the revolving blue light changed the way my father looked at the world: money suddenly became no object. It was like movies I saw at the Sheridan Drive-in that took place in Las Vegas, movies where you could see reflections of neon lights inside the wide eyes of someone who, until then, had been a perfectly normal person. These movies never ended pretty. The guys usually wound up broke or alcoholic, and the women wore makeup that smeared when they cried and they started putting on their wigs crooked. My mother always said to my father afterward, "I don't know why we bring the kids to these kinds of movies," and my father would say, "It's not like it's going to kill them." This, I came to realize, was my father's bottom-line: if what we were doing wasn't going to kill us, then he was fine with it. Time and again, my father would ask my mother, "Are they dead? No? Then I don't see why you're getting so worked up!"

I never actually saw reflections of the swirling blue light inside my father's eyes, but they might as well have been there. I knew he was weak in these moments, but I asked for the money, anyway. What I was doing was wrong, but I couldn't have said exactly why it was wrong. I just felt it in the pit of my gut, was all. One thing I did know was that I needed the Icee more than he needed his dollar. That's the way I saw things, at least.

The Icee machine was located at the front of the store, across from Customer Service. I loved everything about the Icee machine. I loved the plastic Icee display—a gigantic three-dimensional cup with a heaping pile of red Icee, all of it illuminated from the inside, causing the cup to glow. A huge red-and-white straw poked up out of the fake mound of ice. I loved how each letter in the word "Icee" was covered in snow, and how the colors alternated blue-red-blue-red. The cup was raised high enough that I could see it from distant parts of the store, causing me to salivate as far away as the fish hooks or radiator fluid. The only flavors to choose from were blue and red. I never knew what the flavors actually were, so I ordered them by color. I preferred red.

I was also in love with the girl who worked the Icee machine. She had long blonde hair, but her eyebrows were dark, and she had a tiny dot of a mole on the side of her cheek, like Ginger on *Gilligan's Island*. The mole wasn't always in the same place, though, which worried me. It traveled up and down her right cheek. One time it was even on the left side of her face. I wanted to ask her about it, but I was so in love with her that I could barely bring myself to speak in her presence. More often than not when I opened my mouth, nothing came out.

"Look who's here," she said the day my father was loading up on L'eggs. "Let me guess," she said. "You want the red one. Right?"

I nodded.

She pulled a cup from a contraption that held all the cups. When it came time to work the Icee machine, she always made a serious face while placing the cup beneath the spout and pulling down the lever. While she did this, I stared into the Icee machine, which kept the colored ice inside swirling, round and round. The swirling hypnotized me, and I couldn't stop staring at it until the girl touched my hand with the ice-cold Icee she'd made for me, and then I'd involuntarily jump.

"I made an extra-big one for you today," she said, even though she always made an extra-big one for me.

While I was busy uncrinkling my dollar bill, she reached out and ruffled my hair. She was the only cashier I knew who liked to touch me. It both startled and pleased me. It made me want to reach out and touch the mole on her cheek, but I didn't. I ducked my head and mumbled, "Thank you."

Icee in hand, I headed for the exit to wait for my dad. In the shadows of the giant Kmart sign above the store, I slowly sucked down my drink, but even when I took measured sucks, the brain freeze usually came after my third or fourth mouthful. The pain arrived like a knife rammed into my forehead, or like a truck running over my head, backing up, and running over it again. I'd never experienced anything so awful in my life. I would fall against one of Kmart's windows as soon as the pain struck. Any shopper who happened to be near the window, circling a clothes rack, looking for the perfect pair of back-to-school pants for their kid, would jump back and scream. Next, I would lean forward, clutching my head while still holding onto my Icee. Tears would fill my eyes. Finally, I would slump to the ground and sit with my head between my knees, waiting for the blaze of pain to pass. When it did—and it always did—I would slowly, nervously, bring the straw back up to my lips and suck in another tentative mouthful of Icee, until the brain freeze came back, causing me to lie on my side and moan.

This was how my dad often found me, curled on the ground, my face contorted.

"Brain freeze?" he'd ask, and I'd nod. One time he said, "It's a sign of superior intelligence, you know. Me and you, we're alike that way. Now, I'd never criticize your mother or your sister, but you know what? They don't get brain freezes. Neither of them. I'm not going to draw any conclusions for you, but I think you can see where I'm going here, Hank. The thing is, we need to stick together. Me and you, buddy."

Today, I was about to suck in my third mouthful of Icee when two high school boys, Vik Schwingel and Bobby Smidowicz, walked up to me.

Vik Schwingel said, "You look familiar."

"You go to Kennedy?" Bobby Smidowicz asked.

I nodded. I knew who Vik Schwingel and Bobby Smidowicz

were. They had graduated from my school. About half the time the school's p.a. came on, one or the other (or both of them) was being called to Principal Santoro's office, where a bloodied student (either Vik's or Bobby's victim) waited nervously for his mother to come get him.

"I want that Icee," Vik Schwingel said.

"My lips already touched the straw," I said.

"What's that supposed to mean?" Bobby Smidowicz asked.

Vik said, "Did I ask you where your lips have been?"

"No," I said.

"Didn't your mommy teach you to share?" Vik asked.

I raised the straw to my lips and sucked in another mound of ice. That's when it hit me: the worst brain freeze ever.

Bobby said, "Look at him, Vik. He's gonna start crying."

"You gonna start crying?" Vik asked. "Hey, Bobby. You got any Kleenex on you?"

"Kleenex?" Bobby asked, patting himself down.

"For the kid," Vik said.

"Oh," Bobby said. "Nope, I don't. I'm clean out."

Vik, staring into my eyes, said, "Bobby here, he's all out of Kleenex. Now, give me that Icee."

I wasn't sure what came over me, but I had made up my mind that I wasn't going to give it to him. But I also knew that I couldn't keep it, either. I took off the lid and turned the cup upside down. At first, nothing came out. Then a giant blob of red ice came out all at once, hitting the ground and splattering all three of us. The upside-down cup started dripping, as if it were bleeding.

Bobby balled up his fists, but Vik asked calmly, "Now, why did you do that?" Then he gritted his teeth and pushed me hard against Kmart. The back of my head hit the window and I dropped the cup, which Bobby needlessly stomped on, crushing it.

Vik held up his palm and said, "See this?" When I nodded, he smacked my nose hard with his open hand. The nerves inside my nose seemed attached directly to my eyes, which instantly sprang tears. I clutched my nose. What I hadn't expected was for the physical pain of getting punched to smother the brain freeze, but that's what happened, and I was suddenly grateful for the arrival of Vik and Bobby and for the violence they had doled out to me. In fact, getting beaten up was almost a comfort. When I moved my hand, I saw that my palm was covered with what I thought at first was Icee juice. I looked down and saw that the entire front of my shirt was streaked red. *Blood*, I thought, and my knees started going soft.

"Next time," Bobby said, "when Vik asks for something, you just give it to him. You hear me?"

Pinching shut my nose, I nodded.

Vik gave me one last shove that knocked me to the ground. My head bounced once, twice against the sidewalk. When I looked up, I saw Vik and Bobby holding open the double-doors for a couple of senior citizens, who thanked them. And then they disappeared inside.

I lay on the ground, my head next to the quickly melting Icee blob, my nose still gushing. I was about to sit up when one of the doors opened and my father stepped outside carrying four large Kmart bags, two in each hand. He glanced around, expecting to find me standing upright, but then he looked down to where I lay struggling to right myself.

"Brain freeze?" he asked.

"Sort of," I said.

"I'd give you a hand," he said, "but as you can see…" He motioned with his head toward all the bags he was carrying.

"I'm okay," I said and pushed myself up. I stood and brushed off my pants, then I caught up to my father, who was already heading toward his pick-up truck.

"Damned bags are heavy," he said. He glanced over at me and said, "Must have been a bad one."

"What?"

"Brain freeze," he said.

I wiped my nose with the back of my arm. I could feel the side of my head swelling from where it had smacked the sidewalk.

"I bought your mother a hell of a lot of pantyhose," he said, laughing as though startled by his own lack of control.

"She's going to be mad," I said.

"Why?" he asked, stopping abruptly, glaring down at me. "If I want to buy her pantyhose, who's she to tell me I can't? Huh?"

I shrugged, and we started walking again.

"The worse they are," he said, "the smarter you are."

"Girls?" I asked.

"No. Brain freezes. Did I ever tell you about the one that sent me to the emergency room?"

"No," I said.

"Really? I haven't?" He looked over at me, as though I might be lying. He swung all four bags up and over the side of the truck's bed. I wasn't sure, but I thought I heard a few eggs crack when the bags landed. He pulled a pack of Lucky Strikes from his shirt pocket, smacked it on the top of his head for a while, like a crazy man, then opened the pack and pulled a cigarette out with his teeth. As my father lit his cigarette, cupping the match and ducking his head, I thought, *How many times have I seen him doing this? How many times have I seen him in this exact same position?* And then I felt as though I were floating outside my own body, looking down on a scene that had happened to me a dozen times before, playing out exactly as it did today. It was the first time I'd ever felt déjà vu, and for a second or two it might as well have been last summer or the summer before last summer, but then the pain in my nose came back, and the only moment I could possibly have been standing in was this one right here, the summer my father and mother yelled at each other about money and I was in love with a dark-eyebrowed girl with a drifting mole.

My father, taking a long drag off his cigarette, pulled a handkerchief from his back pocket and wiped his nose, then began telling me the story of the brain freeze that landed him in the hospital. "It's a doozy," he began, blowing an astonishing amount of smoke toward me. I stood there patiently and nodded, covered in my own blood, my eyes filling with tears again, listening to every other word as the blinding sun beat down on us.

3

One cold, drizzly day in November, Ralph came springing nonchalantly toward me on the playground. "I finished that list," he said.

"What list?"

"You know," he said, growing impatient. "The *list*."

And then I remembered. On the last day of seventh grade, all the way back in June, he'd told me about a price-list he was working on, prices he charged to do bodily harm to his fellow classmates. For a fee, he could be hired to take care of someone you didn't like. And now, as if the sun had set only once since we'd last talked about it, Ralph was telling me that he had finished it.

I held out my hand, stifling a yawn. I really wanted to see the list, but I didn't want to act too interested. It was dangerous to act too interested in anything that interested Ralph. As I unfolded the sheet, Ralph said, "You want me to take somebody out for you?"

"Maybe," I lied.

Ralph nodded. "Let me know and I'll write up an estimate."

I grunted.

Ralph then launched into the history of the list, how *his* list was the exact same list that the meanest gang in New York City used in the 1880s, a group of thugs who called themselves the

Whyo gang. I was about to ask him how he knew all of this when he unfolded another sheet that clearly had been torn from a book.

"Where'd you get that?" I asked.

"Library."

"You tore up a library book?" I asked. Tearing up a library book ranked right up there with flag burning and swearing in church. I loved the library. I would read a book about anything—Kung Fu, the Incas, silent movie stars with names like Fatty and Buster, the Loch Ness monster. We didn't have any books at home, and so I always felt the stab of anger when, at the library, I found a page scribbled in or a wad of chewing gum holding two pages together. And now here I stood, face to face with the culprit himself. "Don't tell me you tore up a library book," I said.

Ralph shrugged. "I didn't have a library card. Listen. Forget the library, okay? Why are you always distracting me?"

"Why didn't you just get a card?" I asked.

Ralph stepped up so that the tips of his shoes were touching the tips of my shoes. He said, "I don't know *why* I didn't just get a card, okay? Who cares. Listen. My *point* is that the leader of that gang had this exact same price-list on him when he was arrested." He took a step back and said, "I thought about raising the prices, but after thinking about it all summer I finally decided to keep them the same. It'll be part of my selling point. 1978 service at 1880 prices!"

For having been held back two grades, Ralph took great care in his own personal projects. His list—the one he'd copied from the now-vandalized library book—had been carefully typed with only a few blobs of Liquid Paper, raised like Braille, covering the typos.

Punching	*$2.*
Both eyes blacked	*4.*
Nose and jaw broke	*10.*
Jacked out (blackjacked)	*15.*

Ear chawed off	*15.*
Leg and arm broke	*19.*
Shot in leg	*25.*
Stab	*25.*
Doing the big job (murder)	*100. and up.*

"Wow!" I said. "Fifteen bucks for a chawed off ear?"

"Ask around," Ralph said. "You won't find it any cheaper."

I handed the list back to him. I was impressed with it, but it also gave me the creeps to hold. I didn't know why Ralph and I were friends. The best I could figure, we were friends because I was taught to be polite. Everyone else was too afraid of Ralph to stand around and listen to what he had to say. But the more I listened to him, the more I liked him. If I were any smarter, though, I should have done what the other kids did—run full-tilt in the opposite direction. For better or worse, it was too late for that.

"Hey," Ralph said. "You want to get an ice cream cone later and terrorize some kids?"

"Nah, I gotta get home," I said. "I'm supposed to go somewhere with my parents."

"Suit yourself," Ralph said, "but all week long I've had a craving."

"For ice cream?" I asked.

"Nuh-uh," he said. "For terrorizing kids." I expected him to grin, but he didn't. He folded the price-list and tucked it away. Then he cracked his knuckles, one at a time, and took his place in line with the rest of the eighth graders.

Before I could shut the front door behind me, my sister, Kelly, yawned at my arrival, then delivered the news: "Grandma's been arrested." She said this without inflection, as if she were merely telling me what was on TV today, a new show called *Grandma's Been Arrested*. She was two years older than me, a sophomore in high school, and about as exciting as a fuse box.

In our family, Kelly was always the bearer of bad news. I was starting to think she *liked* delivering bad news, that bad news traveled through her like an electrical current, and to get too close to her was like sticking your finger into a light socket.

"*Our* grandmother?" I asked.

Kelly rolled her eyes. "Uh, *duh*," she said, which had become her new favorite phrase. She'd say this to Mom and Dad, to our aunts and uncles, to our neighbors. I'd heard her say this into phones, into parked cars, to stray dogs and cats, to her stuffed animals, to people on TV. I had heard it through walls, from the floor above and the floor below me, with screen-doors separating us, from the opposite sides of picket fences, around grocery store aisles, and, once, while passing a large bush. Lately, I'd begun to hear it in my dreams, and I was starting to wonder if Kelly was sneaking into my room at night and whispering it into my ear: *Uh, duh…Uh, duh… Uh, duh…*

I said, "What for?"

"What for what?"

"What was she arrested for?"

"Oh," Kelly said. "Stealing shoes."

"Shoes?"

"Yep. Allegedly, she'd go into shoe stores, try on some snazzy shoes, and then when the salesman wasn't looking, she'd walk out of the store wearing them. She was doing it all over town, so the owners set up a sting operation."

"A sting operation?" I said. "For Grandma?"

Before Kelly could answer, the front door banged open, causing me to jump and clutch my chest. Mom and Dad came in, but without Gramsie.

Dad said, "We have to wait until she's arraigned tomorrow

morning, and then the judge will set bail. Bail! I can't believe what I'm saying. *Bail!* Do we have any beer? Kelly, go check the fridge and see if there's any beer in there."

I said, "Maybe we should get a good lawyer."

Dad said, "Is my last name Rockefeller? Do you see me throwing hundred dollar bills into our fireplace to keep the house warm?"

"What fireplace?" I asked.

"Exactly," Dad said, cocking his head and squinting while firing up a cigarette.

Kelly returned with a beer for my father. She popped it open and handed it to him, and my father smiled at her, then poured half the beer down his throat. His eyes turned glassy. He let his knees relax so that he could drop, in one swift motion, into his recliner.

Kelly was the one who fetched things for Mom and Dad, who didn't ask questions, and so my parents liked her best. I was the one who interrogated, who was always setting one or the other of my parents off, and I wasn't so sure what they thought of me. In all of these years I should have learned a thing or two from Kelly, but I didn't.

My mother was busy in the kitchen, making Greek chicken. Gas hissed from the oven and I could smell oregano. My father finished the rest of his beer and said, "Your grandmother, she's really put her you-know-what in a sling this time. She's up crapola creek without a paddle. That woman's made her bed and now she'll have to lie in."

I said, "Finders keepers, losers weepers."

Dad and Kelly looked over at me, as if I'd just materialized in the room. Then he cut his eyes over to Kelly and said, "How's about another beer, sweetheart?" While Kelly played fetch, Dad leaned over and turned on his stereo. With his forefinger he led the record player's arm to the 45 already on the turntable, Elvis Presley's "Suspicious Minds," a song my father played so often that you could barely hear the music over all the snaps and pops, but before long the two of us were sitting there bobbing our heads. When Kelly came in with Dad's beer, she started bobbing her head, too, and if someone who didn't know us happened to walk in at that precise moment, they'd have thought they were looking at three of the happiest people on this side of the planet.

The next morning at school, I buttonholed Ralph and said, "Get this. My grandmother got arrested for stealing."

"Whoa!" Ralph said. "What sort of places does she loot?"

"Shoe stores," I said.

"Shoe stores?" He laughed. "*Shoe* stores?" He thought about it for a minute. Then, narrowing his eyes and nodding, he said, "Shoe stores," as if the idea of robbing shoe stores suddenly made perfect sense.

"She'd get a pair of shoes from the Goodwill for fifty cents, then go over to the shoe store, try on an expensive pair, and when the salesperson wasn't looking, she'd walk out of the store."

"If you're gonna steal shoes," he said, "that's the way to do it—one pair at a time." He rubbed the half-dozen whiskers on his chin and said, "Methodical. Patient. I bet she'd make a good safe cracker."

"I think she's just a kleptomaniac," I said.

"Are you crazy? This woman knows what she's doing. She wants shoes. She's got a plan. Kleptos, they steal stuff, they don't care what. But your grandmother, she's like Clyde Barrow."

I nodded. I didn't know anyone named Clyde Barrow.

A black Monte Carlo rolled up alongside the playground, a smoky window rolled down, and a guy in the passenger seat said, "Hey, you. Yeah, *you*. Are you Ralph?"

Ralph leaned into me and said, "Looks like business. Wait here, okay?" Ralph walked over to the car, sort of bouncing on his way there. I'd always suspected that one of Ralph's legs was an inch or two shorter than the other one, but it wasn't the sort of thing you'd ask a person. Instead, I paid attention to the cuffs of his pants to see if one was higher than the other, but they were both already higher than they should have been, and since Ralph usually wore a different colored sock on each foot, it was difficult to tell *what* his problem was.

The guy in the passenger seat looked about my father's age. I crouched down, trying to get a good peek at the driver, but he was wearing dark sunglasses and staring straight ahead. Ralph pulled his price-list from his shirt pocket and handed it to the passenger. They exchanged a few words, then Ralph took out a tiny spiral pad from his back pocket and wrote something down. He tore the sheet from the spiral and handed it over. The passenger nodded, handed Ralph an envelope, and then the two of them shook hands. As soon as Ralph started walking from the car, the smoky window rolled up and the driver pulled away.

"What did you give those guys?" I asked when Ralph returned.

"An estimate," he said. He sighed. "I wish they hadn't done that, though."

"Who?"

"Kenny and Norm." Ralph's cousins. I liked Kenny better than I liked Norm, but it was like choosing between two cough syrups: they both made the hair on my arms stand up.

"What did they do?" I asked.

"They told a few of their friends about my price-list, then *those* people told more people, and now I've got more clients than I know what to do with."

"I thought you wanted business."

"I do," Ralph said. "The problem is, I don't even know these guys."

"I thought Norm was in jail."

"He copped a plea," Ralph said.

"Oh." This wasn't news I wanted to hear. "So what did those guys in the car want you to do?" I asked.

Ralph shrugged. "They want me to chew off somebody's ear," he said.

"Hey, that's fifteen bucks, isn't is?" I asked, trying to boost his spirits. "Chawed ear, right?"

Ralph nodded.

"So?" I said. "Whose ear?"

"Roark Pile's," he said.

"Roark Pile?"

We both looked over at Roark Pile. Roark was one of our own classmates. Short and hunched, wearing bottle-thick eyeglasses, Roark looked more insect-like than ever as he stood alone at the far corner of the playground. We'd had only one class together, a math class, and he'd had an asthma attack and had to be taken to the school nurse. I'd been going to school with him for eight years but hadn't ever said a word to him, and now that I thought about it, I wasn't sure anyone else had ever spoken to him, either. He was flipping through his *Star Wars* collectors' cards today. He kept the cards rubberbanded together, and whenever there was a break before class, during lunch, or on the playground, he'd take the rubber-band off and shuffle through them. He studied the cards with such intensity that you'd think Princess Leia had just materialized in front of him, whispering, "Oh, Roark Pile. You're my only hope." At least three days a week he wore a T-shirt with an iron-on decal of Chewbacca on the front. He also had a *Star Wars* lunchbox that prominently featured the Wookiee. I didn't care much for Roark, but I didn't care for him in the way that people don't care much for people they don't talk to, which is to say, I didn't know *why* I didn't care for him. I just didn't. I'd never had any desire to chew off his ear, though.

"Roark Pile," I said. "Why?"

Ralph huffed, disgusted with me, and said, "I don't ask *why*. That's part of the deal. I get a job, I do the job. *Why* doesn't factor into it. I like to think I'm more professional than that."

"So," I said, "are you going to bite his ear off right now?" I didn't want to admit it, but I was curious to see how it would happen. Would Ralph walk up behind him, bite down onto his ear, and start yanking on it? Or would he pin Roark to the ground first, secure Roark's hands under his knees, and then try to chew it off?

"Are you crazy?" Ralph asked. "You don't just bite off someone's ear in broad daylight."

"Oh. Have you ever bitten somebody's ear off before?" I asked.

"Not for money," Ralph said, "no."

The first warning bell rang, and Roark Pile began strapping his *Star Wars* cards back together. In a few days he'd have only one ear, but for the time being he was probably unaware that he even had ears, let alone that it was a luxury to have *two*.

"Jeez," I said, shaking my head. Ralph and I joined the line heading back into school. "Who'd have thought someone was out to get Roark Pile?" I asked.

Ralph said, "Don't fool yourself. There's always someone out to get you."

When I arrived home from school, Grandma was in the living room, sitting in the recliner, feet propped up. She wasn't wearing any shoes, and I wondered if the police had gone to her house and confiscated all of them, leaving her barefoot. "Grams!" I yelled, but my father cut me off.

"Don't talk to her," he said. "She's grounded."

Grandma smiled at me, then shrugged. With her forefinger and thumb, she made like she was zipping her own mouth shut. For my benefit, she cocked her head at my father and rolled her eyes. My fear of her as a hardened criminal lessened at the greater fear that she had taken up mime.

Dad said, "She's unrepentant. She says it was an innocent mistake. Jesus Christ Almighty. My own mother, an unrepentant crook!"

I found my sister in the backyard with Mom. They were both sitting on rusty lawn chairs. I said, "Grams is home."

Kelly said, "Better hammer your shoes to the floor."

I was about to tell her to take it easy on the old lady when I noticed that they were both drinking fruity, icy drinks, and that both my mom's and my sister's lips were bright red. "What are those?" I asked. "Slurpees?"

Mom said, "Not quite. Just a little something to take the edge off."

Kelly extended her arm over her head, then wiggled her hand like she was shaking a maraca. "MargaRITA," she said.

"You're drinking *alcohol*?" I asked.

Mom said, "Oh, Hank, it's just a margarita. It's mostly ice."

"Well, then," I said. "Can I have one?"

"No," she said.

"Why not?"

"You're too young."

I looked inside, through the plate-glass window, and could see Dad pointing at Grandma, reprimanding her, but I couldn't hear what he was saying. Grandma sat stock-still, staring straight ahead, looking like a taxidermied version of her own self. Then her eyes began to move, slowly tracking toward me. When she finally spotted me, she started to smile but stopped. I could tell that she was worried that I didn't like her anymore, the way everyone else seemed not to like her anymore, so I smiled to reassure her that this wasn't the case. For lack of anything better to do, I pretended that I was leaning against something, the way a mime would. Next, I acted like a heavy wind had swept through town, and it was all I could do to keep standing while walking into it. For my final routine, I pretended that I was trapped inside of a box, and that the box kept getting smaller and smaller. Grandma was laughing. My dad was in the middle of one of his *tell-me-what-I've-done-to-make-you-screw-up-so-badly* gestures when he turned and saw me outside pretending to be Marcel Marceau. The box that I was inside kept getting smaller and I kept trying to curl tighter and tighter, lying on my side now, pulling my legs up to my chest and starting to convulse, as if the box were crushing me.

Mom turned, saw me, and yelled, "Oh my God, Hank's having a seizure!"

Kelly said, "Put a pencil in his mouth so he doesn't bite his tongue off."

My father, though unable to hear either my mother or Kelly, lunged for the phone in the living room and started dialing.

But it was Grandma I kept watching, and I felt in that moment that we were reading each other's mind, and that she was the only person in this whole crazy family who'd ever really understood me.

Ralph and I spent the weekend trailing Roark Pile. I wasn't sure why I was trailing him with Ralph, except that I was bored and I'd never trailed anyone before. When you trail someone, you learn how dull people really are. I guess I thought we'd be following Roark onto construction sites and into hollowed-out mounds of dirt that no one else knew about, or that he'd have secret knocks for getting into unmarked storefronts, or that maybe he'd have a girlfriend from another school, a girl who reminded him, in some remotely hairy way, of his favorite *Star Wars* character, Chewbacca. But no: the Roark Pile of my imagination had nothing to do with the real Roark Pile. And what we already knew about Roark Pile from school— that he didn't have any friends and that he was obsessed with *Star Wars*—was all that there was to know about him.

"Man oh man," I said. "This is one boring guy."

Ralph poked my shoulder with his forefinger and said, "Follow yourself around one day and see how interesting *you* are."

I wanted to ask Ralph at what point he had started taking Roark's side, but I let it slide. Following someone all day long can make you crabby. After several hours of hiding behind a thorny bush across the street from Roark's house, Ralph and I decided to call it a day.

Ralph said, "Is your grandmother out of the clink?"

"Dad sprung her yesterday," I said.

Ralph nodded. "She staying with you guys?"

"Until we can figure out what to do with her," I said.

At the corner where Ralph and I were to go our separate ways, Ralph said, "Maybe you could set up a meet. You know, me, your grandmother, Kenny, Norm."

"Kenny and Norm?" I asked.

"Sure," Ralph said. "I told them about the old lady. The word *genius* came up ten times. I kept count. Of course, eight of those times Kenny and Norm were talking about themselves, but still…"

"I'll see what I can do," I said.

"You're a good egg," Ralph said, but then he punched my arm so hard that if I really were an egg, I'd have splattered all over his fist.

When I got home, Dad was sitting at the kitchen table with six crushed beer cans in front him and one sweaty can in his hand. Mom was curled on the couch, weeping. Kelly was staring blankly at a fuzzy TV show on the Spanish station.

"Hey, where's Uncle Fester and Cousin It?" I asked.

"Somebody tell Hank," Mom said.

"What?"

Kelly turned from the mustachioed bandito on TV and said, "Grandma's dead."

"She's *dead*?" I yelled. My first thought was that Dad had killed her, and I felt a strong urge to creep to the front door, then bolt for my life.

"She had a heart attack," Kelly said. "One minute she was eating oatmeal, the next she was dead. It was fast. Not entirely painless, but not too bad, I guess."

"Where's she now?"

"What, do you mean like *heaven*?" Kelly asked. "I guess that's where she is, but I don't know. I don't think she went to confession after stealing all those shoes, so she might not be in heaven. She might be, you know, some other place. It's hard to say. I guess we'd have to ask a priest."

I glared at Kelly before saying, "Where's her *body*?"

"Oh. An ambulance came and took her away." She cocked an eyebrow and said, "Any more questions, Sherlock? I mean, we're all a little broken up around here since we were the ones who were here when it happened."

I could tell that Kelly enjoyed having been here when Grandma keeled over. It made her one of the chosen ones. Later, she would probably cite this moment as one more piece of evidence of her superiority over me.

"I guess I don't have any more questions," I said. "Nope, I guess that's it for now."

The next time I saw Ralph, I told him about my grandmother. We were across the street from Roark Pile's house, hiding behind a row of hedges.

Ralph nodded gravely. "They got to her," he said.

"Who got to her?"

"Shoe store managers," he said.

"Actually, it was a heart attack. She was pretty old."

Ralph laughed, shook his head. "Hank, Hank, Hank. Think about it. What are the odds? The old woman goes to the slammer, right? She gets out, but before she has a chance to get back to work, *wham*, she falls over dead. And you think that's a coincidence? Hey, look," he said, putting his arm around my shoulders. "I was born the same day Kennedy was killed. I know about conspiracies. It's in my blood." He removed his arm and said, "When's the funeral?"

"I don't know yet."

Ralph said, "When you find out, let me know. I'd like to pay my respects to the old broad."

"Sure. Okay."

Roark Pile emerged from his house, tugging on his Chewbacca T-shirt. He seemed especially bug-like today, walking with his shoulders hunched and his head down, seemingly without a direction in mind, as though feeling his way across town with a pair of antennas. We followed him for hours—past New Castle Park, where the power line towers buzzed so hard your teeth would start to *zing*; to Haunted Trails Miniature Golf Range, where, on the first hole, you had to putt the golfball between Frankenstein's legs; to Dunkin' Donuts, where I had once vomited across the counter. We ended up at the city reservoir, which was a bone-dry cavern alongside 87th street. Another boy was down there waiting for him. It was the first time, to my knowledge, that Roark had made contact with another human being his own age.

"What are they doing?" Ralph said.

I pulled out my father's binoculars, a fancy pair with zoom that I controlled with my forefinger, only today I couldn't seem to focus and zoom at the same time. I hadn't used them much before except to zoom in on my sister's face at close range and start screaming, causing her to yawn and say, "Puh-*leaze*."

"Look," Ralph said. "They're making an exchange of some kind. I bet he borrowed money from a loan shark."

"I can't see," I said, zooming in and out, trying to focus.

"Roark Pile, gambling addict," Ralph said. "No wonder they want me to bite his ear off. He probably owes money all over town. It's finally making sense."

"Wait, wait," I said, capturing Roark in my sights. "Okay, I got him."

Ralph said, "Well?"

"They're trading *Star Wars* cards," I said.

"Yeah, right. I bet," Ralph said, unconvinced.

"No, I can see them. It's *Star Wars* trading cards."

Ralph said, "Why the hell are they meeting all the way down there then? And who's that kid? Do we know him?"

Across 87th street was a different school district, meaning that there were a dozen more grade schools and another high school, our rival high school, and it was possible that one of their kids had slipped across the border to make this exchange with Roark. I told my theory to Ralph.

"I wish I had a high-powered rifle," he said. "I'd shoot the cards right out of their hands. Scare 'em a little."

"So," I said. "Are you going to bite off his ear or what?"

"I don't know," Ralph said. "I mean, I guess so. I don't have any good reason *not* to bite it off. Something's not right." He stood from his crouch and said, "I wish I knew what, though."

My mother took me to Robert Hall to buy a suit right off the rack, just as the commercial advertised. My last suit was from 1975, a sky-blue leisure deal that my mother had thought looked nice with a dark-blue turtleneck, but every time I put that turtleneck on, I thought that I was going to choke to death.

"Ugh, I can't breathe," I'd say in a raspy voice through labored breaths. Kelly would roll her eyes, and Mom would say, "Hank, cut it out before someone decides to choke you for real."

Turtlenecks always jacked up my body temperature a notch

or two, and my face and ears would turn dark red if I wore one for too long.

Today, Mom pulled a dark-blue leisure suit off the rack and said, "Now, *this* would look nice with a light-blue turtleneck."

"No turtlenecks!" I yelled. "They CHOKE me! You don't BELIEVE me, but they DO! They cut off the circulation to my HEAD and then I can't BREATHE!"

A few customers stopped what they were doing to stare at me. Other kids' mothers looked disgusted that someone my age was whining.

"Okay, okay," Mom said. "Now, keep your voice down."

To quiet me, she pulled off the rack a three-piece forest-green suit and promptly located a matching tie. Suit in bag, we stopped next door at Kinney Shoes for a new pair of patent leather wingtips.

"Hey," I whispered to Mom. "Is this one of the places grandma knocked over?"

"Shhhh," she said. "Quiet."

Since Mom didn't answer me, I had to assume that my guess was correct. When a large man burst through the saloon-style doors that separated the customers from the stock in back, I thought of Ralph's conspiracy theory, how the shoe store managers were probably involved in Gramsie's death.

"I see we're doing a little shopping today," the big guy said. "A Robert Hall suit!" He nodded at the bag. "And what's the occasion? You look a little young to be getting married!" He winked.

"A death in the family," my mother explained. "His grandmother."

"Oh. Oh, well, I'm very sorry," the man said. He cleared his throat. "I didn't know."

How COULD he know? I thought. *Why would he say that he didn't know unless he DID know?* I said, "We think someone killed her."

"Hank!" Mom said.

The salesman cocked his head and squinted at me, sizing up the situation. "Murder?" he asked.

"Maybe you heard of her," I said. "Ruth Boyd." I waited. The man didn't say anything, so I continued. "She got herself mixed up with some people she shouldn't have."

Mom took hold of my elbow, squeezed it as hard as she could, and said, "Enough!" I was about to say more when my mother yanked my arm hard enough to put a dislocated shoulder back into place. With the salesman eyeing both of us now, my mother smiled bravely and said, "What kind of dress shoe do you have in a size eight?"

That night, Ralph and I trailed Roark Pile again, but Roark spotted us and took off running.

"I think he's on to us," Ralph said.

"I don't know why you don't just bite his ear off," I complained.

Ralph said, "How'd you like it if somebody hired me to bite your ear off? Now, let's say they hired me for all the wrong reasons. It seems to me that a little investigative work might save you your ear, right? And that's all fine and dandy if it's *your* ear I've been hired to bite off, isn't it? But not if it's someone else's. No! You want me to bite a guy's ear off without doing any legwork. Who knows what chain reaction I'll set off if I bite somebody's ear off for the wrong reason? Jesus, Hank, your head's so thick I'm surprised it's not in a laboratory being weighed even as we speak."

Ralph was wearing an old turtleneck that had been eaten by moths. I hadn't meant to set him off, so I decided to change the subject. "I can't wear turtlenecks. They choke me."

"Choke you?" he said. "What, like *this*?" He reached out and grabbed my neck, and although he was only joking, he choked me for a good five seconds before letting go. He snickered and, mocking me, said, "*They choke me!* You know what? If I had a little spare time, I'd bring a lawsuit against the school and make a case that *you* should've failed two grades, not me."

I could tell that this business of biting off Roark Pile's ear was troubling Ralph, and that this was why he was snapping at me. I decided not to take any of it personally, but I also didn't want to get choked again, so I said, "I better go, Ralph. People are still grieving back home."

Ralph nodded. "Yeah, well," he said. "It's not like Roark Pile's ear is going anywhere, now is it?"

"Apparently not," I said.

Grandma's wake was held at Vitiriti and Sons Funeral Parlor. I'd never seen a dead person before and I was secretly looking forward to it until I actually saw my own grandmother in the casket. I couldn't help myself. I burst out crying.

My sister, Kelly, came up to me and whispered, "Geez, Hank, are you okay?"

My shoulders shuddered, and I couldn't catch my breath. My crying reached the point that it didn't seem to have anything to do with Grandma anymore. I was feeling lightheaded, the way I felt lightheaded around gasoline pumps, and like those dizzying moments at the Standard Oil with my dad or mom, when I'd suck in the fumes as fast as I could, I started to enjoy the act of crying, the giddy way it made me feel, and I wasn't sure I could make myself stop crying even if I wanted to.

My mother came over and said, "Oh, my poor Hank," and hugged me until her blouse was soaking wet from tears.

My father eventually stomped over and said, "You're scaring everyone, Hank. Go outside and get some fresh air." He nudged me away from the casket.

Outside, in the dark funeral home parking lot, I found Ralph and his cousins, Norm and Kenny. Norm was wearing a tuxedo

T-shirt. Kenny was wearing a powder-blue tux he must not have returned after his senior prom five years ago. Ralph was wearing the same moth-eaten turtleneck he'd worn yesterday.

"Hey, hey! Look at you," Norm said, tugging at my new suit and sniggering. "Somebody die?" Kenny punched him, and Norm said, "Oh yeah. *Sorry.*"

Ralph said, "You forgot to tell me about the wake, Hank. I had to look it up in the newspaper."

I hadn't told him on purpose, but I acted surprised. "I didn't tell you?"

Ralph leaned toward me and said, "Hey, you been crying or what?"

"Nah," I said. "I'm allergic to perfume."

Ralph said, "You look like a blowfish. Doesn't he look like a blowfish?"

"He looks like a blowfish," Norm said.

Kenny nodded. "He looks like a blowfish."

I needed to change the subject, so I asked Ralph if he'd bitten off Roark's ear yet.

"Soon," Ralph said. "Tomorrow, maybe." He nodded, as if imagining the crucial moment that his teeth would sink into the lobe. He said, "You going back inside?"

"I don't think so," I said.

"Okay," Ralph said, "I guess it's time for us to pay our respects then."

Kenny and Norm nodded solemnly. Ralph slapped me on the back. Kenny pinched my cheek. Norm trapped me in a bear hug and said, "Don't ever forget her, man." He smelled like beer and Italian sausage. For a second I thought Norm had fallen asleep on my shoulder, but then he stood, straightened his tuxedo T-shirt, and said, "All right, dudes, let's do it."

•

The next morning at school, Ralph said, "I'm biting Roark's ear off tonight, six o'clock, no matter where he is or what he's doing."

"What if he's using the bathroom?" I asked.

"I don't care," Ralph said. "It's tonight or never."

"Thank God!" I said.

We were on the blacktop, waiting for the bell to ring. Ralph, glaring at Roark, ground his molars so hard, I thought I heard them squeak. When the bell rang—a noise that always made my heart clench—I started making my way toward the eighth grade line, moaning with each step.

"What's your problem, Hank?"

"My mother pitched my old tennis shoes," I said. "She thought they were getting ratty. So until I get some new ones, I have to wear these." I pointed to the wingtips from Kinney shoes.

Ralph said, "Sure your grandmother didn't leave those for you in her will?"

I shrugged. No one had said anything about a will. All Dad ever talked about these days was having to go over to Grandma's trailer and, as he put it, sift through all her junk. Last night, after dinner, he lit a cigarette. Staring at the flame rising from his Bic, he said, "An accidental fire would make my life a hell of a lot easier. Accidental on purpose!" He sucked on his cigarette, coughed a few balls of smoke, then dropped the lighter next to his ashtray.

"Tonight," Ralph said. He reached over and gently touched my ear, and I shivered.

Before meeting up with Ralph, my father took me over to Grandma's trailer. The trailer was in a park across the street from Haunted Trails Miniature Golf Range, and from her bedroom window, you could see the looming head of Frankenstein, the bolts sticking out of either side of his neck. I'd been inside the trailer a few hundred times before, but I'd never noticed until today how small it was or how little she owned.

"Well, hell," Dad said, peeking under the bed, then tipping the cedar chest up to see if anything was underneath. "This won't take much time at all. Guess I won't have to burn the place down after all."

"There's not much *to* burn," I said. But when I opened the closet door, hundreds of pairs of shoes came tumbling out, an avalanche large enough to grip my ankles.

"Holy Mother!" Dad said.

There were slippers, white orthopedics, high-heeled shoes with straps, stilettos. There were clogs, sneakers, even snow boots. I'd never really thought much about shoes before, but looking at these, I sort of understood her fascination. It was no different than my own desire to save every issue of *TV Guide*. There were things you collected for no other reason than that you wanted to collect them. I couldn't explain to anyone why I owned over two hundred issues of *TV Guide*. I just did.

On our way home, Dad said, "Your grandmother sort of lost her mind near the end. Went a little cuckoo."

"I don't think she was all that crazy," I said.

Dad didn't say anything until he'd stopped at a red light. Then he turned to me and said, "What do you know about crazy? Huh? You've never seen anything in your life except civilized behavior. Hell, we're practically the Cleavers. Your mother's June, I'm whatever-the-hell-the-dad's-name-is, your sister's Wally, and you're the Beav. Did they have a dog? I can't remember. Doesn't make a difference for the point I'm making. But here's my point…"

A car behind us started honking. The light had turned green a while ago, and now it was already turning yellow again.

"Okay, okay!" Dad said and punched the gas. We barely made it a block when a cop pulled us over and wrote my father a ticket for failing to yield.

"Have a nice day," the cop said, swaggering back to his cruiser.

I waited until we were almost home before speaking again. "You were about to make a point," I reminded him.

"What?" He seemed startled to discover that I was in the car with him.

"Before that guy honked his horn."

My father looked up at the ticket pinned under the visor, then cut his eyes to me. "A point? What point? I don't know what you're talking about, Hank." He parked the car, snatched the ticket from the visor, and said, "Hold on to your hat, son. Here's where it all hits the fan."

I checked my watch. I was already late meeting Ralph. I walked behind Dad, but as soon as we stepped over the threshold, I turned around and walked back outside, shutting the door between us.

Ralph was waiting at a corner, jabbing the shattered sidewalk with a stick. All along the sidewalk were places where blunt instruments had slammed down, leaving cobweb patterns in the concrete, and I wondered if Ralph came out here at night with a ball-ping hammer and smashed the sidewalk himself.

Ralph said, "Where were you? We're supposed to be at the hardware store right now. My surveillance information leads me to believe that Roark will be there."

"Surveillance information? *What* surveillance information?" I wasn't sure I liked the idea of Ralph having the equipment to listen in on people. I knew he'd tap my phone in a heartbeat if he had the means to do it.

Ralph said, "I don't want to give away all my tricks, but if you really want to know, I took a drinking glass and held the bottom of it up to their living room window last night, and then I stuck my ear to the mouth of the glass. I got all sorts of good stuff, including this business about going to the hardware store." He winged the stick into the neighbor's yard, causing a cat to yowl and run up a tree. He stood and brushed dirt from his already permanently stained pants.

Dellagado's Hardware was all the way across town. For long stretches of the walk I didn't think I was going to make it. My new shoes were chopping away at my ankles, and I cringed each time my foot hit the pavement. Though we got there before closing, the manager was already pushing the last of the marked-down lawnmowers back inside the store.

"You kids better hurry up if you want anything."

Ralph saluted the man, then rolled his eyes at me.

Loitering in the row of pesticides, I asked, "Do you think Roark already left?"

Ralph picked up a box of weed killer and said, "Am I carrying a crystal ball? How should I know?" He set the weed killer down and reached for a can of wasp spray when the bell above the front door jingled and Roark lumbered inside with a man who looked creepily like what you'd imagine Roark to look like in thirty years.

"Is that his *father*?" I whispered.

"Gee, I don't know," Ralph said. "Here, let me get my crystal ball out again." Then he gently smacked my face with a fly-swatter.

"Ouch! *Sorry*," I said.

Roark's father walked up to the manager, and the manager said, "What's new in the world today, Roark?"

Ralph and I looked around for Roark Pile, but he had already abandoned his father.

The father said, "Same ol', same ol'."

"Oh, no," Ralph said. "The old man's name is Roark, too."

"Two Roarks?" I said. "How is that even possible?"

Ralph and I didn't have to say anything more. We both knew the truth: the men who had hired Ralph were after Roark's father and not Roark. I was about to suggest we leave when Roark Jr. rounded the corner and nearly slammed into us. He froze but didn't say a word. A sound came from his throat like he was having a heart attack, but then I realized that it was just Roark breathing.

We were so close that I saw the intricate details of his ears. They were small and pink. The lobes were attached to his head instead of dangling, like mine or Ralph's. I could even see the ear's network of veins and the blue blood that shot through them. He must have sensed that I was looking at his ears, because he reached up and scratched one before turning and leaving us alone in the bug spray aisle.

"What are you going to do?" I asked. "Are you going to bite an ear off of each Roark?"

"Ugh. I don't believe this." And then, without so much as baring his teeth at either them, Ralph walked past the two Roarks and out of the store. I caught up to him.

I said, "I better call home for a ride. My shoes feel like they're made out of razor blades."

Ralph ignored me. He kept walking. When he finally stopped, he said, "If I'd known it was *this* Roark Pile, I'd never have agreed. I have age limits. I won't bite off the ear of anyone eighteen years old or older. I mean, I'd *love* to bite the guy's ear off, don't get me wrong."

"Can't you make an exception?" I asked.

Ralph shook his head. "A man sets up rules, he has stick to them. If I make an exception today, what's to stop me from biting off, say, *your* father's ear. Or your *mother's*, for that matter."

I shrugged. "Nothing, I guess."

"That's right." Ralph sighed. "I don't know. I was thinking of getting out of the business, anyway." He took his price-list from his shirt pocket and said, "Here. Maybe you'll want to take it over. The money's good and the hours are flexible."

"I don't think anyone's afraid of me," I said.

Ralph said, "You're right. People aren't afraid of you. But once they know you've got this price-list, that'll all change."

"Thanks," I said. I tucked it into my pants pocket. Ralph started walking away, but I couldn't bring myself to follow, limping instead to the nearest phone so that I could beg my mom for a ride home.

The next morning at school, a long dark sedan rolled up alongside the playground, a tinted window crept down, and a man with dark sunglasses motioned Ralph over.

Ralph said, "Time to break the news." He sauntered over to the car, crouched, and poked his head through the open window. I could see a lot of hand gesturing, but I couldn't hear anything.

"So?" I asked when Ralph returned.

"They weren't happy."

"It was a misunderstanding," I said. "I mean, how were you supposed to know there were two Roarks, right? What are the odds?"

"Actually," Ralph said, "I spent their money."

"They paid you up front?"

Ralph nodded.

"It's only fifteen bucks," I said. "Can't your cousins loan you fifteen bucks?"

"The problem," Ralph said, "is that they gave me a hundred."

"A hundred?" I said. "For chawing off an ear?" I pulled out the list that Ralph had given to me. I was right: *Ear chawed off. $15.* One hundred dollars was for doing the big job. *Murder.* I looked back up at Ralph.

Ralph said, "They didn't say *exactly* what they wanted, so I was going to mix it up a little, make it come out to a hundred bucks' worth of service. You know, chew his ear off, then punch him forty-three times."

"And you think that would have been okay with them?" I asked.

Ralph shrugged. "Probably not," he said.

My feet continued to ache from the new shoes. In a spiral notebook I charted their metamorphosis, how they went from being baby soft feet to bloody stumps, from slightly toughened feet to bloody stumps again, from callused feet to bloody stumps again, and so on. The garbage can next to the washer and dryer was stuffed with bloody socks.

Mom said, "I thought you'd eventually break them in, but I guess that's not going to happen. You're costing me a fortune in new socks."

And so, in the end, it wasn't the pain so much as the cost that resulted from the pain that finally persuaded my mother to give me ten bucks for a new pair of sneakers. She was too embarrassed to go with me after our last adventure together, so one Saturday I limped all the way to Kinney Shoes by myself. Aisle after aisle, I picked up sneakers and tested their durability by bending them toe to heel. For fun, I imagined how much it would hurt if my foot were inside and someone were bending my foot the same way that I was bending the shoe. I was making the face of someone in excruciating pain when the big salesman from my last visit appeared behind me and said, "You want to give it a whirl? Try it on for size? See how it works for you?"

"Sure!" I said.

I tried on both shoes, walking up and down the aisles, first bouncing on my toes, then walking on my heels. I was about to tell the salesman that I'd take them when the front door opened and Roark Pile walked in with a woman who must've been his mother.

"What kind of dress shoe do you have in a size eight?" the woman asked the salesman, and it was like a fist jabbed square in my gut, hearing the same question my own mother had asked when we were looking at shoes for Grandma's wake—and though it was possible that Roark and his mother were here for no other purpose than to buy shoes, I couldn't help wondering if the men who had hired Ralph had contracted someone else to take care of the problem. Because of this, I really didn't want to be in the same store with Roark and his mother. It didn't seem right.

I was at the far end of an aisle, watching from the greatest distance possible. Roark began looking around, so I stepped out of sight, hiding behind a tall shelf of shoes.

The salesman said, "Let me round up a few choices," and I heard his feet slapping the carpet, the slap getting louder and louder, until he was upon me. "How're those sneakers working out?"

"They're pretty nice," I said. "Comfy."

"It's your lucky day," he said. "They're on sale. Nineteen ninety-nine."

I nodded. I had only ten bucks, not a penny more.

"Genuine leather," he added before heading for the back room to search for dress shoes.

I peeked around the corner. Roark was heading down my aisle. I walked one aisle over so that a tall shelf of shoes separated us. I could feel his presence, so I tried miming his moves, taking a step when I heard him take a step, moving slowly toward the exit while Roark moved slowly toward the stock room. It was like some kind of magnetic force pulling us together, and midway down the aisle I knew that he was directly opposite me, standing on the other side of that shelf. I tried not to breathe, hoping he wouldn't know that I was there, but then I saw him looking at me through a cluster of perforated holes in the shelving unit, the way a fly looks at someone with its many eyes.

"Why do you keep following me?" he whispered. "Everywhere I go," Roark said, "you're there."

I wanted to explain, but to say anything in my defense would only prove Roark right: I *had* been following him. Maybe not today, but on all those days with Ralph, I'd trailed Roark's every move. So I didn't say anything. I tiptoed away, toward Mrs. Pile, toward the entrance, and the magnetic grip started to loosen. Each step became easier than the last.

Mrs. Pile had parked herself on a bench. As soon as I reached the door and turned to nod at her, the salesman came out of the stock room holding several shoe boxes. He froze when he saw me at the door, as if fearing he had lost a customer, but then he looked down at the new pair of gym shoes on my feet and realized what was about to happen. Roark was still looking through the perforated shelf, waiting for me to answer his question, not realizing that I was no longer there. Mrs. Pile was watching her own curious son, as if trying to figure out how he had become what he had become. The salesman, eyes narrowing, didn't say or do anything. Nobody said or did anything, and I realized that whatever was going to happen next hinged on my next move.

"Roark!" I yelled, startling myself. Roark looked up, confused to see me now by the door. "Is that you?" I asked, smiling and looking around. Everything that happened next seemed beyond my control. I strode over to Roark, trapped him in a hug, and said, loud enough for everyone to hear, "Where've you been hiding? I haven't seen you in ages!" As Roark tensed in my embrace, I peeked over my shoulder. The salesman had resumed delivering the new shoes to Mrs. Pile, and Mrs. Pile was staring at Roark and the friend she didn't know he had. Clearly, I had made her day. Her son had friends! Who'd have guessed?

I turned back to Roark, patting his shoulder. I was about to let go when I felt him relax. His grip on me, however, tightened. I wanted to say something, a word of comfort, but when I opened my mouth, nothing came out. I just stood there holding the poor kid. Was he crying? I wondered. I couldn't tell. "Here, here," I said, but it was more for myself than for Roark, because suddenly *I* was the one who felt like crying. I didn't know why, either. For my grandmother? For Roark's father? For standing in this shoe store, not knowing what would happen next? I really couldn't have said. I patted Roark and listened for the telltale signs, the sniffles, the sobs, but the only sounds I could make out were Roark's asthmatic breaths and my own thumping heart, as if one depended upon the other to keep the two of us alive.

4

Mom said she needed to talk to me—"this minute," she said—
that it was really important and couldn't wait, but I said,
"Not now." I opened the sliding glass door, walked outside, and
found my dog Tex, who'd spent this week digging up the backyard,
holding a bone lengthwise in his mouth, his fourth one today. He
dropped it onto a small, neat pile next to the grill. He licked my
hand, and I pointed at his nose and said, *Sit! Give me a paw!* but he
tilted his head, then ran away.

We had found Tex two weeks ago during a downpour, this
wet dog the size and color of a meatloaf. He was lumbering across
the expressway, his dark head hung low, too depressed by the rain
and lightning to care about the cars and trucks speeding toward
him. Dad pulled over and Mom opened her door, and together we
lured him into our car and into our lives with the promise of a good
home and table scraps.

"He *smells* like a dog," my father had said. He snickered and
called him a dog's dog—a joke I didn't get, though I liked how it
sounded.

"Tex!" I yelled now, but Tex was busy in the backyard, digging
where I couldn't see him. Our house was small, our front lawn tiny,
but the backyard stretched away forever—one of the few in the city

that did so, but only because if you kept walking you'd run into a fence, and beyond that fence was an industrial park that nobody wanted to live near.

I sat on the crooked chaise lounge, just beyond the rim of the bug-light's light, and I watched and listened to the moths and June Bugs and what-have-you touch down on the bulb, then flap crazily to get away from it. In the mornings I liked to walk outside barefoot and check the yellow bulb, see the wings glued to the glass, and touch what's left of these bugs who wanted too much of a good thing.

I was beginning to focus too intensely on the bulb, a dim yellow hole burning into my field of vision, when I caught Kelly, my sister, glaring at me from the kitchen. She slid open the glass door, glared harder, and said, "Hank, is that you?"

"No," I said. "It's John Gacy, serial killer!"

Kelly stared blankly in my direction. She never laughed at my jokes, never thought what I said was funny. Dad called her a literalist. A dog's dog, I thought. She stepped outside, leaving Mom alone at the kitchen table, and shut the door behind her.

"Where's Dad?" I asked.

"Va*moose*," she said.

"Bowling?"

"Sure," she said, as if she knew things about Dad that I didn't, but I decided not to press. Kelly walked over to where I was sitting, and without looking at me, she said, "I'm depressed."

"Me, too," I said, smiling.

"No you're not," she said. "*I'm* depressed." From her back pocket she pulled a folded, soggy sheet of paper. She handed it to me and said, "I'm manic-depressive."

What she'd given me was a photocopy of a page from the dictionary, the definition for *manic-depressive*.

"Wow," I said, impressed by the size of the words, the jumbo letters blurry on the paper.

"It's chemical," she said.

"So," I said. "You're a depressed maniac."

"A manic-depressive, you clod."

"Who knows," I said. "Maybe I'm a manic-depressive, too."

She rolled her eyes and said, "I don't think so."

"How would you know?"

She sighed and took back her definition. She folded it carefully and stuck it into her back pocket. "A manic-depressive can always spot another manic-depressive," she said. "And you're *not* a manic-depressive."

"Maybe not," I said. "But I'm double-jointed." I showed her my knuckles and began popping one in and out of place.

She groaned and said, "Goodbye," though it had come to mean something far more than *goodbye*—a word so weighted, it was meant to send me off somewhere far away from her.

"*Adios*," I whispered, and Tex, collector of bones, walked into the semicircle of light, another one clamped in his jaws, his eyes glowing red like the sole demon from a bad family snapshot.

Ralph hopped a fence whose gate he could've simply opened. He walked over to the chaise and nudged me with his foot. He was starting to grow wispy sideburns. The shadow of a weak mustache clung to his upper lip. Today he was wearing a skintight lime-green T-shirt that said South Side Irish, though technically we lived on the southwest side of Chicago and Ralph was Lithuanian.

"Ralph," I said. "The fence has a latch."

"Latch snatch," he said, speaking a language I knew and didn't know at the same time. He walked over to the sliding glass door to peek in on my mother who was staring at the table. Whenever she did this, she reminded me of Superman boring holes through steel with his eyes.

"What's wrong with her?" Ralph asked, serious now, backing slowly away from the house.

"I don't know," I said. "She's probably a manic-depressive or something."

Ralph nodded as though he'd heard of such things before. He shut his eyes and let the full impact of my mother's life soak into him like a hot breeze. Then he pulled a fluffer-nutter sandwich wrapped in cellophane from his back pocket, peeled back the plastic, and stuffed half of it into his mouth.

"My sister is a manic-depressive," I said. "Do you believe that?"

Ralph's jaw went slack, and in the dark hollow of his mouth, I saw swirls of marshmallow fluff and peanut butter and long strings of spit connected like cobwebs from his tongue to his teeth.

"Unless she's pulling my leg," I added.

"Oh," Ralph said and shut his mouth, as if amazement and disappointment were the pulleys working his jaw. "You want to know something?" he said. "I wouldn't mind getting to know your sister better."

Ralph was always talking about getting to know my sister better—this was old news—so I yawned and said, "What's the game-plan tonight, Ralph?"

"Well," Ralph said, "my aunt and uncle and their idiot kid are on vacation, and they asked me to feed their dog."

"They asked *you*?"

He stuffed the last of his sandwich into his mouth, wiped his palms onto his jeans, and said, "Yeah. They asked *me*. What're you sayin'?" He pushed me hard with both palms.

"Nothing," I said.

"What's wrong with somebody askin' *me* to take care of their ugly, mangy, flea-infested pet, huh?" He pushed me again.

"Cut it out, Ralph."

Ralph smiled now and winked at me. He was like that. He'd

beat you up one minute, buy you an ice cream cone the next.

"Let's go," he said.

It was seven o'clock and dark, the last splotch of light disappearing even as we spoke. Ralph and I headed down Menard, walking fast as always, hands jammed deep into our pockets.

We walked to the part of town where people left junk all over their yards and porches—washers and dryers, Big Wheels with broken handlebars or cracked seats, roofing shingles piled against houses—a part of town where things were either missing or broken.

Ralph bent over and picked up two rusty nuts and a screw. He gave me one of the nuts, and I began rubbing it between my two palms.

A small boy approached on a Schwinn Continental, his legs barely long enough to reach the pedals. When he got close enough, Ralph stepped in front of him and raised his palm up, the way a traffic cop would. Then he took hold of the kid's handlebars and said, "Hey. Where'd you get this bike?"

The boy said, "It's my brother's."

"Uh-uh," Ralph said, shaking his head. "It's *mine*, and I think it's time you give it back." Ralph walked behind the boy, looped his arms under the boy's armpits, pressing his palms firmly against the boy's neck, then lifted him off the bike. It was a smooth move, and though I didn't think Ralph should have done it, it was as impressive as anything I'd seen lately on Sunday afternoon wrestling.

Ralph sat on the bike, squeezed the brakes twice, and said, "Hey, Hank. Watch this." He pedaled hard up and down the street, yelling, "*Look! I'm Evel Knievel!*" He popped a wheelie, rode it high for a long time, then fell completely backwards, off the bike, cracking his head against the asphalt. The Schwinn wobbled a ways before smashing into a parked car.

"I think I've got a concussion," Ralph said. He stood and brushed himself off. His hair was matted to the back of his head. Silently, without any warning, he started walking away.

The boy, still on the ground, kept sobbing. I wasn't sure why, but I gave him the nut I'd been holding.

Ralph scratched his head several times where a dark stain had begun to grow. I kept up with him, in case he died. Ten blocks later, I said, "You shouldn't have done that."

"Done what?"

"Scared that kid."

"What kid?" Ralph asked. "I don't remember any kid."

"No one likes a bully," I said.

Ralph said, "Are you still talking about that kid?"

We walked until we ended up in the alley behind Lucky's Tavern. Lucky's was on the far edge of town—"a *dive*," my mother called it, "a dive where nothing but a bunch of ignorant rednecks go." Whenever Mom said this, Dad laughed. Dad spent a lot of time at Lucky's, and the idea of rednecks going there apparently cracked him up. I'd never been inside Lucky's, but every time we drove by I stared through the dark-tinted windows, beyond the beer advertisements, hoping to see what a bunch of ignorant rednecks looked like. The few times I could see—hot nights when the door was propped open—what I saw were two old men sitting at opposite ends of the bar along with the bartender perched on a wooden stool next to the cash register, his head tilting back to watch the TV suspended above him, nobody moving. It reminded me of something I might have seen behind glass at the Field Museum downtown, a moment in history frozen in time and place: *Lucky's Tavern*, the sign would have read. *A bunch of ignorant rednecks. 1979.*

When Ralph and I arrived at Lucky's tonight, the alley was empty.

"Not much happening," I said.

"Take a load off," Ralph said, and he sat next to the Dumpster, hiding behind a stack of flattened boxes and a large wire rack of some sort, a magazine rack, probably.

Ralph said, "Give me the lowdown on your sister. We're practically the same age, you know." Ralph shifted on the gravel, stretching his legs, trying to get comfortable. When it came to Kelly, Ralph believed anything I told him, and normally I told him the truth. Today, however, I decided to make things up, saying whatever came to mind.

"She's got only one kidney," I said.

"Really?"

"She wet her bed until my mother bought her a rubber blanket."

Ralph said nothing, savoring the thought.

"She sleeps on her back and snores like a pig."

"I wouldn't mind listening to that sometime, if you can arrange it," Ralph said.

I said, "She's really only my half-sister. We've got different fathers. Mom married some other guy first. Then she fooled around with my dad, and *whammo*, she got knocked up."

Ralph said, "So what happened to Kelly's dad?"

I shrugged. "Who knows. He was a drifter."

Ralph said, "Now that you mention it, I can see your mother with some drifter freak. No offense, but she's the type."

"Yep."

"Wow, Hank," Ralph said. "Your family's more twisted than mine."

But then I couldn't go on. I couldn't keep the lie inside, smothered where it belonged. So I told Ralph that I was lying, smiling as I confessed. He reached over and grabbed my neck. He choked me harder than I expected, pushing his thumb into my windpipe, blocking the passage of air. When he let go, he said, "You shouldn't lie about your mom." And that was all he said.

My throat kept throbbing, phantom fingers squeezing my neck between heartbeats, giving me the creeps. Then, at long last, the back door to Lucky's creaked open, though all that appeared at first were four fingertips clutching the door's edge.

"I should go over there and bite them," Ralph whispered. He bared his teeth like a werewolf and moved toward my forehead. I yelled, and the man stepped around the door, a beer bottle dangling next to his leg from the tips of his fingers, a cigarette bent upward from his lips, the way FDR smoked. It was my dad. He stood there in the light, squinting at us, until he recognized us and smiled.

"Hey, guys," he said. "What's going on?"

"Hi, Dad," I said.

Ralph said, "Hey, Mr. Boyd."

Dad didn't seem a bit surprised to see us there, all the way across town, half underneath a Dumpster. He said, "How're you boys doin'?"

Ralph said, "Just hanging out. Looking for drifters."

Dad chuckled, but I doubt he knew what Ralph meant. No one ever seemed to know what Ralph meant.

Dad shook his head and flicked away his cigarette butt—a long, high arc, soaring like a bug on fire, landing in somebody's backyard. Whenever Dad did this, I was afraid he was going to set the whole city on fire, the way Mrs. O'Leary's cow had set the city on fire a hundred years ago. Dad said, "Petey pulled a straight out of nowhere. Do you believe that? Out of *nowhere*. And to think, I *dealt* it to him."

I didn't know anyone named Petey. In fact, I never knew any of the people Dad mentioned.

"Snake-eyes!" Ralph yelled. "The doctor! Bingo!"

"A straight!" my father said, wagging his head.

"Yowza!" Ralph said. He raised his palm into the air, as if to high-five, and said, "My main most man!"

My father pointed his forefinger at Ralph and fired it like a gun. Then he looked at me and said, "Are you gonna be home later tonight?"

It was a stupid question: I'd never *not* come home for the

night. But I nodded and said, "Yeah. Sure."

"We need to talk, son," he said. He raised his arm to wave goodbye and said, "We'll talk tonight," then stepped back into the bar, the heavy door slamming hard behind him.

"I don't get it," I said. "Everyone wants to talk to me."

"You're like Ann Landers or something," Ralph said.

"I don't think so," I said. "I don't think they want my advice."

We took alleys to Ralph's aunt and uncle's house, and when we reached it, we approached from behind. At the back door Ralph tried the doorknob, then jerked a screwdriver from his pants.

"What's that for?"

"They forgot to give me a key," Ralph said. He jammed the screwdriver between the door frame and the door, and started prying.

"Hey," I said. "Don't do that. You'll bust up the woodwork."

"Listen, Einstein," he said. "What do you think they'll be more upset about—a broken door or a dead dog? Huh?" Ralph continued wiggling the screwdriver back and forth, pushing with all his weight, until the door finally popped open. He stepped inside and said, "*Voila!*"

Ralph switched on a light and began searching the house. I stood in the kitchen, looking around for the dog food bowls, the dog food, and the dog. I checked the kitchen countertop for a note, directions on dog maintenance, but couldn't find one. I went to the living room and said, "Here, pooch. Here, poochy pooch."

The house looked exactly like all of my Italian friends' houses—furniture covered in see-through plastic; bisque figurines decorating the end-tables; a three-dimensional Last Supper hanging above a humongous TV console.

"You sure we're in the right house?" I yelled. "Nothing

personal, Ralph, but this doesn't look like the sort of place where one of your relatives would live. It's too clean."

I stepped into the bedroom to keep giving Ralph a hard time, but he wasn't listening: he was rifling through drawers, pulling everything out, and throwing it over his shoulder. He stood up and said, "What a dump."

"You're the one messing it up," I said.

Ralph walked back into the living room, picked up a figurine of an old man wearing a straw hat and holding a fishing rod, and said, "Look at this crap. A house full of junk. And how much does this TV weigh? A gazillion pounds, probably. At least a gazillion."

"I can't find the dog," I said. "What kind of dog is it?"

Ralph pulled a newspaper clipping from his pocket, uncrumpled it, and said, "Hey. Go out front and tell me what the address is. We might be in the wrong house."

"You're kidding. Wrong house?" My heart began pounding.

"Hank," he said, looking at me for the first time since we'd entered the house. "You see anything that looks good?"

"What do you mean?"

"Cassette deck, turntable, ham radio?"

"Ham radio? What's a ham radio?"

"Forget it," Ralph said. "Just go check the address, okay?"

"Ralph," I said. "Where's the dog?"

"What dog?"

I pointed to his newspaper clipping and said, "What's this?"

He handed it to me and said, "Here. I'm gonna look around some more. Now, go outside and see if *this* address matches the address outside. Is that too hard for you? Jeesh."

Ralph walked away, and I smoothed out the clipping. It was an obituary for a woman named Nadine Lorenz. I studied the dead woman's address, looking for a mistake, but there was no mistake: we were inside her house. If the clock on the wall could be trusted, visitation hours were in full-swing this very second.

When Ralph returned, he said, "So what's the verdict?"

I waved the clipping at him. "This is *her* house?"

Ralph said, "Technically, no. Not anymore."

"Ralph," I said. "We should leave."

He let out a long, disappointed sigh, the kind of sigh my father liked to make, and said, "You're right. There's nothing here but a bunch of old lady crap." On his way out, he picked up a waffle iron and said, "How much you think these things go for?" He lifted it high into the air, over his head, and said, "This would make a great weapon. Someone screws with you, you pull this baby out and say, 'Hey. You want a waffle?' Then *boom*. You smash the dork in the face with it."

We stepped into the fresh air, and Ralph shut the now-busted door.

"She was dead," I said. "You broke into a dead woman's house. That's the lowest thing I ever heard of."

"I've heard of lower," Ralph said.

The waffle iron dangled beside Ralph's leg, and every so often he chuckled, but I didn't feel much like talking anymore. Each time he chuckled, I had a gut feeling Ralph wasn't long for this world. Soon, I would have to make a decision: keep hanging out with Ralph or cut my losses. There were pluses to both sides. *With* Ralph, no one would mess with me; they'd know better. *Without* Ralph, I might stay alive longer, and my chances of doing any serious jail time would be kept to a minimum. These were the benefits, short- and long-term, and though it should have been an easy decision, I knew it wasn't going to be. I liked Ralph. That was the sad part.

Ralph stopped in the middle of the street, as though he'd read my mind, sensing his own mortality, and he touched his hair, sticky now from the blood where he'd fallen off the Schwinn. He said, "I got hit on the head once with a sledgehammer."

"Really," I said. "Did it hurt?"

"Nuh-uh."

When we got to Ralph's house, he opened the gate and shut it without offering to let me come inside. I'd never been any closer than where I stood today, and I'd never seen his mother, though I always suspected she was peeking out from between the thick crushed velvet curtains, watching our every move. He lived in a small house with gray, pebbly shingles covering the sides, and black shingles on the roof. The lawn was mostly dirt.

Ralph said, "You know why it didn't hurt?"

"Why?"

"It knocked me out cold," he said. "You know that tunnel of light everyone talks about? Let me tell you, pal, it's true. I saw it. I kept walking deeper and deeper into this bright light, and then I started getting pulled back, away from it, and the next thing I knew, I was awake and in bed. It changed my life, Hank. No kidding. From that point on, I decided to be a different person."

"What kind of person was that?"

He grinned and said, "A mean one."

Ralph walked away, and as he reached for the screen door, I said, "How old were you Ralph?"

"Eight," he said. He waved at me with the waffle iron, then disappeared into his house.

I wasn't feeling so good anymore. I held my gut and walked quickly along the dark streets. I was back in a part of town that made me queasy, an area my mother always told me to stay away from. When I was in the first grade, a high school boy was killed on this very street, clubbed to death with a baseball bat by one of his own classmates, a bully named Karl Elmazi. But the scary part of the story wasn't that a guy had gotten beaten to death with a Louisville Slugger. It was that the bully had ten of his buddies with him, and none of them, not a single one, tried to stop the beating.

For my mother, this was a powerful story with a good moral.

"Pick your friends carefully," she liked to say, especially after one of Ralph's visits.

The dome light was on inside Dad's car when I got home, and Kelly was slouched in the driver's seat, her palm cupped over the mirror on the door. I crept up on her, hoping to scare her, but I didn't. In fact, she moved only her eyes, as if my being there constituted only the barest of movements.

"You still depressed?" I asked.

"After looking at you," she said, "I've never been more depressed in my life."

"What're you so depressed about, anyway?"

She reached over to the ashtray and picked up a lit cigarette I hadn't noticed. She said, "Everything and nothing. But I don't expect you to understand that."

I nodded; I didn't understand. It didn't seem possible.

I reached into the car and placed my palm on top of my sister's head, just to feel it. I'd heard that ninety percent of a person's body heat escapes out the top of their head, and this was what I felt: searing heat rising like a ghost from Kelly's scalp.

Kelly, ignoring my hand, snuffed out the cigarette in the ashtray.

I took my hand away and said, "What're you doing out here?"

"Waiting for Mom," she said, and this time I *did* understand. It was nearly midnight; Dad had been home only a short while. I could tell because the car's engine was still ticking. "We're going for a ride," Kelly said. "She says she wants to talk to me about something important." She rolled her eyes.

"Good luck," I said and made my way around the house, to the backyard. From a safe distance, I watched Mom and Dad through the sliding glass door. As usual, they were arguing. Tex came up behind me, his paws crunching the grass with each step. He was lugging a long, bent bone in his mouth, thin at one end, thick at the other.

"Tex," I said. "Holy smoke. What's *that*?"

Tex dropped the bone and jogged away, the way he'd been doing all week. I picked it up and held it close to my face to get a good view. It looked like a leg.

I walked over to the pile of bones next to the gas grill, crouched, and spread them out before me.

"Tex," I said, but I was whispering. I was too close to the house, too close to the bug-light, the swarm of bugs, too close, it seemed, to everything. I made my way across the backyard, looking for Tex, listening. The yard was large, and I couldn't see him or hear him. No doubt he was flat in the high grass, resting, listening to crickets, distant dogs, and the high power lines sizzling above us.

My parents were still arguing, but they looked so small out here, this far away, that it was impossible to take them seriously. If only they could've seen themselves, they might actually have laughed. Instead, Dad pointed at Mom, and it looked as if he were saying, *Sit! Give me a paw!* And Mom, as though she'd read my mind or sensed what I had sensed, lifted her purse from the floor and left the house. A moment later, the car started. Dad stood alone in the kitchen while Mom revved the engine too hard, gunning it, trying to blow it up. When she finally let up on the gas, she backed out of the driveway, headlights spraying across our house before she aimed her car down the road that would eventually take her away from us for good.

"Tex," I said. But Tex wouldn't answer.

Dad opened the sliding glass door and walked outside, and I took a step back. He was staring right at me, but he couldn't see me. He pulled a pack of cigarettes from his shirt pocket and smacked the pack against his palm. I'd seen him do this thousands of times before, but only now did it register that here was a man smacking a pack of cigarettes into his palm, and I had no idea why.

Dad stood on the back porch, exhausted, lighting a cigarette, the weight of everyone's life crushing his head, this man I both knew and didn't know—a dad's dad, I thought and tried snickering, but I'd never snickered before and couldn't do it now. Dad looked deeper into the backyard, searching for the sound he had heard, my half-snicker. He tried to see but couldn't and gave up. He looked down. Leaning forward, he rested his hand on the gas grill for support. At first I thought he was fainting, collapsing from stress. A heart attack, I thought. A stroke. I was about to run toward him, to help him, then realized he wasn't dying at all—not yet, at least—but looking down at the bones Tex had found. He eased himself onto his knees and began messing with them, arranging them the way you would a puzzle. Then he leaned back and studied what he'd done. I couldn't see it, not really, but I knew that he was crying. There was something about his posture, and about the way he touched the bones and simply stared.

He said something I couldn't hear, and I stepped back further into darkness. I sensed Tex close by, behind me, and I stepped back again, but I fell this time, my leg suddenly deep inside a hole.

Tex nudged my arm with his cold nose, his gesture of need. I pulled my leg from the hole and reached into the ground.

"Dad," I whispered, but Dad couldn't hear me.

Dad was sitting now, resting against the grill, moving his hand through the air. He was petting the ghost of a dog he'd once known, and all the way across the yard I was touching that same dog's skull, still lodged in the earth. I tried to imagine the sorts of things firing inside Dad's head, and so I looked at Tex, concentrating on the bones beyond his fur and skin, beyond the Tex I knew—the dog *beneath* the dog—but I couldn't imagine anything at all. There was no dog beneath the dog. There was only Tex.

When Dad finally looked up from the bones, he peered out into the dark of the backyard and called my name. "Hank? Is that you out there?" he asked. "Hank. What are you doing?"

I didn't say anything. I was already filling in the hole, clawing frantically, trying to cover the skull.

"You okay?" he asked. "You hurt or something?"

I flattened out, placing my head against the ground, remaining as still as possible.

"They're all against me, Hank," he said, more to himself than to me. "Not you, too." He took a long drag off his cigarette, and while smoke escaped his nose and mouth, momentarily blanketing his face, he shook his head, then stepped back into the nervous quiet of our house.

5

The Sheridan, at the corner of 79th and Harlem, was our nearest drive-in movie theater. It was a dusty parking lot with a few hundred metal posts poking up out of the gravel. Each post held a cast-iron speaker. At the center of the lot was a low-to-the-ground concrete bunker where concessions were sold and where the projectionist ran the movie. When my parents took me and Kelly to the Sheridan, we sometimes had to drive around to find a speaker that worked. My father, cursing each time one wouldn't click on, would eventually say, "I'll try one more, and if *that* one doesn't work, I'm getting a refund." But the last one always worked, maybe because the odds were leaning in our favor with each bad speaker, or maybe because we would end up parking several rows behind everyone else and the speakers back there hadn't been used much.

When we first started going to The Sheridan, my parents owned a Rambler. My father didn't like to run the heat during the movie—"We'll burn up all our gas," he'd say—so on cold nights we'd bring blankets and pile them up on top of us. Kelly would kick me under the blankets and then blame me for starting it.

"*Both* of you better cut it out," my father would say, "or this is the last thing we'll ever do together as a family, you hear me?"

The truth is, it was the *only* thing we ever did together besides live in the same house, but the threat always hinted to other, more interesting things, all of which would vanish if we didn't cut it out. I wanted to ask if there were things that I was forgetting, but I knew that this question would set my father off. I was always setting one or the other of my parents off with questions I'd ask before I really thought them through.

During our dozen years of going to the Sheridan, we saw probably fifty or sixty movies, but the ones I remembered best were *Easy Rider, Planet of the Apes, The Chinese Connection, Beneath the Planet of the Apes, Buster and Billie, Escape from the Planet of the Apes, Walking Tall, Conquest of the Planet of the Apes, Enter the Dragon,* and *Battle for the Planet of the Apes.* The few times that I made the mistake of going with someone else's parents, I saw *The Love Bug* and a movie called *Gus* about a mule that played football.

Every night was a double feature. The first movie was always the one that everyone in the world wanted to see, but I liked going to the Sheridan for other reasons. For starters, I liked intermission. A black-and-white movie of a clown pointing to a ticking clock played on the screen to show how much time you had left to buy hot dogs. On those rare occasions when my father would give me money to get everyone a hot dog, I would walk by the projectionist's booth and look at the man inside. It was the same man each time, an old guy with a pencil thin mustache, the kind of mustache Bud Abbott had, and he would always be smoking a cigarette and reading a magazine. One time I walked in front of the concession stand and jumped up with my arm in the air, and the shadow of my hand appeared on the screen, magnified to at least twelve feet high and three feet wide. When I got back to the car, I wanted to ask if anyone had seen my incredibly big hand, but my father was complaining about how little ice was in the cooler, and how his beer, sitting on top of everyone else's drinks, was now too warm to enjoy. Kelly, sound asleep or pretending to be sound asleep, was nothing more than a lump under the covers. I handed over to my mother the hot dogs, each one slipped into a shiny aluminum bag so that they looked like miniature rocket ships.

"If Kelly doesn't wake up," Dad said, "I'll take her hot dog. She'll never know, right?"

The other thing that I liked about going to the Sheridan was the second movie because they were often about women in prison, and sometimes the women weren't wearing any clothes. My parents liked to believe that I had fallen asleep by the time the movie had gotten to the racy parts, and I'd even go so far as to shut my eyes.

"Are they asleep?" my father always asked at the appearance of the first half-dressed woman.

My mother'd turn around and say, "Kelly's asleep. I can't tell about Hank. He's still sitting up." And then she'd call out to me in a heavy whisper: "*Hank. Are you asleep? Hank. You're not watching this, are you?*"

As soon as she turned back around, I'd open my eyes just a little so that they were narrow slits through which I could watch the movie. Usually, the movies were about women who'd gone bad, women who were in prison at the very beginning of the movie, or women who weren't bad to begin with but who ended up bad in prison anyway. I imagined girls from my school—Mary Polaski or Peggy Petropulos—handcuffed and put together in a dark jail cell. I imagined myself as a prison guard, smacking my billy club against my palm, walking back and forth in front of their cell.

No matter how hard I tried not to, I always fell asleep at some point during the movie, dreaming of girls from my class, all of them now in prison, and when I woke up, I was either slung over my father's shoulder or I was already in my own bed, my body curled like a fist. Only once did I wake up during the movie itself, and my mom and dad were in the front seat kissing. I'd never seen them kiss like this, on the mouth, the way men and women kiss in movies. On the screen behind them was a woman who, having escaped from prison, was being chased by a pack of vicious dogs. I couldn't actually see the face of the woman being chased because we were seeing everything through her eyes. The dogs were barking behind us, getting louder, catching up to us, while jagged tree branches scratched our arms and fallen tree trunks caused us to trip and stumble. My mother said to my father, "Okay, that's enough," and my father leaned back away from her. Without a word, he rolled down the window and returned the speaker to its hook. Then he started the car and backed out of our space.

Was this what they did each time Kelly and I fell asleep at the drive-in? Did they kiss until my mother said they'd had enough?

As Dad circled the parking lot, I could still hear the tinny barks and growls of angry dogs. I had to swivel in my seat to keep watching the movie, but as my father pulled out of the Sheridan and turned onto Harlem Avenue, the screen got smaller and smaller, until finally it all disappeared, leaving the four of us alone—me; my sister the lump; my mother picking up trash and stuffing it into a too-small bag; and my father behind the wheel. My father's eyes kept darting up to the rearview mirror, and I imagined that the pack of dogs, having jumped from the screen, was following us, gaining on us, and that my father was doing what needed to be done to save us, but you could tell by the haunted look in his eyes that he feared he would fail.

6

Ralph ran a hand up and over his head, flattening his hair before some freak combination of wind and static electricity blew it straight up and into a real-life fright wig.

We were standing at the far edge of the blacktop at Jacqueline Bouvier Kennedy Grade School, as far away from the recess monitor as we could get. In addition to being a foot taller than the rest of us, Ralph was starting to sprout sprigs of whiskers along his cheeks and chin, scaring the girls and prompting the principal, Mr. Santoro, to drop into our homeroom unexpectedly and deliver speeches about personal hygiene.

"Boys," Mr. Santoro would say. "Some of you are starting to look like hoodlums." Though he addressed his insult to all the boys, everyone knew he meant Ralph.

Today, Ralph pulled a fat Sears catalog out of a grocery sack, shook it at me, and said, "Get a load of this." The catalog was fatter than it should have been, as if someone had dropped it into a swamp and then pulled its bloated carcass out a few days later.

"I don't think they sell that stuff anymore," I said. "That's a 1974 catalog, Ralph."

"Quiet," Ralph said. He licked two fingers, smearing photos and words each time he touched a page to turn it. "I'll show you

Patty O'Dell."

"You found it?" I said. "That's it?"

Ralph nodded.

Rumor was that Patty O'Dell had modeled panties for Sears when she was seven or eight, and for the past two years Ralph had diligently pursued the rumor. If there existed somewhere on this planet a photo of Patty O'Dell in nothing but her panties, Ralph was going to find it.

"Here she is," Ralph said. Reluctantly, he surrendered the mildewed catalog. "Careful with it," he said.

Ralph stood beside me, arms crossed, guarding his treasure. His hair still stood on end, as if he had stuck the very fingers he had licked into a live socket. I looked down at the photo, then peeked up at Ralph, but he just nodded for me to keep my eyes on the catalog.

I had no idea why Ralph and I were friends. I was a B+ student, a model citizen. Ralph already had a criminal record, a string of shoplifting charges all along Chicago's southwest side. He kept mug shots of himself in his wallet. The first time I met Ralph, he had walked up to me and asked if he could bum a smoke. That was four years ago. I was nine. I didn't smoke, but I didn't tell Ralph that. I said, "Sorry. Smoked the last one at recess."

The photo in the catalog was, in fact, of a girl wearing only panties. She was holding each of her shoulders so that her arms criss-crossed over her chest, and though I saw a vague resemblance, the girl in the photo was not Patty O'Dell. Not even close. After two years of fruitless searching, Ralph was starting to get desperate.

"That's not her," I said.

"Of course it's her," he said.

"You're crazy," I said.

"Give it to me." Ralph snatched the catalog out of my hands.

"Ralph. Get real. All you need to do is look at Patty, then look at the girl in the photo. They look nothing alike."

Ralph and I scanned the blacktop, searching for Patty O'Dell. It was Halloween, and I couldn't help myself: I looked instead for girls dressed like cats. All year I would dream about the girls who came to school as cats…Mary Pulaski zipped up inside of a one-piece cat costume, purring, meowing, licking her paws while her stiff, curled tail vibrated behind her with each step she took. Or Gina Morales, actually down on all fours, crawling along the scuffed tile floor of our classroom: up one aisle, down the next, brushing against our legs and letting us pet her. The very thought of it now gave my heart pause. It stole my breath. But only the younger kids dressed up anymore, and all I could find on the blacktop today were Darth Vaders and Chewbaccas, C-3POs and R2-D2s. The occasional Snoopy.

The seventh and eighth graders were already tired of Halloween, tired of shenanigans, slouching and yawning, waiting for the day to come to an end. Among us, only Wes Papadakis wore a costume, a full-head rubber *Creature From the Black Lagoon* mask, suctioned to his face. Next to him was Pete Elmazi, who wore his dad's Vietnam army jacket every day to school, no matter the season. There was Fred Lesniewski, who stood alone, an outcast for winning the Science Fair eight years in a row, since everyone knew his father worked at Argonne National Laboratory—where the white deer of genetic experiments loped behind a hurricane-wire fence, and where tomatoes grew to be the size of pumpkins— and that it was Fred's father (and not Fred) who was responsible for such award-winning projects as "How to Split an Atom in Your Own Kitchen" and "The Zero Gravity Chamber: Step Inside!"

There were all of these losers, plus a few hundred more, but no Patty. Then, as a sea of people parted, Ralph spotted her and pointed, and at the far end of an ever-widening path I saw her: Patty O'Dell. We stared speechless, conjuring the Patty who'd let a stranger snap photos of her for a department store catalog while she stood under the hot, blinding lights in her bare feet. It was a thought so unfathomable, I might as well have been trying to grasp a mental picture of infinity, as complex and mysterious as the idea of something never coming to an end.

"You're right," Ralph said, shaking his head. "It's not her." He tossed the catalog off to the side of the blacktop, as though it were a fish too small to keep. He shook his head sadly and said, "I thought I found her."

After school, Ralph told me to meet him outside my house at eight, that his older cousin Norm was going to pick us up and take us to a party. Norm had just started dating Patty O'Dell's older sister, Jennifer, and with Norm's help, Ralph and I hoped to get to the bottom of the panty ads, maybe even score a few mint condition catalogs from Jennifer, if at all possible.

"You got a costume?" Ralph asked.

"Of course I do," I said. "I've got all sorts of costumes. Hundreds!"

I had lied to Ralph; I didn't own any costumes. In fact, I'd had no plans of dressing up this year. But now I was trapped into scrounging up whatever I could, piecing together a costume from scratch.

My sister, though disgusted by my choice and unable to conceal her revulsion, expertly applied the make-up.

"Of all the costumes," Kelly said.

"What's wrong with Gene Simmons? What's wrong with KISS?" I asked.

"One day," she said, smearing grease paint from my eye, all the way up to my ear, and back. "One day you'll look back on this moment, and you'll change your identity."

"Okay," I said.

"You'll move to a different country," Kelly said.

"Whatever."

I found hidden at the back of my parents' closet a stiff black wig hugging a Styrofoam ball. I sneaked a dinner roll out to the garage, spray-painted it black, then pinned it to the top of the wig, hoping it would look like a bun of hair. My parents didn't own any leather, but I found a black Naugahyde jacket instead, along with a pair of black polyester slacks I wore to church. For the final touch, my sister gave me her clogs. She was two years older than me, and her feet were exactly my size.

In the living room, in the shifting light of the color TV, my parents stared at me with profound sadness, as if all their efforts on my behalf had proven futile. My mother looked for a moment as though she might speak, then turned away, back to the final minutes of *M*A*S*H*.

Outside, I met Ralph. As far as I could tell, his only costume was a cape. A long black cape. One look at Ralph, and I suddenly felt the weight of what I'd done to myself. Ralph said, "What're you supposed to be? A clown?"

"I'm Gene Simmons," I said. "From KISS."

Ralph reached up and touched the dinner roll on top of my head. "What's that?"

"It's a bun," I said.

"I can see *that*," Ralph said. "But why would you put a hamburger bun on top of your head? And why would you paint it black?"

"It's not *that* kind of bun," I said.

"Oh."

"At least I'm wearing a costume," I said. "Look at you. Where's *your* costume? All you've got on is a cape."

Ralph smiled and pulled his left hand from his cape. Butterknives were attached to each of his fingers, including his thumb.

"Holy smoke," I said. It was the most impressive thing I'd ever seen.

"I'm an Etruscan," he said, pronouncing it carefully while rattling his knives in front of my face.

"A what?"

"An Etruscan," Ralph said. "I've been reading a lot of history lately."

"History?" I said. This was news to me. Ralph hated school.

"Yeah," he said. "Stuff about the Romans."

"Romans," I said. I didn't tell Ralph, but I knew a little something about the Romans myself. I wrote my very first research paper in the sixth grade on them, though all I remembered now were bits and pieces: the Gallic War, The Ides of March, some creep named Brutus stabbing Caesar to death. The idea of Ralph picking up a book and actually reading it was so preposterous, I decided to lob a few slow ones out to him, a quiz, and test what little he knew against what little I knew.

"So," I said. "What do you think about Caesar?"

"A great man," he said. "He brought a lot of people together."

"Oh really. How'd he do that?"

"Violence," Ralph said. I expected him to smile, but he didn't. His eyes, I noticed, were closer together than I had realized, and his eyebrows were connected by a swatch of fuzz. Ralph glared at me, as though he were thinking about punching me to illustrate what he'd just said. But the thought must have passed, and he said, "Etruscans were the original gladiators. Crazy, but smart. Geniuses, actually. Very artistic."

"How'd you get the knives to stick to your fingers?"

"Krazy Glue," Ralph said.

I nodded appreciatively. I had always feared Krazy Glue, scared I'd accidentally glue myself to my mother or father, or to a lamppost. I'd seen such things on the news, men and women rushed to the hospital, their fingers permanently connected to their foreheads.

"What if they don't come off?" I asked.

Ralph said, "I thought of that. That's why I glued them to my fingernails. My fingernails will grow out, see. And then I can clip them."

"You're a genius," I said.

"I'm an Etruscan," he said. "Very brilliant, but violent."

Ralph's cousin Norm pulled up in a Chevy Impala and motioned with his head for us to get in. He was twenty-five years old and ghoulishly thin, but the veins in his arms were thick and bulged out to the point you'd think they were going to explode right there…a spooky guy with spooky veiny arms, but he worked at the Tootsie Roll factory on Cicero Avenue, along with Ralph's other cousin, and he gave me and Ralph bags of Tootsie Pops each month, which made up in part for the spookiness.

I took the backseat; Ralph rode shotgun. Norm said nothing about our costumes. I reached up and made sure the bun on top of my wig was still there. Norm gunned the engine, then floored it. Blurry ghosts, clowns, and pirates appeared and disappeared along the sidewalk. Pumpkins beamed at us from porch stoops.

A mile or two later, Ralph said, "Where we going, Norm?"

"I've got some business to take care of first."

"What kind of business?"

"I've got a trunk full of goods I need to unload."

Ralph cocked his head. If he were a dog, his ears would have stiffened. He loved the prospect of anything criminal. "Goods," Ralph repeated. "Are they stolen?"

"What do you think?" Norm said.

Ralph turned around, smiled at me, then looked at Norm again. "What kind of goods?" he asked.

Norm lifted his veiny arm and pointed at Ralph. "None of

your business," he said. "The less you know, the better."

Ralph nodded; Norm was the only person who could talk to Ralph like that and get away with it. A few minutes later, Norm pulled into a White Hen Pantry parking lot.

"I need some smokes," he said, and left us alone with the engine running.

Ralph turned around in his seat. "So what do you think's in the trunk?"

"I don't know," I said.

"Guns," Ralph said. "That's my guess. Bazookas. Maybe some grenades." He turned back to the White Hen to watch his cousin. He rested his hand with the knives onto the dashboard and began drumming them quickly.

Norm returned to the car, sucking on a cigarette so hard that the tip turned bright orange and crackled. Then he filled the entire car with smoke and said, "I ran into a little trouble two nights ago. Serious trouble. I'll admit, I screwed up. But hey, everyone screws up every now and then, right? Huh? Am I right?"

"Right," Ralph said.

"Right on," I said. I lifted my fist into the air, a symbol of brotherhood, but nobody paid any attention.

"I had to get on the ball," Norm said. "Think fast. Figure out a way to come up with some money, pronto."

"What happened?" Ralph asked.

Norm looked at Ralph, then looked down at Ralph's fingers with the attached butterknives, as if he hadn't noticed them until this very second. He turned and looked at me, squinting, raising his cigarette to his mouth for another deep puff. "Just what the hell are you guys supposed to be anyway?"

Ralph said, "I'm an Etruscan."

"And I'm Gene Simmons," I said. "From KISS."

"The Etruscans," Norm said. "I never heard of those guys. They must be new. But KISS," he said and snorted. "That's lame.

You should've gone as Robert Plant. Or Jimmy Page. Or somebody from Blue Öyster Cult. Now *that* I'd have respected."

Norm put the car in drive and peeled out.

The longer we sat in the car, the more I thought of Patty O'Dell posing for a Sears catalog. The more I thought of Patty O'Dell posing, the more I wanted to roll down the window and howl. I wasn't sure why.

Norm wheeled quickly into the parking lot of a ratty complex called Royal Chateau Apartments and said, "Give me a few minutes, guys. If the deal goes through, we'll party. If not, I'm in serious trouble. Big time," he said, opening the door and getting out. He slammed the door so hard, my ears popped.

Ralph turned around and said, "How's it going back there?"

I gave him the thumbs up.

Ralph said, "Let's take a look and see what he's got in the trunk."

"I don't think that's a good idea," I said.

"C'mon," Ralph said. "Pretend you're Gene Simmons. What would he do in a situation like this?"

I leaned my head back and stuck my tongue all the way out, but the bun on top of my wig flopped over, cutting short my impression. A pin, apparently, had fallen out.

"I got the Krazy Glue with me," Ralph said. "You want me to glue it down?"

"I'm fine," I said.

Ralph reached over, turned off the car, and jerked the keys from the ignition.

"Hey," I said. "What're you doing?" But Ralph was already outside, leaving me with no choice. I got out, too.

By the time I reached the trunk, Ralph had already inserted

the key into the lock. "Ready?" he asked. He turned the key and the trunk hissed open. Slowly, he lifted the trunk's lid, as if it were the lid of a treasure chest and we were seeing if the mutiny had been worth the trouble.

"Holy crap!" Ralph said. "Would you look at that!"

My heart paused briefly before kicking back in, pounding harder than ever. I'd never seen anything like it. The entire trunk was packed full of bite-size Tootsie Rolls. There must have been a few thousand. I dipped my hand inside and ran my fingers through them. Ralph scraped his knives gently across the heap, as if it were a giant cat wanting scratched.

"Norm," Ralph said, frowning and nodding at the same time, clearly impressed with his cousin. "He's a real thinking man's man. He knows when to steal and when not to. Don't you see? This is perfect. I mean, when's the only time people start thinking bulk Tootsie Rolls? Halloween, man."

"Halloween's almost over," I said.

Ralph pointed his forefinger/butterknife at me and said, "That's the point exactly. People are running out of candy. They're getting desperate. Here's where Norm comes in. Bingo!"

"We better shut the trunk," I said.

"Not yet," Ralph said. "I'm hungry. Give me a hand. Start stuffing some of these babies into my pockets."

Ralph and I scooped up handfuls of Tootsie Rolls and dumped them into Ralph's cape pocket. Then Ralph shoved as many as he could into his jeans pockets. Twice, he accidentally poked my head with a butterknife.

"Watch it," I said. "You're gonna put my eye out."

"Count yourself lucky," Ralph said. "An Etruscan would've chopped off your head or thrown you to a lion by now."

We shut the trunk and waited for Norm. Using only his teeth and one hand, Ralph unrolled Tootsie Roll after Tootsie Roll, cramming one after the other into his mouth until his cheeks bulged and chocolate juice dribbled down his chin. He started talking, but his mouth was so full I couldn't understand a word he was saying.

Out of the corner of my eye I spotted Norm. I nudged Ralph. Norm was walking toward us, along with a fat guy decked out in a red-white-and-blue sweat-suit. The man's hair was sticking up on one side but flat on the other, as if Norm had woken him.

When Norm saw us, he shot us a look and said, "Get off the trunk, you punks." To the guy with him, he said, "All I need are the keys…"

"I got 'em," Ralph said. "Here."

He tossed them to Norm; Norm glared at Ralph, a look that said, *We'll talk about this later.*

"Didn't want to waste gas," Ralph said. "Remember when they had that shortage?"

The fat guy said, "I ain't got all day. Let's take a look."

Norm nodded, popped the trunk.

Where there had once been a mound of Tootsie Rolls was now an obvious trench. I didn't realize we'd taken that many. I looked at Ralph, but he just pulled another Tootsie Roll from his cape pocket and unrolled it with his teeth and weapon-free hand.

The fat guy said, "These are the small ones. I thought you were talking about the long ones."

"They're the same thing," Norm said. "One's just smaller than the other."

The guy shook his head. "Look, Slick. To make a profit I got to sell a hundred of these for every twenty of the big ones I'd've sold. You see what I'm saying? Kids want the ones they can stick in their mouths like a big cigar."

"That's true," Ralph whispered to me.

"Okay," Norm said. "All right. You want to haggle? Fine. I respect that."

But the guy was already walking away, back to his Royal Chateau, saying, "No can do, Slick. No business tonight."

After the man rounded the corner, I looked up at Norm, afraid he was going to yell at us, but he was holding two fistfuls of his own hair and yanking on it. "I'm screwed," he said. "Do you hear me? I…am…*screwed*."

Ralph made a move to offer Norm a few Tootsie Rolls, but when I nudged him, he thought better of it, slipping the stolen goods back into his own pocket, keeping them out of Norm's sight.

For an hour we sat in Norm's car and said nothing while Norm drove. Ralph started running his butterknives through his hair, giving himself a scalp massage. "Hey, Norm," Ralph finally said. "What do you know about Patty O'Dell posing for a Sears catalog?"

Norm said, "Would you mind shutting up a minute and letting me think?"

"Sure," Ralph said. He twisted around to face me and said, "Hey, Hank. Quit talking. Let the man think."

"What am *I* doing?" I asked.

"Both of you," Norm said. "Shut the hell up."

Norm drove us in circles, a loop that kept returning us to 79th and Harlem, a corner Ralph and I knew well because it was the home of Haunted Trails Miniature Golf Range, where Ralph and I enjoyed chipping golf balls over the fence and into heavy traffic, and behind Haunted Trails was the Sheridan Drive-In, where we could sneak through a chopped-out part of the fence and watch Bruce Lee on a screen the size of a battleship.

The seventh time Norm made the loop, I gave up any hope of ever making it to a party. When Norm finally deviated from his endless loop, he jerked a quick right into Guidish Park Mobile Homes. He stopped the car, killed the lights, and turned back to look at me.

"I need a favor," he said.

It was so dark, I couldn't even see his face. "What?" I said.

"I want you to take something to number 47—it's about a half-block up there—and I want you to give it to whoever answers the door and tell them I'll get the rest of the money tomorrow. Okay?"

I didn't want to do it—my bowels felt on the verge of collapsing—but I was awful at standing up for myself, unable to tell someone older than me *No*, if only because my parents had trained me too well. I was dutiful to the end. So I told Norm okay, that I'd go, and when I stepped out of the car, he unrolled his window and handed over a cardboard cylinder. It was about a foot long. I shook it but couldn't hear anything inside. Only when I passed under a streetlamp did I see what I was holding: a giant Tootsie Roll bank. It had a removable tin cap with a slit for depositing coins. I shook it again but couldn't hear any change.

At number 47, I knocked lightly on the door, two taps with a single knuckle. I was about to give up when the door creaked open and a man poked his head outside. He narrowed his eyes and inspected my costume. Without looking away, he reached off to the side and asked, "You like Butterfingers or Milk Duds?"

"Milk Duds," I said. "But actually I've got something for *you*. It's from Norm."

Before I could smile and surrender the giant Tootsie Roll, I was yanked inside the trailer by the scruff of my Naugahyde jacket. He shut the door behind us and said, "Who are you?"

"His cousin," I lied.

"Uh-huh," he said, nodding. "So you're the famous *Ralph* I've heard so much about."

"I guess so," I said.

"My name's Bob. Can you remember to tell that to Norm? *Bob.*"

"Sure," I said.

"I'm Jennifer's brother," Bob said.

"Jennifer O'Dell?" I asked.

"That's right."

"So you must be Patty's brother, too." I glanced quickly around the room for catalogs. Bob kept his eyes on me, then squeezed the giant Tootsie Roll, as if it were my neck, until the lid popped off. He emptied it onto a card table. The best I could tell, there were three tens and a twenty, along with a note folded into a tight triangle, the kind we used in homeroom as footballs.

"Maybe I should go," I said.

Bob put his hand out, as if he were a traffic cop, and said, "Not yet. Follow me." We walked down a short and narrow hallway to a door at the far end of the trailer. When Bob opened the door, he motioned for me to join him inside the room.

It was dark, almost too dark to see, the only light coming from the room now behind us. Two women were resting in bed, and at first I wanted to laugh, because one of the women looked like she was wearing Wes Papadakis's *Creature From the Black Lagoon* mask, and the thought of a grown woman lying in bed in the dark wearing a stupid rubber mask struck just the right chord in me tonight. Bob was trying to scare me, his very own Halloween prank, but I wasn't falling for it. I started snickering when Bob flipped on the light and I saw her face. I wanted to look away, but I couldn't. It kept drawing me in, like a pinwheel: *eyes so puffy she could barely see out...lips cracked open and swollen...the zigzag of stitches along her nostril.*

The other woman sitting on the bed was a girl my age, and when I realized who it was, that it was Patty O'Dell, I quit breathing. She was wearing a long white T-shirt that she kept pulling over her knees, trying to hide herself from me. I knew it was the wrong time to think about Patty posing in the catalog. I couldn't help myself, though. But each time I got to the part where Patty would take off her socks, I would look over at her sister—I couldn't not look— and the Patty of my imagination would dissolve into something dark and grainy.

When I finally gave up, I raised my hand and said, "Hi, Patty," but Patty turned her head away from me and stared at the wall.

"How much did he bring?" Jennifer asked.

Bob huffed. "Fifty bucks," he said.

The woman looked down at her hands.

"There's a note, too," Bob said. He unfolded the triangle and said, "Oh, this is classic. You'll love this. He spelled your name wrong. He doesn't even know how to spell your name. Hey. Big surprise. The man's illiterate." Bob laughed and shook his head. "Says here he'll try to get you the rest of the money tomorrow."

"Figures," she said.

Bob crumpled the note and said, "So what should we tell Gene Simmons? We can't keep an important man, a man of his *stature*, tied up all night."

"Tell Norm it's too late. He had his chance. That was the agreement. A thousand dollars or I'd call the police and file a complaint."

Bob looked at me. "You got that?"

I nodded.

"Good," Bob said. "Tell him to expect the police at his door in, oh, let's say an hour, two at the most. Maybe that'll teach him not to hit a woman."

My clogs clopped hollowly against the asphalt all the way back to the car. The night was officially ruined. I might not have been able to hold infinity in my mind, but I sure knew the end of something when I saw it.

My stomach cramped up, as if it had been punctured, as if my body were somehow poisoning itself. I was angry at Norm, certainly, angry at Norm for beating up Jennifer, angry at Norm for driving us around and acting like it was nothing, a mistake, a mistake anyone could make...but I was also angry at Norm for how Patty had looked at me, then looked away, angry because I was close to something, I wasn't sure what, but each time I got within reach, I looked over at Jennifer, I saw her face, and it all disappeared. Norm had ruined it for me, whatever it was. For that I wanted to hurt Norm myself, but the closer I got to him, the more unlikely that seemed. I was thirteen. Norm was twenty-five. What could I possibly do?

Near the Impala, I heard someone gagging, trying to catch his breath. I dashed around the car and found Ralph bent over, a pool of vomit next to a tire. Ralph's door was open, and the dome light inside the car lit up half of Ralph's face. Norm was slumped down in the driver's seat, his hand drooped over the steering wheel, a cigarette smoldering between two fingers. The radio was on low. Ralph's fingers clanked together, and I thought of Brutus, his knife plunging into Caesar, again and again.

"What did he do to you?" I whispered to Ralph. "Did he punch you in the stomach?"

"Who?" Ralph asked, still bent over, not looking at me.

"Norm," I said.

Ralph peeked up now, fangs of vomit dripping from his chin. "Why would Norm punch me in the stomach?"

"You're throwing up," I said.

"I know. I ate too many Tootsie Rolls," Ralph said. "Besides, it's a Roman ritual. Eat 'til you puke. I wanted to see if I could do it. You should congratulate me."

After Ralph cleaned himself off with handfuls of loose dirt and the inside of his cape, we slid back into the car. Ralph said, "The first vomitorium on the South Side of Chicago. People will travel from miles away to yak their brains out here."

Norm revved the engine. He said, "So? What did she say?"

"She wants to talk to you," I lied.

"Oh yeah?"

"She wants you to go home," I said, thinking of the police at his door later tonight, knocking with their billy clubs. "She said she'll be there in an hour," I added.

"Really," Norm said, sticking the cigarette in the corner of his mouth and pounding the steering wheel with his palm. "Well, what do you know about that? She's forgiven me."

"You bet," I said.

Norm shook his head and put the car in reverse. Back on Harlem Avenue, he said, "So where do you boys want to go?"

"Home," I said.

"Home it is!" Norm said. He said *home* as if it were an exotic place, like Liechtenstein or the Bermuda Triangle.

And so we drove in silence the first few miles. Then Norm said, "You think I should buy her some roses?"

"Nah," I said. "No sense wasting your money."

I could see Norm's eyes in the rearview mirror. He was watching me, but I couldn't tell if he knew that I was lying. At a stoplight he turned around and said, "Gene Simmons, huh?"

"Gene Simmons," I said.

"From KISS," Ralph added.

Norm said, "When I was in high school, I went to a costume party dressed as Jim Croce. I glued on this big hairy mustache and walked around with a cigar and sang 'Operator.' Chicks dug it." He smiled nostalgically until people behind us started honking. The light had turned green. "All right!" he yelled. "I'm *going* already!"

Not far from the junior college, a pack of men and women wearing togas trudged along a sidewalk, hooting and raising bottles of liquor above their heads. "Whoa! Would you look at that," Norm said.

Ralph cranked down the window for a better view. He said, "Stop the car."

"What?"

"Stop the car, Norm. I need to join them."

"Why?"

Ralph, peering out the window at the throng of bedsheets and olive-wreaths, said, "My people."

"What people?" Norm asked.

"Romans!" Ralph got out of the car and yelled to the passing crowd: "Greetings!" He raised his hand with the butterknives in salutation, and the Romans went wild. They beckoned Ralph over, and Ralph loped across the street.

Norm shook his head. "He's something else, ain't he? Half the time I forget we're related."

I had turned back to Norm, but Norm was still watching Ralph, amazed. I studied Norm but found no clues, no trace of what I was looking for, so I decided to ask him, to see what he'd say. "Why'd you do it?"

Norm's eyes moved slowly from Ralph to me, focusing, his pupils growing, adjusting to the difference in light. His brow furrowed, and he looked like he really wanted to answer me, as if the reasons were somewhere on the tip of his tongue. Then he shook his head and said, "Hell, I don't know. You lose control sometimes." He rubbed his hand up over his hair in such a way that it stood on end, the way Ralph's hair had stood on end this morning…a family gene, I suspected, a whole genealogy of screwed-up things inside him that he didn't understand, would *never* understand… and I thought, *Of course Norm doesn't know. Of course.* Not that the answer to my question was any comfort. Just the opposite, in fact.

Slowly we drove on, though a block away, as the last goblin of the night floated past us, I couldn't resist. I turned and looked out the back window again.

The Romans were holding Ralph aloft, over their heads, and chanting his name. Ralph, floating above them, looked so content, so pleased, you could almost be fooled into believing he was leading his people into Chicago, as Caesar had gone into Gaul, to bring us all, by way of murder and pillage, together as one people, one tribe.

7

The power company that serviced Chicago and its suburbs wanted to do something nice for the kids, so they constructed parks where their power line towers sat. Where I lived were three of these parks, each with a two-hoop basketball court, a swing-set, a merry-go-round, a slide, and a couple of giant cast-iron insects that sat atop industrial-sized springs, all of this in the shadows of wires, hundreds of them, strung from tower to tower like garland at Christmastime. Every few hours the power lines surged, and the buzzing, growing louder, was the sound I imagined a man in an electric chair heard as his own sour spirit detached from his body, the way a humongous Band-Aid would sound peeled from a really hairy leg.

I wasn't much of an athlete, but I liked throwing my basketball around at New Castle Park, one of the three parks with the power line towers. Everyone I knew watched the Harlem Globetrotters on TV, and for a while it seemed that every kid in town owned a red, white, and blue basketball. At least once a day you'd see some poor kid trying to dribble a figure-eight between and around his legs. It was embarrassing to watch—their bulging-eyed concentration, their rigor mortus legs forming an upside-down U, the slippery ball flipped into the street, sometimes in front of a speeding car. My favorite Globetrotters were Meadowlark Lemon and Curly Neal, but I knew I'd never be able to do what they could do, and so I was satisfied with banging the basketball off the backboard, occasionally making a basket, all under the constant hum and crackle of the power lines. I threw that ball again and again, trying to empty my head of all thoughts. It wasn't as easy as it sounded, draining away your own past and future, trying to exist in whatever moment you happened to be in—not a second before and not a second after. This was how I imagined insects spent their days. I had stared hard into the eyes of a fly once, wondering if it had ever, even for a second, thought about what it had done the day before. One time I stared at a grasshopper for thirty minutes, hoping for a sign, a look of reflection, but I wasn't so sure that it even remembered what it was doing when I first began looking at it. One thing I learned was that it was difficult to *not* think about anything because thinking about *not* thinking was actually thinking about *something*. The idea of *nothing* fascinated me. I loved the idea of nothing because it didn't seem possible. How could there ever be *nothing*? There couldn't! And so I'd throw the ball, again and again, until I'd get a splitting headache trying to think of nothing but thinking about everything else instead. I always got a headache playing basketball, and I always took this as my sign to go home.

One November day, I saw Ralph trudging along New Castle Avenue, dragging a burlap bag behind him.

"What's in there?" I yelled from the basketball court.

Ralph stopped, then looked up and around, into the air, as if he'd been hearing voices his entire life.

"Over here!" I said.

Ralph turned, saw me. He didn't smile. He didn't wave. He nodded, which was about as friendly of a greeting as a person could expect from Ralph, then he made his way over. His wallet was connected to a long, drooping chain that rattled when he walked, and he was wearing a hooded sweatshirt with the hood up. The bag slid up the curb, then bounced across the park's grass.

He said, "What're you doing? Playing basketball by yourself?"

"You want to play some Horse?" I asked.

"Horse?" He narrowed his eyes, as if the game that I had suggested involved one of us riding the other one around the basketball court. I hadn't really thought about it before, but I'd never seen Ralph in possession of any kind of sporting equipment. Since Ralph was two years older than the other eighth graders, the principal wouldn't let him take gym class with us. I wasn't even sure what he *did* during that period. He said, "You come here a lot? By yourself?"

"All the time," I said.

Ralph nodded. He said, "My cousins, they know a guy who knows a guy who knows something about electricity. See these power lines? This guy, the one who knows this guy that my cousins know, he said that if you spent too much time around these things, you'll end up sterile."

"Sterile?" I said. I suspected that the look I was giving him was the same look that he'd given me at the suggestion of Horse. I knew that being sterile meant that I would never have kids and I knew roughly what part of my body it had to do with, but I wasn't sure about the specifics. How, for instance, could something that didn't even touch me make me sterile?

"*Who's this guy?*" I asked.

"He's some guy who knows a guy who knows my cousins."

"And he's an expert on electricity?"

"So I've been told," Ralph said.

We stood there a moment without saying a word. The power lines sizzled above. I looked down at Ralph's burlap bag—a gunny sack, my mother would have called it. There was a lump in it about the size and shape of a small animal, like a possum.

Ralph said, "I better not stand here long. I normally don't even walk on this street."

"Afraid of getting sterile?" I asked.

I expected Ralph to laugh or at least smile, but he didn't. He nodded. "Don't want to risk it," he said.

Ralph, heading back to the street, dragged the lump behind him. I was about to yell out to him, to ask again what was in his sack, but a sharp pain tore through my head, causing me to drop the basketball. The ball bounced once, twice, a third time, each bounce closer together than the last, until it was vibrating against the ground, then dying and rolling toward the fence. To stop thinking about the searing pain inside my head, I tried imagining what was inside Ralph's sack. A cat? A bucket's worth of sand? A couple of meatloafs? I shut my eyes and concentrated hard, harder than I had ever concentrated in my life, and while the power lines started to surge, its buzz growing so loud I was afraid that the towers themselves were going to burst into flames, an image of what was in the sack finally came to me: a baby, *my* baby, and Ralph, like some ghost from the future, rattling chains but spooked by his own sad mission, had come to show me what would never be.

8

One week before Christmas in December of 1969, when I was four years old, the Santa Trailer finally arrived at the Scottsdale Shopping Plaza. Three weeks late, it sat parked alongside the curb outside Goldblatt's Department Store. Back then, the sky was always grey around Christmastime, the clouds heavy and low, expectant with snow. But that Sunday morning was particularly dark as Mom drove us down Cicero Avenue, the clouds swirling, almost black. I was in the passenger seat, unbelted and pressing my face against the cold glass so that my nose looked smashed— and then I saw it: a banged-up mobile home with Santa's gigantic smiling face painted on the side of it.

I was five years old. I screamed as loud as I could and yelled, "*Santa!*"

Mom swerved, as though Santa had appeared in front of us, and we hit the median doing fifty. The front tire blew out, and Mom almost sideswiped a semi while trying to move three lanes to the right. She pulled into the parking lot of a competing department store across the street, where there was no Santa trailer.

After she had safely parked the car, Mom sat with her head on the steering wheel. It felt strange sitting there in silence and watching Mom. I wondered what she was going to do next. I was starting to think that the reason she was slumped forward was because her back was broken, so I reached out and poked her hard with my forefinger.

"Not now, Hank," she said. "I'm trying to settle my nerves."

Mom spent about as much time settling her nerves as I spent playing with my Hot Wheels. I didn't really know what "settling nerves" meant except that I wasn't supposed to bother her while they were being settled.

Our breath had fogged up the windows, so I started drawing Santa Claus with my finger on the glass. When I was done, I was surprised by how much it actually looked like him. Normally, whenever I tried drawing something with my crayons, the pictures ended up looking nothing like what I was trying to draw. A cat looked like a four-legged animal with the head of a man wearing a long mustache. My houses looked like boxes that had been left out in the rain, drooping to one side, seconds away from collapsing.

"I need to call your father," Mom said. "Zip up your coat."

"I don't want to go," I said.

"*Hank*," she said, her voice low, almost a growl. But then she did something she almost never did. She gave up. "Okay. Fine. Wait here. Keep the doors locked."

"My door *is* locked," I said. "See?"

"Well, keep it that way," she said. "And don't touch the keys in the ignition. I'm leaving the car running. You'll freeze to death otherwise." She pointed to the stick shift. "Don't touch this, you hear?"

I nodded.

"Promise me," she said.

"Promise."

She took a good, long look at me and sighed. "You're getting more and more like your father every day."

I liked my father, so I smiled.

Mom got out, locking her door before slamming it shut and

causing my ears to pop. And then I watched her get smaller and smaller. I held up my forefinger and thumb so that she fit into the empty space between them, as though I were holding her—and then, as she continued to shrink, I pretended that it was because I was pinching her. Before she reached the door, I pushed my forefinger and thumb together, crushing my mother so that I couldn't see her any more, and then I started to fake-cry, pressing my face against the window, my shoulders shuddering.

But then I stopped. I was bored. What interested me most inside the car was the lighter. My father and mother were always pushing it in and waiting until it popped back out, and then they'd light their cigarettes with it. Whenever I asked if I could light a cigarette, they'd shake their heads, as if they'd barely heard me, or they'd give me a funny look, as though a cigarette were dangling from my mouth too, before telling me no.

Alone now, I pushed in the lighter. Just when I thought it wasn't ever going to pop back out, it did. I pulled it from its slot. It was heavier than I'd imagined, and I almost dropped it. Inside was a series of circles inside of circles. The circles were bright orange and giving off heat. I held the lighter in one hand, but with my free hand, I pointed my finger at the glowing circles and started moving the tip of my finger toward it. As the orange circles grew dimmer, I wanted to touch them to see what they felt like, but I couldn't bring myself to do it. I finally returned the lighter and sighed.

What now? I wondered. *What now?*

And then I saw Santa's trailer through Mom's window.

I opened my door and stepped out. It was colder than I realized, and my nose started to run. I locked the door and slammed it shut. I walked to the back of the car and stood by the tail-pipe where grey clouds of smoke from the still-running car surrounded me. After the smoke had completely wrapped itself around me, I stepped out from it, a little dizzy, hoping someone would see me and think that I was a genie who had appeared magically from the car's tail-pipe.

I coughed a few times and walked to the corner. Cars and trucks flew past, one after the other. Snow whipped around my ankles, crawling up my pant legs, above my socks. I shivered. My snot froze as soon as it left my nose. I couldn't stand there all day—Mom would eventually come back—so I started walking across the street.

Cars honked. Another car, trying to stop, lost control and fishtailed. A man rolled down his window and yelled, "What the hell do you think you're doing, kid?" I waved at him. I'd never walked across a street this wide before. It was fun—it was certainly better than sitting in Mom's car—and I was already thinking about more streets I could cross.

On the other side of Cicero Avenue, in the Scottsdale Shopping Plaza parking lot, I had to weave in and out of parked cars to reach the Santa Trailer. A few times, I lost sight of it and started to panic, but then I'd walk into a place where there were only a few cars, and there the trailer would be again.

"Santa!" I said, bleary-eyed from the cold, my toes and fingers almost entirely numb.

I expected to see a long line when I approached the entrance, but no one was there, and the door was shut. There were two doors, actually—one to go into and one to go out of.

I walked up the three steps to the first door and knocked. When Santa didn't answer, I tried the knob, but the door was locked. I was about to knock again, harder this time, when I heard around the corner someone begin to cough loudly, then clear his throat and spit. Although I couldn't see the actual person, I saw the spit. It flew out from behind the trailer, as if shot from a gun, and landed in some snow-covered shrubs next to Goldblatt's Department Store.

"Santa?" I called out and walked to the back of the trailer.

Santa was sitting on the trailer's bumper, smoking a cigarette, and eating a Milky Way.

"Oh," he said when he saw me. "Hey." He took one last long

pull on the cigarette, then flicked it out into the parking lot, where it sizzled in a pond of grey slush and died.

"Santa!" I yelled.

Santa raised the candy bar and said, "Hold on. Mouth's full."

"Can I tell you want I want for Christmas?" I asked.

Santa grimaced as he swallowed the last bite, then he tried tossing the rest of the candy bar into a garbage can but missed it. He looked around, making sure no one other than the two of us saw what had just happened. Two giant blackbirds appeared from the roof of Goldblatt's. They must have been the last remaining birds in all of Chicago. They fought over the candy bar, until one managed to hold it in its beak and fly off. The other bird squawked, as if to say, "Damn you!" and followed.

"Thing is," Santa said, "trailer ain't open yet."

I stared at him. I couldn't believe that I was actually talking to Santa Claus. I walked over and put my arms around him, burying my face in his soft velvet belly.

"Whoa!" he said. "Easy there."

I squeezed him harder.

A young woman, with hair piled up in what my mother called a beehive and wearing a long coat with leather fringe around the bottom, came up and said to Santa, "Where the hell were you last night? Were you with Midge?"

I let go of Santa and backed up.

Santa shrugged. "I dunno. Out? Playing pool?"

"Bull. I'm sure you were with that…"—she looked over at me—"…you-know-what."

"C'mon. Do we have to do this today?" Santa asked.

The woman cut her eyes over to me again, then back to Santa. She said, "Maybe I should call her husband and ask him."

"Don't do that," Santa said.

Walking backwards, the woman said, "Yeah, maybe that's what I'll do," then headed back to the parking lot and climbed into a VW Van with a giant peace sign painted on the side.

"Was that Mrs. Santa?" I asked.

"What? Oh, yeah. Yeah." He yanked up his velvet pants and coughed, then looked around the parking lot, distracted.

I gave his jacket a few tugs and asked, "Want to know what I want for Christmas?"

"Hunh?" he asked, looking down. "Right, right. Christmas. Maybe we outta go inside the trailer. But we gotta make this fast, okay?" I followed him around to the door.

"Where are your reindeer?" I asked.

"Good question," he said. "Probably went around back to do their business. They're a little shy about that. Especially what's-his-name. You know. The one with the big red nose?"

"Rudolph's here?" I asked.

"Yeah, him. Rudolph. The whole gang's here. Donald and Blister, too." Santa crouched, felt around underneath the trailer until his eyes widened, and then he smiled. "Ah-ha!" he said, showing me the key. He unlocked the door and flipped on the light, and we walked inside.

A half-eaten hamburger lay on a small dinette table. A crushed soda can sat next to it. It was freezing cold in the trailer, too. Each time I opened my mouth, I saw my breath. In fact, it seemed colder inside than outside, but maybe it felt that way because I was expecting the trailer to be warmer. I started shivering. My teeth clacked together.

"Hey, man, sorry about the mess," Santa said and kicked a crumpled paper sack out of the way. In the middle of the trailer sat a large, overstuffed chair with foam poking out of its holes. Santa fell back into it and sighed.

I started climbing up onto his knee when the door opened and a woman entered. It was a different woman from before. She looked from Santa to me and then back to Santa.

Santa looked at his watch. "You're early," he said. Lowering his voice, he said, "We've got a situation."

The woman said, "What kind of situation?

Santa said to the woman, "Give us a second?" He looked down at me and said, "Quick. Name one thing you want."

"I want Rock 'Em Sock 'Em Robots, and I want…"

"Groovy," Santa said. "Consider it done." He lifted me off his knee, reached into a plastic laundry basket next to us, and pulled out a red sucker. "Here you go. Now, scoot."

I took the sucker and headed for the exit. At the door, I turned for one last look. The woman was sitting on Santa's lap now. When Santa saw me lingering, he shooed me with his hand. The woman raised two fingers, flashing me the peace sign.

I left the trailer.

Back at the busy intersection, sucker in mouth, I saw Dad in the parking lot across the street. He was on his hands and knees, peeking underneath cars. Mom was standing by Dad's pick-up truck, and although I couldn't tell for sure, I had a feeling she was crying. She kept covering her face with her hands and shaking her head.

"Mom!" I yelled.

She couldn't hear me, but then I heard my own name: "Hank!" It was Dad, standing at the corner. "Don't move!" he yelled. "Wait right there!" He ran all the way across the street without anyone swerving or honking. "Where the hell did you go?" he asked. Before I could tell him, he said, "You really threw us for a loop, you know that? I was looking everywhere for you, kiddo. Come on," he said. "Hold my hand."

His hand was as hard and cold as a frozen chicken thigh, but I held onto it anyway. After we crossed the street and started approaching our cars, he yelled, "Hey, look who I found!"

Mom uncovered her face. I expected her to be thrilled to see me, but her eyebrows pushed together, and I knew I was going to be in trouble.

"Mom!" I said. "Guess who I met!"

"I don't care if you met the Pope," she said.

Under his breath, Dad said, "Ease up, huh? The kid's alive."

Mom glared at Dad, then shook her head and turned around.

Dad said, "You locked Mom out of her car, Chief. Good thing your old man has a key." He walked over to the car, reached into his pocket, felt around, but came up empty. Then he turned toward his pick-up and stared at it. Smoke rolled out of the tail-pipe.

"Crap," he said.

"What?" Mom said, turning around.

"I locked my keys in the truck," he said.

"How could you?" Mom asked.

"Habit, I guess," he said. "It's not like I normally keep the truck running, you know."

"Now what?" Mom said. "What the hell do we do now?"

"Hey, hey. Don't jump all over *me*," Dad said. "I'm warning you." He looked like he was grinning, so I grinned, too.

"Warning me?" Mom said. "*Warning* me? Or *what?*"

Dad looked around, kicking snow out of the way, until he found a large stone. He picked it up, carried it over to Mom's car, and pounded it against Mom's window three times until the window shattered.

"There," Dad said, dropping the stone. "It's unlocked."

"*Perfect*," Mom said. "Just *perfect*." She walked over to the driver's side, brushed the broken glass of the seat with her gloved hand, and slid inside.

"Just give me your keys now," Dad said, "so I can unlock my door."

Mom shifted the car and drove away, leaving the two of us behind. We stood there watching her until we couldn't see her anymore.

I cleared my throat.

Dad said, "That woman. I swear."

I pointed at the stone. "You want that?" I asked.

Dad said, "Yeah, in a minute." He pulled a pack of Lucky Strikes from his coat pocket, shook it a few times, and extracted a cigarette with his teeth. "Here. Stand in front of me. Help me block the wind," he said, ducking his head while striking the match. "Dammit," he said each time the match blew out, but I didn't mind. I liked how the smell of the burnt match tickled the inside of my nose, and I liked feeling needed. To block the wind even more, I held both of my hands up near my father's face, as if his head were a balloon that I was about to pick up. The match stayed lit this time, and Dad managed to get the cigarette going. Smoke surrounded me, and when I backed up and wiped my stinging eyes, Dad said, "Don't cry, kid. Your mother just gets beside herself sometimes. That's all."

I wasn't crying, but I didn't tell Dad that. Instead, I wiped my eyes some more and sniffled loudly, and then I crouched down and picked up the stone. Dad stared at me a while and then took the stone.

"Thanks," he said.

With the cigarette in the corner of his mouth and smoke blowing through his nose, he wound back his arm, as though the stone were a baseball. I looked across the street and saw Santa Claus. He was in a headlock and getting punched repeatedly by a tall man. The woman who had flashed me the peace sign was trying to pull the tall man away from Santa.

"Look!" I said to Dad.

"Yeah," Dad said, "it's beautiful, ain't it?" He was looking up at the sky. The grey clouds had begun delivering snow. It was as though a hatch had opened, and down it came. It arrived in large, wet flakes, and Dad started to laugh. He opened his mouth, letting snow pile up on his tongue.

I looked back across the street. The tall man, pulling the woman by her elbow, was walking away from Santa, who was on his knees. I raised my arm and flashed Santa the peace sign. Santa stood slowly and brushed himself off. Then he walked closer to the street to see who I was, holding his hand up to his brow to block the snow.

"*Merry Christmas!*" I yelled.

Dad, thinking I was talking to him, said, "Merry Christmas, son," and winged the stone at the window as hard as he could. The window shattered. "Sweet mother!" he said, laughing. "What a day." He looked down at me, grinning, and said, "Hey, listen. I want you to tell me what you want Santa to bring you. It's only a week away, you know. Christmas, that is."

"I already told him," I said. "He's over there."

"Who?"

I pointed, and Dad turned around. Santa was bent over, hands on his thighs, vomiting in the snow.

"Oh," Dad said. He stared for a while at Santa before flipping away his still-smoldering cigarette. "Good enough, then," he said. He ruffled my hair with his big palm, and then together we brushed the broken glass from the truck's front seat, climbed inside, and braced ourselves for the bitter-cold ride home.

9

Our neighborhood was pinched on two of its four sides by factories. My father worked at the 3M plant, the one that made tape. I couldn't have told anyone exactly what it was my father did there, but every few weeks he'd bring home rolls of scotch- or packing-tape or a box of packing peanuts, in case we ever needed to mail something fragile, which we never did. One year he came home with six hundred rolls of shrink-wrapped duct tape. "Bastards don't give us a Christmas bonus," he said, "so I thought I'd give one to myself. What the hell, right?" Since it normally took us two years to use up a single roll of duct tape, my parents doled out the extra rolls to our friends whenever an occasion to give gifts came up, but even doing this left us with over five hundred rolls. As far as I knew, nobody had that many friends.

I'd never really thought much about the things my father brought home until the winter of '78, the year I was in eighth grade. That December, three weeks before Christmas, my father came home with a large but severely crooked pine tree he'd found poking up out of a Dumpster behind Dunkin' Donuts, where he stopped off each morning for coffee on his way to 3M.

"It's a perfectly good tree," he said, standing with the front door wide open and pointing to it on the sidewalk. In Chicago, during winter, opening the front door was like opening the door to a walk-in freezer, and the first icy gusts of wind caused me to shiver. Snow whirled into the house as my father retrieved the tree and dragged it inside. A few dozen branches caught on the door frame and snapped off along the way. He said, "I figure somebody took an early vacation and threw this baby out."

Mom said, "You found it in a Dumpster? It's probably crawling with vermin, Frank." Instead of helping with the tree, she headed for the kitchen. Whenever she was mad, she loved to pretend that she was cleaning the cabinet that held the pots and pans. She could clang around in there for hours.

"Vermin?" Dad called out over the racket. "In *December*? I didn't see any *rats*, if that's what you mean." Dad rolled the tree across the living room and into a corner. He sat on the edge of the sofa, lit a cigarette, and stared into the tree. "First real tree we've ever had," he said, "and your mother's putting up a stink."

My sister had begun walking everywhere barefoot. I almost always heard her before I saw her, and tonight it was her voice I heard first ("What's all the noise down there?") followed by stomping. And then Kelly appeared, tromping down the stairs. The living room carpet was jungle-dense green shag, and when her bare foot met the main floor, a pine needle inserted itself into her sole. She screamed and fell to the carpet, as if she'd stepped on a landmine, only to have another needle jab her knee when she landed. "Oh my God," she said, afraid to move, staring up at us, frozen in place. And then she started bawling.

Mom ran into the living room, looked at Kelly, and said, "Did something bite her?"

Dad didn't answer. He blew smoke out his nose and shook his head.

•

The next night, my father came home with a set of plastic reindeer. One reindeer was completely flat, as if a semi had run over it. Another was missing a head. All had been smeared with a mysterious dark soot.

"Where on earth did you find those?" my mother asked.

"Oh, next to the highway. They were just lying there, so I pulled over and threw them in the back of the truck."

Kelly came downstairs wearing combat boots she'd bought earlier that day from an Army surplus store. She took one look at the reindeer and said, "They're deformed."

"You're getting gunk all over the carpet," Mom said, testing the soot by touching it with her forefinger, then holding her finger under a hundred-watt bulb to get a better look.

"Okay, okay," Dad said, dragging the reindeer, which I realized now were connected by wire, out of the house. "Hank," he yelled to me. "Give me a hand here. I want to put these on the roof."

"Are you sure?" I asked.

"Of course I'm sure. It's Christmas!"

The next night my father came home empty-handed, but the night after that he showed up with a long, rectangular piece of sheet metal that was curled on one end and spray-painted red.

"What's that?" I asked.

"Whaddya mean, *what's that*? It's a sleigh. Haven't you ever seen a sleigh before? Me and some of the guys at work, we were screwing off on our break when I spotted some scrap metal. Next thing I knew, we had ourselves a sleigh. Want to give it a whirl?"

"I don't think so," I said.

"Want to watch your old man give it a whirl?" He smiled and waggled his eyebrows.

I shrugged. We lived on a flat street on the southwest side of Chicago, and the only incline anywhere around would be the city's empty reservoir. In winter, once it started snowing, the reservoir became the closest thing to a ski resort that we had, and although no one I knew owned skis, they used sheets of corrugated cardboard or metal garbage lids, anything that could be sat on, to slide down the slope. Chances were that I would see kids I knew there, and I didn't want my father joining them with his curled-up piece of sheet metal.

"What's wrong with you people, anyway?" my father asked, smiling. "Where's the holiday spirit?" He wagged his head. It was the look of a man who'd stepped off a plane only to find he'd taken the wrong flight. "Okay, give me a hand putting this on the roof behind the reindeer then. You can do that, can't you?"

Over the next week and a half, my father brought home all kinds of garbage he'd found at the side of the road or in a trash can or behind the factory where he worked: J-shaped plumbing pipes that he claimed looked like silver candy-canes; a couple of foot-high Troll dolls with pug noses and rainbow-colored hair that could double as Santa's helpers; and a piece of chicken-wire that he bent to look more or less like a camel.

"A camel?" I asked.

"You know," he said. "The Three Wise Guys? The Gift of the Rabbi? *You* know the story. They were sort of like the first Federal Express, only they used a camel instead of a truck."

"Have you been drinking?" Mom asked.

Dad said, "It depends on what you mean by drinking."

Thursday night, after he'd come home from work and eaten dinner, Dad suggested that we search our neighbor's trash to see what we could find. It was the night before garbage pick-up, and the streets would be lined with fresh trash.

"You'd be surprised to see what people throw out," he said.

Mom said, "You're *not* letting our son pick through other people's garbage."

From another room, I heard Kelly say, "Gross," and then she appeared, combat boots on. She pulled a pair of binoculars from behind her back, looked at me through them, and said, "No telling what kind of bacteria you'll find. You better burn your clothes when you're done, Hank."

Dad draped an arm over my shoulders and said, "We're not going to be tearing into garbage sacks, if that's what you girls think. We're just going to see what they've left by the curb. The *bigger* items. Isn't that right, Hank?"

I nodded. It was easier to agree than to disagree, so I found myself agreeing to all kinds of things I really didn't want to agree with.

After leaving the house, and after the two of us settled into the pick-up's ice-cold cab, Dad pulled a can of beer from his coat pocket. I'd always liked the sound it made when he popped one open. He said, "Women," and took the first loud slurp.

Unlike other dads I knew who bought plastic holders for their drinks, the kind that hung from inside their car-door window, my father used a roll of duct tape. The duct tape sat next to him on the seat, and he placed the can of beer inside the tape's hole. It was heavy enough so that the drink wouldn't slip around, and the can was a perfect fit—not too tight, not too loose. Using the roll of tape as a drink coaster was ingenious, really, and I wondered how a man who could think up something as brilliant as this could come up with some of the other harebrained ideas he had.

When my father lifted the beer for another sip, I asked, "What if people don't want us messing with their trash?"

My father laughed. He set down the drink and dug into his shirt pocket for a cigarette. Cigarette smoke always burned my eyes, but whenever I mentioned this to my father, he'd tell me to crack a window. It was so cold tonight, though, that I needed to keep the window up to keep my teeth from chattering.

My father puffed several times to get the cigarette going. He said, "Listen. Garbage is fair game. You throw it out, it's no longer yours, pal. The United States has some of the best garbage in the world. You're living in junk heaven and don't ever forget it."

At first we stopped to examine only the big stuff, as promised, but when the big stuff wasn't panning out, Dad made me untie garbage sacks while he used a flashlight and a tire iron to poke through them.

"Good God," he said. "The things people eat!"

"I don't think this is a good idea," I said. "Why don't we go home?"

"Maybe you're right," he said. "Looks like a bad week for garbage. But don't go thinking that's a poor reflection of our fine country."

A block from our house, my father spotted three white beanbag chairs. They were next to a trashcan, piled one on top of the other. "Bingo!" he said.

"They're losing their beans," I said. "They look sort of, I don't know, *deflated*."

"Don't you see what they look like, though?" he said.

"What?"

"It looks just like a freaking snowman!" he said. "You can't see that?"

"Not really," I said. "No, I guess not."

"Use your imagination," Dad said. "Don't they teach you to use your imagination in school? A little paint for a face and it'll look just like a snowman. And the great thing is, it won't melt. All of our stupid neighbors will have to worry each and every time the sun comes out, but not us, no sir."

And so while my father revved the engine, I heaved each beanbag chair into the bed of the pick-up, where they looked, lying on their sides, more like a giant albino insect from a horror movie than a dozing snowman. A radioactive ant, I thought. The sort of thing that might push open our front door, shimmy inside, and eat our whole family alive.

·

Friday night, my father came home with a copy of the *Southtown Economist* and opened it up so that it covered the food Mom had put on the table. He said, "Look at this, ladies and germs." Steam from a plate of chicken legs was starting to make the paper sag, but Dad just snapped the paper back into shape and said, "A contest for the best holiday decorations on the South Side!"

Kelly said, "I can't get to the rolls, Dad."

Mom, frowning, said, "Where'd you find that paper?"

"Huh?"

"The paper? Where'd you get it?"

It was a good question; Dad never read the newspaper.

"Lucky's," Dad said.

Lucky's was the neighborhood tavern, and this past year my father had earned enough points from all the beer he'd bought that the bartender presented him with a wooden stein with his name on it. I'd never seen it because the stein, according to my father, remained at Lucky's on a shelf behind the bar along with all the other steins presented to those who earned the right. It was, Dad said, the highest honor Lucky's bestowed upon its customers.

"That paper's probably filthy," Mom said, "and now it's touching the food we're about to eat."

"Huh? Oh." Dad raised the paper higher, but one of its corners curled over, as if trying to lick Dad's plate.

"Look," he said. "The deadline's next Friday. The winner gets five hundred bones. Now, I don't want to knock our good neighbors or anything"—here, my father snickered; he hated our neighbors—"but the way I see it, any frickin' idiot can go to the Kmart and *buy* decorations." He looked at me. "Am I right, Hank? Sure I am. But not everyone can turn *nothing* into *something*. Which is what we're doing. The entry fee is only, let's see…" He rattled the paper a few times, leaning over and squinting. "Ah, here it is. Twenty-five bucks." He looked up and said, "Not a bad investment for a five hundred dollar payday. But me and Hank, we've got a hell of a lot of work to do before next Friday, don't we?"

I nodded.

Dad reached over the table and cuffed my shoulder. "My little apprentice," he said, then rolled up the dirty newspaper and swatted the top of my head with it.

Early Saturday morning, before anyone else was awake, I looked out my bedroom window and saw Ralph standing in the middle of the street. He wasn't wearing a coat. He was staring at our house, squinting and nodding, but I couldn't tell what he was thinking. Ralph lived in a shingled shotgun house with his mother, but since I'd never actually seen his mother, I sometimes wondered if he lived there alone, coming and going as he pleased. It was possible, I supposed. I wasn't going to ask, though. I was too polite to ask. Politeness, I was realizing, was my downfall.

"Ralph," I said after stepping outside, bundled up in my snorkel parka, the hood pulled up and unrolled so that it funneled out from my face at least a foot, narrowing into a small porthole and ending in a wreath of fake fur. "Is everything okay?" I asked through the hood's long tunnel.

"What?"

"IS EVERYTHING OKAY?" I yelled.

Ralph nodded.

I realized that I was standing next to the beanbag snowman, but I pretended not to notice it. I expected Ralph to ask what was happening to our house, but he didn't say a word. He lumbered quietly toward me, but his eyes were busy recording everything my father and I had done. A slight wind whispered past, and three dangling candy canes made out of plumbing pipes banged over my head. My father brought home red book-binding tape from work, and he wrapped the tape around each pipe to create the swirls and make them look more like candy canes, but they still looked like plumbing supplies.

Ralph said, "I'm broke, Hank. Dead broke. And then last night I saw some Christmas carolers going door-to-door and I had an idea."

I cringed. I always feared Ralph's ideas. I pictured myself, Ralph, and Ralph's two creepy older cousins, Kenny and Norm, knocking on people's doors and singing "Jingle Bells" for money. I didn't want any part of it.

"Look," I said. "I can't really sing, Ralph. I'm sort of tone deaf, if you want to know the truth."

Ralph said, "What are you talking about? We're not *singing*. Are you crazy?"

"Good," I said. I rolled back the tunneled hood so that I could see and hear Ralph better.

Ralph said, "Actually, I was wondering if you wanted to help me *jump* them so we could take their money."

"You want me to help you mug the Christmas carolers?" I asked.

Ralph shrugged. "Mug. Jump. *Whatever.*"

"Do people give money to them?" I asked.

"Sometimes," Ralph said. "Tips and whatnot. Plus, they probably have a little spending money of their own. You know, for juice or candy bars."

I wasn't going to help Ralph mug Christmas carolers, but when I asked how old they were, Ralph perked up. "Fourth graders," he said. "Fifth grade, tops. I promise. Now, the way I see it, we'll be outnumbered—there's got to be at least six of them—but two of them are chicks, and all of them are at least three years younger than you and five years younger than me."

Going door-to-door and shouting "Jingle Bells" off-key suddenly didn't sound so bad after all. "I don't know," I said. "I don't think it's a good idea."

Ralph said, "Yeah, well, maybe you're right. I guess six of them could do some damage to us, especially if they're carrying weapons."

"Weapons? What kind of weapons would a bunch of carolers have?"

"I don't know," Ralph said. "Could be anything. Steak knives, corkscrews, ice picks. Kids these days'll turn anything into a weapon." He sighed and shook his head. He seemed to be reconsidering the plan.

Relieved, I leaned against the beanbag snowman, which I realized was a mistake. Ralph's eyes had followed my elbow, stopping at the snowman's head. He reached out and, using his fingernail, scraped the face my father had painted yesterday after a late night at Lucky's. The paint was too thick in places, dripping at the corners of the snowman's eyes and mouth, causing it to look like a beanbag version of Alice Cooper. After chipping off some of the thicker clumps of paint, Ralph tucked his hands into his pockets.

I said, "Dad's entering the house in a Christmas decoration contest. The winner gets five hundred bucks."

Ralph, frowning and nodding, said, "So *that's* what's going on here."

"What did you think was going on?" I asked, acting offended.

"No, no," Ralph said. "I can see it now." He was walking backwards so as to take in the whole house at once. He said, "It looks like something Picasso would do."

Only last week we'd taken a school field trip to the Chicago Art Institute downtown to see the Picasso exhibit, but everyone was bored out of their skulls and no one really paid much attention. The next day at school, our art teacher said, "You should be ashamed of yourselves. All of you. You were looking at the work of a genius, but what did you care? You were bored, right?" and I made the mistake of nodding.

I assumed that Ralph, who had failed two grades, would have

been even more bored than the rest of us, but apparently this wasn't the case.

"Picasso?" I said. "You think so?"

"Absolutely," Ralph said. "Your father's a genius."

"*My* father?" I said. "A *genius*?"

Ralph nodded. He said, "But don't expect the judges of the contest to recognize that. That's the whole deal with being a genius. No one realizes you're one until you're dead."

I turned around and looked at the house. I wasn't sure that I saw what Ralph saw, but then I wasn't sure what the big deal was about Picasso, either, so what did I know?

Ralph said, "Listen. About the mugging. If you change your mind..."

"I don't think I'll be changing my mind," I said.

"You never know," Ralph said. "All I'm saying is, if you decide that you *do* want to jump a bunch of little kids who can't sing worth crap, come and get me."

It was getting colder out, so I rolled the snorkel parka hood out again and yelled, "WILL DO!"

The week before Christmas I asked my art teacher, Mrs. Richards, if I could borrow one of her books about Picasso. She eyed me suspiciously but then she looked anyway, digging through a pile of brushes, crepe paper, chunks of plaster and globs of clay until she found the book. "I expect this to be returned to me in the condition I'm giving it to you," she said.

That entire week, I had a hard time staying awake in school. I normally had problems staying awake, but this week I couldn't keep my eyes open because I was up until at least midnight every night helping my father.

Dad brought home sheets of plywood from work—"They'll

never miss it!"—but since we didn't own the appropriate tools for doing fancy edge-work, like curlicues, everything we made looked as though it had been attacked by a drunk man swinging an ax. But this, I was starting to realize, was part of Dad's genius.

"There!" he said. "Now, why don't we paint a holiday message on one of these. Not your usual holiday message. Something original."

I said, "What about 'Happy Christmas and Merry New Year'?"

Dad narrowed his eyes at me. He could tell that there was something wrong with what I'd said, but what I'd said wasn't so different from the original that he couldn't immediately tell what was different about it. A dozen empty Schlitz cans sat along a saw horse. Artists, I'd read in the Picasso book, were tortured by demons, and they often sought the company of alcohol and other substances. This explained why Dad had earned the beer stein at Lucky's. He was a tortured artist.

"No, no," Dad finally said at the suggestion of my holiday greeting. "Here. Hand me the spray-paint."

Before I could offer another suggestion, Dad started shaking the can.

"Tell me, kiddo," he said after he'd stopped shaking. "What's the first thing that comes to mind when you think of Argo."

Argo was two towns northwest, our football arch rival and home to Argo Corn Starch factory. On a day with only the slightest of breezes, the wind picked up the stench and carried it from town to town, causing those who didn't live with the corn starch smell on a daily basis to gag and run inside. It was the sort of smell that lodged itself into your nose and stayed there for days.

"It stinks," I said, "if that's what you mean."

"Exactly." He ruffled my hair, then started spraying. He sprayed so close to the board that the first letter looked like a blazing sun of hot tar, but then he backed up and tried again. "What do you think?" he said when he'd finished. In large block letters, the sign read: JINGLE BELLS, ARGO SMELLS!

"You sure you want to put this outside?" I asked.

"Absolutely," Dad said. "What this shows is town pride. That's always good for a few extra votes."

"Okay," I said. I helped Dad drag the enormous sheet of jagged-edged plywood out to the curb, and we leaned it against the mailbox.

Dad stood in the street to take a look. "That aughta do 'er," he said.

I imagined whole books written about my father and his art, each book including a chapter about his son, Hank, and how he was the only one in the entire Boyd family who understood the old man, and how much that had meant to the genius on his deathbed.

The next night, Dad said, "What have I been thinking? We keep checking the garbage in our own neighborhood when what we *should* be doing is checking out the hoity-toity neighborhoods."

"You're right!" I said, nearly yelling to show my enthusiasm.

We waited until dusk before tooling around Beverly, a Chicago neighborhood I didn't even know existed. Some houses were smeared in stucco and had roofs made of orange tiles instead of shingles, the kind of tiles that looked like flower pots cut in half. I'd seen houses like these on TV shows that were set in California or Florida, but I'd never seen any in Chicago before. The streets had been plowed all the way to the concrete, the excess snow lugged away. I couldn't imagine where it had been taken, though. The curbs were lined with garbage cans—large, squarish plastic cans placed neatly side-by-side. No slumping Hefty bags. No punctured Glad bags oozing intestines of spaghetti. But there were also no large items here—no appliances, no bicycles. Did these people buy things that didn't break so easily? Or had someone already beaten us here, someone who knew the best time to swoop in and pick through the hoity-toity's trash?

Dad said, "We better take a closer look. No telling what they're storing in those trash cans."

"Really?" I said. "You think?"

"Absolutely. I didn't burn all this gas to come here and admire their lawns."

"I don't want to pick through garbage anymore," I said, a whine creeping into my voice.

"Oh, okay," Dad said. "I see. You're embarrassed to be with your own father."

"No, that's not it," I said.

Dad held up his hand, palm out, as if to say, *Halt!* He said, "I didn't think it would ever come to this, but then, I don't know why not. I was embarrassed by my old man, too. He was senile and sometimes went out in public without his pants on, but maybe I should have gone a little easier on him, the crazy old coot."

The knife-stab of guilt punctured me. Who was I to thwart my father's project? Picking through garbage was a small price to pay for being in the company of genius, so I told him okay, that I would do it.

"No, you don't have to," he said. "I wouldn't want to embarrass you."

"Stop it," I said. "I said I'd do it."

Can after can, I raised the lid while my father aimed the flashlight inside. Each and every bag was neatly shut with twist ties, so my father gave me his Swiss Army knife with the pair of minuscule scissors for me to snip the heads off, allowing my father to poke about with his trusty tire-iron. The tire-iron was such a useful tool, I was starting to wonder why I didn't own one myself. I was about to ask my father if I could have one for Christmas when a police cruiser rolled up and flipped on its swirling lights.

My father's face alternated between blue and red.

The cop got out, shining a flashlight into our faces, and said, "How are you gentleman doing tonight?"

My father lifted his flashlight, shined it into the cop's face, and said, "Just fine. And yourself?"

"Put your flashlight down, sir!" the cop called out, squinting. "*Now!*"

Under his breath, my father said, "They don't like it when you do to them what they do to you." He lowered the flashlight.

The cop came over, took a good long look at me, then looked down at the Swiss Army knife in my hand. He cut his eyes to my father and said, "Looking for food?"

My father laughed. "What, do we look like hobos? Do we look like vagrants? Ha! That's a good one. No, my son and I are looking for *junk.*"

"Junk? What kind of junk?"

"The kind of junk a person can use to decorate his house."

The cop nodded. It was clear he didn't know what my father was talking about. He said, "Look, sir, I'm going to let you go with a warning. But you can't be coming here, rooting around other people's trash. The people here, they don't like it."

"Tough," my dad said. "The law says that once you throw something out, it's fair game. Isn't that the law where *you* live, too? I bet it is. Unless, of course, you live in one of *these* houses. Hank, do you think the officer lives in one of these houses?" Though the question was directed at me, my father didn't move his eyes from the cop. He snorted and, before I could answer, said, "Nope, I don't *think* so."

"Don't get smart," the cop said.

I snickered. Little did he know that he was telling a genius not to get smart.

The cop said, "I see you're raising your kid well, too."

While the cop lectured my father, I reached into one of the garbage cans and pulled out a photo of a family. The photo had been glued onto a piece of artificial wood so that it would look like a slice of tree. In the photo was a father, mother, daughter, and son. Amazingly, the family looked like my family. It was dark out and I couldn't see it all that well, but I could tell that the boy was about my age and the girl was about Kelly's size and shape. The parents, though better dressed, could have been my parents. I looked at the house where the photo had come from, but the lights were out and I couldn't see anyone moving around inside.

"Ah, forget it," my father said to the cop. "We'll go. There's no good junk around here, anyway. Isn't that right, Hank?"

I nodded.

The cop wrote up a warning and handed it to my father. He told us that he didn't want to see us around here again.

"Not a problem," my father said. As the cop walked back to his cruiser, my father looked down at the photo that I was holding and said, "What the hell's that?"

"A family portrait," I said, handing it to him. "Look familiar?"

Dad studied it a moment. "Nope," he said and tossed it back in the trash.

Inside the truck, my father handed the warning to me and told me to stuff it in the glove compartment. I popped it open and a dozen other warnings sprung out onto my lap. My father said, "Don't make a mess, you hear? Just cram everything inside and slam it shut."

I couldn't sleep that night, so I stood up and touched my toes a few times. Our gym teacher had told us that a good way to keep in shape was to do some sort of exercise whenever you were bored, and since I was bored all the time, I was always touching my toes. There were times when my mother or my father would be talking to me, and I'd reach down and touch my toes. Lately, every time my sister opened her mouth to say something, I'd reach down and touch my toes before she could get the first word out. Tonight, I touched my toes three times. When I raised up the third time, I saw Ralph standing across the street and taking notes. I had no idea how long he'd been there. It was two in the morning. I knocked on the window. Ralph looked up, saw me, and quickly folded his pocket notebook.

I put on my snorkel parka and shoes, then tiptoed downstairs. "What are you doing here?" I asked, shivering in the street.

"The house is looking sweet. How's Pablo?"

"*Who?*"

"Your dad," Ralph said.

"Oh. He's okay." Since Ralph seemed to know so much about art, I decided to impress him by quoting a line of Picasso's that I had committed to memory. I cleared my throat. "You know," I said from inside the cave of my snorkel hood. "We all know that Art is not truth. Art is a lie that makes us realize the truth, at least the truth that is given to us to understand."

"Whatever," Ralph said. "Hey, listen, I was wondering if you'd thought anymore about jumping those carolers. We're only a few days away from Christmas, so our window of opportunity is, you know, shrinking by the second."

"That's why you came by?" I asked.

"Naw. I came by to check out the house, see how it's coming along. But now that you're out here, I figured I'd see where you were leaning on the issue of the carolers." Ralph grinned, waiting.

"I don't think I'm up to it. I've been working a lot of late nights." I nodded toward the house.

Ralph said, "Yeah, well, I figured as much. The thing is, I've got a back-up plan to make some money. It's a long-shot, though. Not like the carolers. The carolers were a sure thing."

My fingers were starting to feel like icicles attached to larger blocks of ice. I said, "I better go inside."

Ralph nodded. "Go ahead. I'll only be a few more minutes."

Back in my bedroom, I peeked out my window again and saw Ralph scratching out a few more notes. What was he writing? Before I could shut the curtain, though, he caught me watching him. I started to wave, but he quickly tucked the pad into his pocket and headed toward home.

The day before the judges were to drive around and evaluate the houses, my father stayed home from work to put on the final touches. My parents' voices occasionally floated up through the vents, and I heard my mother say at one point, "Frank, you can't afford to stay home from work."

"Don't worry about it," Dad said. "I've got enough sick time built up to get a brain transplant. Trust me. It's no biggie."

I had woken up that morning coughing and shivering, unable to concentrate on any one thing for more than a second. The flu had come to visit me in the night. I tried touching my toes, but halfway over I felt like puking. I ran to the bathroom and locked myself inside. Eventually, Dad came pounding at the door.

"Ready to give me a hand, big guy?" he asked.

"I don't feel too good," I said.

"Very funny, Buster," Dad said. "The judges'll be here tonight. I need your help." When I opened the door, my father took a step back. "Whoa!"

"It's the flu," I said.

Instead of offering words of comfort, he was out of the doorway and yelling down the stairs, "Hey, Momma Bear, your son's got the flu! He looks like death warmed over!"

When Mom finally came up to check on me, she was carrying a bowl of hot soup and four Flintstone chewable vitamins. She pulled out a thermometer, shook it a few thousand times, then stabbed the underside of my tongue with its silver point. When she slid it out, she said, "Poor kid. One hundred and three." I groaned. Mom said, "Here, drink your soup and take your vitamins. I've got to make sure your father doesn't set the house on fire. That man's driving me to an early grave, I swear." Before she left, she said, "Call me if you need something." As I popped two Freds, a Barney, and a Wilma into my mouth, I heard Kelly say, "You're faking it," and then she appeared to appraise my illness. She was still wearing army boots, but she also had on a camouflage jacket and matching pants. All she needed was some green and black make-up for her face, and we could throw her into a jungle somewhere. "What excuse did you and Dad cook up today?" she asked. "The flu?"

"Listen, G.I. Joe," I said. "I don't have to prove to you that I'm sick. I have a fever of one hundred and three."

She rolled her eyes. Then she took a step closer and said, "Why aren't you outside helping Dad destroy the house we live in?"

"Destroy?" I said. I laughed. It wasn't worth explaining to her about Picasso, about the tortured nature of artists, about how great art always goes unappreciated at first.

Kelly, without any inflection in her voice, said, "I've always wanted to be the laughing stock of the neighborhood. I'd like to thank you and Dad for helping me to achieve that goal."

"No problem," I said. "Anytime. But you didn't really need our help," I added.

Kelly stuck both hands into her camouflage jacket. I worried that maybe she'd bought an army-issue pistol, a sleek black job with a silencer, but she kept her hands hidden and backed out of the room, ghostlike, leaving me to shiver and hallucinate in peace.

Periodically, I'd peek out the window to see what Dad was up to. Twice, a black Monte Carlo with tinted windows crept slowly past the house. A judge, I thought.

All day I drifted in and out of sleep, freezing one minute, boiling the next. Mom occasionally poked her head into the room to check on me, though I was pretty certain that I had hallucinated some of those times, especially when the door opened slightly and I saw only an eye, part of an arm, and the first few inches of a foot, her body broken apart like one of Picasso's paintings, nothing whole, nothing as it should have been.

It was after midnight when my father finally finished with the house. I waited for Dad to come get me so that we could look at it together. I waited and waited, but apparently they thought I was too sick. Everyone had already gone to bed by the time I made my way downstairs in my pajamas. "Hello?" I whispered. "Anybody awake?" I was dizzy from the flu, dizzy from being in bed all day, dizzy from not eating as much as I should have, but I really wanted to see the house so I put on the first coat I found—it turned out to be one of my mother's coats, knee-length and insulated—and I slipped on a pair of my father's too-big muck-lucks.

As soon as I stepped outside, wind blew sheets of snow at me, pelting my face, and I had to duck my head just to make it out into the street. Snow blew up the legs of pajamas, causing me to shiver, but I still had a fever and the cold air felt sort of good, too. I shut my eyes and turned around, preparing myself to take in the whole house at once, and then I opened my eyes. The moon, full and low, lit up our house.

"Holy smoke," I said. I shivered harder, but it wasn't from the cold this time. Dad had transformed our house into a masterpiece. And like most masterpieces, it was hard to put into words *why* it was a masterpiece; it just was. I remember reading in the Picasso book that Modern art wasn't scientific and it wasn't intellectual; it was visual. And when it came from the eye of a genius like my dad, any fool should have been able to see that they were looking at the real deal. As best as I could tell, Dad's vision was this: Christmas gave everyone a good beating—the way the flattened reindeer leaned against the TV antenna, or the way that the plumbing pipe candy canes swung heavily in the wind, or how the trolls that could barely be seen appeared to be climbing down the drain pipe at the corners of the house, as if escaping the long, brutal hours of Santa's workshop.

It was chilling, really, and I found myself wanting to weep right there at both the beauty and the sadness of it all, but before I could squeeze out the first tears, the black Monte Carlo with its smoky windows came rolling up to the house. The judges could finally look at Dad's vision of Christmas and see for themselves how great it was, but when the windows rolled down, I saw that the people inside weren't judges at all. It was a group of high school punks.

The doors opened and all four guys got out. They walked over to our Christmas greeting, and the driver said, "Jingle bells, Argo smells." He looked up at me. "Argo smells, huh?"

I wasn't sure what to say. It *did* smell. I said, "Sort of."

"*Sort of?* Well, *we're* from Argo and *we* don't think it smells." He kicked our sign.

I was about to tell him how sometimes you couldn't smell something bad when you were standing in the middle of it, and I was going to give him a few examples when one of the guys pushed me.

"Look," he said. "He's wearing a woman's coat. He's making fun of the place we live and he's wearing a woman's coat."

"It's my mother's," I began explaining, but a fist met my stomach with such force that I was knocked clean out of my father's muck-lucks. Before I could plead with them, I was surrounded by the rest of the punks and more fists landed against my ribs and my back. Oddly enough, it wasn't as bad as I'd expected, and after they had sped off in their car, I didn't feel hurt so much as sleepy. One minute, I was sitting in a mound of snow, leaning against the now-busted ARGO SMELLS sign, considering taking a nap. The next minute, the police were at our house, I was inside with a blanket wrapped around me, and some guy with a stethoscope was shining a penlight into my eyes. My father was pacing the living room and yelling about how he was going to kill the jerks who broke his sign.

"What's wrong?" I asked.

"Oh, honey," Mom said. "Oh, sweetie. Are you okay?"

"I'm fine," I said.

My father said, "I want blood!"

A short and stocky cop who looked like he might have been a high school wrestler said, "Mr. Boyd. You're going to have to calm down, sir."

Another cop, this one older and with a walrus mustache, came inside, blowing into his palms to warm up. He said something, but you couldn't see his lips moving because of the thick mustache bristles. He looked around, as if maybe he'd stepped into the wrong house, then said, "There's another little problem we'll need to discuss."

"What's that?" my father asked.

"It's a matter of the, uh, *junk* you've got lying around."

"Junk? What junk?"

"Let's see." While he looked at his notepad, he tapped around the bottom edge of his mustache with the tip of his tongue. I'm sure it was an old habit, checking for crumbs, and I could imagine his wife saying, *Honey, you've got a chunk of cake on your...right there...good...you got it!* He said, "Those three old beanbag chairs? That violates the upholstered furniture ordinance. That loose sheet of metal up on the roof is a hazard. A good wind could take that down and slice somebody's head off. As for that huge wooden spool, that appears to be the property of the telephone company. Do you work for the telephone company, Mr. Boyd?"

"I don't see your point," Dad said.

"The point," the cop said, "is that I have a list here. It's about four pages long. There are ordinances about maintaining your property, and you're in violation of most of them."

"Maintaining my property?" my father said. "What, are you *crazy*? Those are decorations!"

The cop looked down at his notepad again. "I think maybe we're talking about different things here," he said. "What I'm talking about is all that *junk* out there. I can show you the list, but I don't think you need to see it. I called the department, and according to our records we issued a warning last week."

"You did?"

The cop nodded. "It's supposed to be cleaned up by tomorrow. There's a stiff fine if it's *not* cleaned up." He stuck out his tongue again, as if to do some more checking, but then thought better of it. He nodded, looked around the house, same as he did when he first arrived, then walked backwards to the front door and let himself out. It was like watching a movie in reverse.

"Clean it up?" I yelled. "You *can't* make him clean it up. My dad's a genius! What's wrong with you people?"

The stocky wrestler-cop pivoted his torso toward me, sizing me up. He said, "The poor kid's still delirious."

My father, using a stage whisper, said, "Hank, take it easy there, pal."

"He must have suffered some brain damage." This came from Kelly. She was sitting in a corner, knees pulled up to her neck, wearing an army helmet I'd never seen before. Had she been there the whole time?

My mother said, "What about my son? What are you going to do about that?"

"Oh yeah. Right. Well, sounds like a bunch of teenagers from another town and, well, there's not a lot you can do. If you see them again, though, give us a call."

My mother nodded but her fists were clenched.

After they left, my father said, "Cops! I bet both they have their own houses entered in the contest. You just watch when the results come in," he said, putting on his coat and heading outside with a crowbar. "Wouldn't surprise me one bit, no sir."

When I woke up the next day—the day that the judges were to visit each house—I thought that I had dreamed all that had happened the night before, but when I stood up and felt the bruised muscles, the ache in my ribs, I realized that all of it had really happened. I opened my curtains and gasped. Next to the curb were all the decorations that Dad and I had carefully selected. Piled the way it was, it looked like what it really was—*junk*.

Downstairs, I asked Mom where Dad was.

"Work."

"Work?" I said. The idea of Dad doing something as ordinary as going to work depressed me.

"He gets time-and-a-half today," Mom said. "That's nothing to sneeze at."

"I need to go somewhere," I said.

"Oh, no," Mom said. "Yesterday you had a temperature over one hundred. You're not going anywhere today, mister."

I wanted to argue, but I knew who'd win. The more you argued with Mom, the harder she dug in. Before you knew it, you'd be locked in a room and chained to a bed, wishing you'd kept your mouth shut.

"Okie doke," I said.

I waited until Dad had come home, until we'd all finished eating, before sneaking away. While everyone thought that I was calling it an early night, I slipped out the back door and put on my snorkel parka, which I had dumped behind some bushes earlier that day. What I hadn't counted on was the parka becoming frozen from being outside. The arms were stiff, and I was colder with it on than with it off. I might as well have tied it to a rope and stored it in Lake Michigan.

I kept it on, though, hoping that my shivering would generate some heat, which it did. I needed to see Ralph. He was the only other person who'd understand what an outrage it was that my father was forced to ruin his masterpiece.

As I rounded the corner of Ralph's street, the first thing that I saw was Ralph's cousin's Nova. Both cousins, Kenny and Norm, were sitting on the trunk and drinking beer. They each lived in apartments that were furnished with things they'd made in shop class in high school. Kenny had a lamp whose shade was a Budweiser can with the top sliced off. Norm had a plywood coffee table that had been covered with pages from *Hot Rod* magazine and then lacquered.

When I got closer I saw that Ralph had decorated his mother's house for the contest. What wasn't immediately apparent was what holiday he had decorated the house in honor of.

Oil drums with ten foot flames shooting out of them lined the sidewalk. A glowing six-foot statue of Jesus held a Roman Candle. I was about to yell out to Ralph, but a Roman candle shot from Jesus' hand and whistled into the sky. Ralph then removed a bedsheet to reveal a life-sized manger. Painted on the side of the manger was what appeared at first glance to be an angel but what, on closer inspection, was actually the logo that Led Zeppelin used for their Swan Song record label.

"I did that," Kenny said, pointing.

Inside the manger was a statue that used to stand outside of a Big Boy restaurant. Next to it was a blow-up Frankenstein doll.

Norm said, "Now *that's* the real spirit of Christmas, folks."

"What's it mean?" I asked.

Kenny said, "It means that life is screwed up. It means that life is weirder than any of us'd ever imagined." He finished his beer, tossed the can into a neighbor's yard, and said, "Hand me another one, little man."

Four more Roman Candles whistled into the night sky, but when one of the still-sizzling fireworks came spiraling back down and hit the manger, the whole thing went up in flames.

"Holy crap," Kenny said. "Get a fire extinguisher."

Norm said, "No, no, man. It's working. This is the way it should be."

By the time the firetrucks arrived, the manger had burnt to the snow and the fire had all but extinguished itself. Ralph stood next to me while the firemen hosed off the oil drums.

"I figured it'd come down to me and your father for first and second place," he said. "Your old man's stiff competition, though."

"Not anymore," I said, and I explained to Ralph what had happened.

I expected Ralph to get more worked up, but all he did was shake his head. Then he slapped me on the back and said, "At least it's good to know that genius runs in your family. From what I've read it skips a generation, but think about your kids, Hank."

Two cops, the same from last night, walked over to Ralph and handed him a ticket. "You're lucky we're not taking you to jail, pal." The cop with the walrus mustache squinted at me and said, "Haven't I arrested you before?"

"No, sir," I said, but the cop didn't believe me. Twice, on his way back to the patrol car, he turned to look at me, as if trying to remember my crime.

"Now what am I going to do?" Ralph said. "I sort of counted on that prize money." He shook his head and sighed. "Give your old man my regards. From one genius to another."

I nodded. "Will do," I said. Ralph and I shook hands, then Ralph wandered over to Kenny and Norm, who were taking stock of the frozen but still smoking lawn.

On my way home, I passed house after house with their strings of blinking lights, the occasional illuminated Santa waving from a front stoop. I hadn't realized until now just how dull people were, how utterly dull and unimaginative. I was so mad that I wanted to break every window sprayed with fake snow. I wanted to set fire to every wreath on every door. I started packing a snowball when I heard them—their voices glorious, angelic—and then I saw them: pudgy faces red from the cold but beaming, their eyes shining in the moonlight, these eight boys and girls at the height of their musical powers. Carolers! I was at one street corner; they were at the other. My arms went limp, and the snowball fell from my hand. I'd thought that they were going in my direction but then they turned, heading where I had just been, marching joyously toward the smoke and the smell of sulfur. I wanted to warn them about Ralph and his cousins, but as soon as one song ended, they began belting out another without pausing to catch their breaths. Their singing was mightier than ever, and the smallest of the eight children, ringing his bell loud enough to rouse even the shyest of ghosts, turned and waved at me, and I waved back.

10

The truth was that before Ralph, I didn't really have any friends. Real friends. Until the middle of first grade, I'd had two imaginary friends, Raymond and Krogerly. Raymond was the friend who always did things I might get in trouble for doing, like wetting my pants. "Raymond did it," I told my mom the first time it happened, as if I were stating something that was simply a fact and, therefore, out of my hands. "There *is* no Raymond," she said, and I tilted my head and silently stared up at her, the way you regarded people who were clearly crazy. "Oh-*kay*," I said, slowly backing away from her.

Raymond was also my middle name, but I chalked this up as nothing more than a coincidence.

My other imaginary friend was Krogerly. My mother did all of her grocery shopping at Kroger, and I suspect Krogerly was born during one of those torturously long and soul-crushing afternoons when I begged my mother to let me sit inside the shopping cart. "You're too big," she told me. "Plus, you've got legs. If you didn't have legs, I'd let you sit in the cart, but you've got legs, so you can walk." Krogerly was the *good* imaginary friend, the one who played Hot Wheels with me, who told jokes that made me laugh so hard I shot milk out my nose.

"What's so funny, Hank?" my father asked one night at dinner.

"Krogerly just said something funny," I said.

My father looked over at my mother, who shrugged and said, "It's his imaginary friend." My father, who didn't have any friends, real or imaginary, nodded. He resumed eating but occasionally glanced up in case Krogerly happened to materialize.

My sister, Kelly, who was nine years old at the time, reached over and punched the empty space beside me.

"Hey!" I yelled. "You're *hitting* him!" She punched again. And then again. "*Mom*," I yelled. "Kelly's punching Krogerly!"

"Both of you had better cut it out," Mom warned, "unless you each want an enema."

Neither of us knew what an enema was, exactly, but we'd seen the equipment under the sink—a giant deflated rubber pillow with a long tube. Mom knew that we didn't know what it was, but she also knew that it scared us. I had assumed that the red rubber pillow would be filled with hot water and then, after the tube had been tied off so that water couldn't leak out, Mom would chase us around the house, swinging it at us. At the mere mention of the word enema, Kelly quit punching my best friend and silently ate the rest of her TV dinner.

I wish I could say that their deaths, Raymond's and Krogerly's, were peaceful, that one day I woke up while they continued to sleep, drifting away into nothingness, but this was not the case. The real problems began when I started taking them to school with me, both at the same time. Even while Raymond was busy wetting my pants, Krogerly would tell a joke out loud, except his jokes had stopped being funny. In fact, they weren't really jokes at all; they were insults, like "Look at his nose!" or "Good Lord, the *face* on that woman!" Krogerly must have been hanging around my father since these were the exact same things Dad always said about people. Where my father said these things out of earshot, Krogerly preferred saying them mere inches from the people he insulted, most of whom were my teachers.

"Mr. Boyd!" Mrs. Waterman yelled one morning before school, gripping my shoulder and pushing me to the side of the playground. "I want you to go to the principal's office and tell *him* what you said about my—what did you call them?—my *big, ugly feet.*"

The ghost-pinch of Mrs. Waterman's fingers remained on my shoulder all the way to Mr. Santoro's, and by the time I reached his office, Raymond had peed my pants again.

"Oh, no," said Mrs. Rokitis, the office secretary, when I entered. "Poor little guy."

"Who stinks in here?" Krogerly asked even as tears streaked my face. "Somebody's perfume smells like a dead skunk."

Mrs. Rokitis cocked her head, squinting, as if she too were hearing voices. "Okay, young man," she finally said. "In the office. But don't sit down. The chairs aren't upholstered in plastic." She resumed typing.

Standing alone in the principal's office, face and crotch both wet, I felt betrayed by my imaginary friends. Why had they turned on me? What had I ever done to them? When Mr. Santoro finally came in, he took one look at me and said, "Who turned the fire hose on, son?"

I didn't know what he was talking about, so I started crying loudly. I cried so hard, I couldn't catch my breath. Each time I tried slowing my breath, I would suddenly suck in all the air I could, sounding like something inhuman. It reminded me of the time I tried talking while breathing in and my mother ordered me to stop. My voice, she claimed, was making the hair on her neck stand on end.

Mr. Santoro took a step toward me, and I screamed. I was seven years old, and adults scared me. Not just teachers, either. *All* adults. The crossing guard lady who was going bald and touched my earlobe every time I walked by her. The employee at Certified

Grocers who swatted at me with his broom when I took down a
can of creamed corn to look at it. Old guys in New Castle Park
who wanted me to sit with them. My aunts who pinched my cheeks
too hard, leaving small bruises. My uncle who ordered me to pull
his finger, which inexplicably caused him to fart loudly. I was even
afraid of my own parents, who hated my aunts and uncles and who
didn't know about the old guys in the park or the crossing guard or
the broom guy. It didn't make a difference who they were. Adults
were adults. They all said and did things that didn't make any sense
to me, each and every one of them, and they always looked mad,
even when they laughed—a series of loud, barking *haw-haw-haw*s
punctuated by explosive coughs that turned their faces bright red.

"Okay, okay," Mr. Santoro said. "That's enough for now. Easy,
boy. Easy."

The next day, instead of going to Mrs. Waterman's class, I was taken
to a small office in the wing of the school where the older kids'
classes were held. There, I met a fat man in a dark suit. He had a
thick gray-and-black beard and eyebrows that curled out from his
head as if they were trying to escape the body from which they
grew. He wheezed when he breathed.

"Hello, *Hank*!" My name came out high and pinched at
the end, like a man stricken by an unexpected and sharp pain. I
imagined someone hiding under his desk, punching him hard in
the gut. "My name's Dr. Stump. Like a tree." When I didn't so much
as blink, he wheezed, "*A tree stump*."

I didn't know what he was talking about and wanted to cry,
but I held back. "Tree stump," I repeated.

"Good!" he yelled. "Good! Good!" Squinting, he put the tips
of his fingers together and peered over them. He said, "I'm not the
kind of doctor you go to when you have a cold, Hank. No siree. I'm

the kind of doctor you see when, well, when you've got too much on your mind and need to talk." He pointed to his head. "When your noggin's all filled up and you need to let something out of it."

"Oh," I said.

"Can we talk about your friends?" he said. "Raymond? Is that right? And who's the other fellow with the funny name?"

"Krogerly?" I asked flatly. I didn't see anything funny about Krogerly's name.

"Ah, yes. It was *Krogerly* who made fun of Mrs. Waterman's feet yesterday, wasn't it? That's what you told Mr. Santoro, am I correct?"

I nodded.

"She *does* have pretty big feet, doesn't she?" Dr. Stump said.

"I think she's beautiful," I said.

"Oh, really? Hm. Okay." He cleared his throat. "So, tell me about this Krogerly fellow. Unless you'd rather begin with Raymond. Are you better friends with one than the other? Do you spend as much time with Krogerly as you do Raymond? Talk to me, Hank. Don't be shy. You can trust me. I'm sure I'm not as charming as Raymond and Krogerly, but don't let that stop you. Tell me all about them, Hank. Tell me everything."

And so I did. I told him everything about my two best friends.

"And then there was this time," I began at the top of our third hour together, but Dr. Stump, whose eyebrows had begun to fold over, like two furry hands clutching the edge of a cliff, raised his palm up to stop me.

"I've heard enough, son," he said.

My feelings were hurt, but I didn't say anything. He was right. He *wasn't* as charming as Raymond or Krogerly, and Krogerly wanted to tell him so, but I managed to stop him in time.

What Dr. Stump did was set up daily meetings with me. Every day, for the next two weeks, I trudged to his office and did what he asked me to do. I put round pegs into holes. I answered questions about everything I'd ever done or thought about in my life. I stared into his penlight, following it with my eyes without moving my head. When he showed me a blotch of ink on a sheet of paper and asked me what came to mind, I told him that it looked like a spider. When he showed me another one, I told him that it, too, looked like a spider. He showed me three more. Spider, spider, spider, I told him.

"Are you afraid of spiders?" he asked.

"Nope."

He leaned toward me. "What *does* scare you, Hank?"

"You," I said, and Dr. Stump leaned back quickly.

"I thought we were friends," he said, sounding hurt.

"Why?" I asked.

"I don't know," he said. "You opened up to me. You told me all about Krogerly and Raymond."

"Do *you* have friends?" I asked.

"Not many," he confessed. "Not as many as I would like."

"Is Mr. Santoro your friend?"

Dr. Stump snorted. "Ha!" he said. "Who's asking, you or Krogerly? Hey, listen, I could tell you a thing or two about that man. You want to talk about your delusions of grandeur? You want to talk about your displaced anger? He's a walking time-bomb. He's a human landmine." I was nodding, trying to take it all in, when a dark look crossed Dr. Stumps's face. "No, seriously," he said. He leaned forward, fat arms stretched across the desk, and said, "I used to be his shrink. I did." He wagged his head. His double chin jiggled. "How do you think I landed this sweet gig? Knowledge is power, Hank. Knowledge is power." He quit talking and stared at me for a good while, the only sound in the room his tortured breathing. He finally leaned back and said, "But why am I telling *you* all of this? Who's the doctor here? You or me?"

I shrugged.

"You'd better go, little man," he said. "I think we've covered enough for one day, don't you?"

I opened the door to leave, and there stood Mr. Santoro. He put his hand on top of my head then moved it to the space between my shoulders and said, "Go back to class, Hank." He didn't look down at me. He was staring into the dark, tiny room at Dr. Stump. "Go on now," he said, gently shoving me away.

The rest of my appointments with Dr. Stump were cancelled. The next time I saw someone walking out of his office, it was the janitor pushing Dr. Stump's desk out the door. The desk lay on its side, and the janitor cursed under his breath the whole time he pushed it. Watching him trying to fit the desk through the door reminded me of all those pegs I was given, and how Dr. Stump had started writing something as soon as I'd put that first round peg into a round hole. While he furiously scribbled away in his notebook, I pocketed three of the pegs, one for me and one each for my best friends, and when Dr. Stump finally looked up at me, I placed a square peg into the square hole and smiled at him, and he smiled back.

Not long after Dr. Stump disappeared, my imaginary friends' days were numbered. It was one of those Chicago winter days where the wind whips up snow that's already on the ground, sending it into everyone's faces and causing them to go blind. I was putting on the snowsuit that my mother had bought me at the Sear's Outlet store near Midway Airport. I liked going to that part of the city because it looked like a ghost town with all of its old crumbling hotels, but my mother always insisted that I lock my doors. "Nothing but hoods around here," she'd say. I knew she meant criminals, but I also thought she meant criminals who *wore* hoods, and so for years, whenever I saw someone wearing any kind of hood, I feared they were going to club me over the head and take whatever I had in my pockets. My snowsuit from Sears Outlet had been sewn all wrong, which was why it was so cheap. I could barely walk in it. The entire puffy attire twisted around me, strangling my body's trunk, like an inflatable python.

"I'm *choking*," I gasped when I had put it on that snowy day. "I can't *breathe*."

When my father saw me, he asked my mother why she didn't buy him one, too.

"How am I supposed to know what in God's name you want me to buy you when you won't even come along?" she asked.

"I'm just saying," my father said, but then he quit talking. He put on his thin jacket and stocking cap, but before he left, he said, "To hell with you people," and walked out the door.

"Maybe he needs an enema," I offered.

Mom looked down at me. "Maybe *you* do, if you keep complaining," she said.

I quit complaining. I wobbled outside and onto our front lawn. We lived in the smallest house on a street of mostly small houses. Across the street, however, sat a large, old house—the largest and oldest on the block—but it wasn't a nice house. My father called it an eye-sore, and whenever my mother saw someone going into it or leaving she would say, "How can people *live* like that?" Wind sucked trash out of their lidless garbage cans and sent old Kleenex, newspapers, and hamburger wrappers orbiting their house like bewildered ghosts. The lawn was mostly dirt, and broken toys lay scattered about for years at a time. Though I was only seven, I was certain that the handlebars to a bicycle, minus the bike, had leaned against a cellar window since the day, cradled in my mother's arms, my eyes had first come into focus. Each year the handlebars got rustier, serving no purpose to either man or machine. I finally asked my father about them one day.

"What handlebars?" he asked.

"Those ones there," I said, pointing.

"Never saw 'em before," he said.

The day my father told us all to go to hell, I decided to walk across my mysterious neighbor's snow-dirt lawn and touch those handlebars. My mother and father had never told me I couldn't go over onto their lawn and touch their stuff, so once I had set my mind to do it, I didn't hesitate.

While crossing the street, I saw my sister biking toward our house. Why she was riding her bike in the snow, I didn't know. I paused respectfully to let her by, but Raymond told me to walk in front of her, so I did.

"Hey, watch it, bub!" she yelled, swerving, almost falling. She biked up the slick driveway, disappearing into the garage that was too small for a car. Krogerly, who found everything funny, snickered into my ear.

When I reached the first patch of snow and dirt, I pretended that I was stepping onto the moon. I was almost four years old when men landed on the moon, and I'd watched it on TV, sitting in a chair that rested on its back so that I could pretend that I was inside the capsule along with them. I'd had a glass of Tang within reach, and I chewed a chalky chocolate stick for nourishment. Moon food. Ever since then, I loved all things about the moon, and whenever the opportunity presented itself to me, I pretended that I was walking on the moon. I even tried to make myself light, walking on my toes and moving in slow-motion. And that's what I was doing that day, stuffed into my misstitched snowsuit, wind blowing so hard I could barely keep my eyes open: I took unbearably slow steps, and each time a foot touched the ground, my arms floated up from my sides and then down again. Up! Then *down*. That's when I noticed a boy, maybe three years older than me, staring at me from the open doorway. Next to him was a much older kid smoking. Why they had the door to their house open on a day as cold as this one was a mystery to me.

"What're you supposed to be? A giant bird?" the older boy asked.

"I'm an astronaut," I said.

"What're you doin' on our property?" he asked. I could tell someone older had taught him to ask this, the way my father had taught me to ask the cashier at White Hen Pantry for a carton of Lucky Strikes so that he, my father, could sit in the car and keep the engine running.

"I wanna see those handlebars," I told the boy.

"What handlebars?"

When I pointed, he walked all the way outside to take a look. He wasn't wearing a shirt or shoes. His bellybutton stuck out like the stem of a pumpkin, but it looked more fleshy, almost like someone's finger, and I imagined a smaller kid inside him, trapped and sticking his pinkie out, trying to get someone's attention. He peered around the corner of his own house. He shrugged at the sight of the handlebars.

"You from around here?" he asked.

I pointed at the house across the street, but the way he looked at it, there might as well have been nothing there at all.

"Gotta name?" he asked.

"Hank," I said.

"I'm George. And that's my brother Pig," he said, pointing. I wanted to ask him how he got the name Pig, but then I saw that Pig's nose was weirdly flattened so that you could see directly inside his nostrils. From what I could tell, his nose was the only pig-like thing about him, but who knew? "Pig and I are watching TV," George said. "Want to come in?"

My parents had told me never to go anywhere with adults I didn't know, but they never said anything about not going somewhere with other kids, so I climbed the stairs and followed George into his house. I could feel Raymond and Krogerly walking behind me, but they said nothing.

"You want the door shut?" I asked. No one answered, so I left it wide open, as it had been.

The first thing I noticed was the smell. On the one hand, I wanted to escape the smell, whatever it was; I wanted to run back outside, where the air smelled like air. On the other hand, the smell was so bad it fascinated me. It held me in place, and I couldn't stop breathing it in; I couldn't get enough of it.

It was like the time my mother bought a carton of milk that had already gone bad and she made everyone take a whiff. "Does this smell bad to you?" she asked, passing it under our noses, and we each jerked quickly back, but then Kelly and I smelled it again and again. My father said, "Why the hell are you making us smell it if it's bad?" but Mom didn't answer. That's how she was, always wanting us to smell bad things. "Come here," she'd say to me or Kelly, "and smell these leftovers," or "Smell these clothes. Do they smell funny?" When we drove through Argo, home of the eye-watering Argo Corn Starch factory, she would take a deep breath and make a tortured face: "Eww. Smell that," she'd say, rolling down her window. I imagined my mother inside George and Pig's house right now, taking a deep breath through her nose and squinting, forcing each of us to do the same.

I unzipped my snowsuit, and George motioned to a big padded chair. He said, "Sit down." The chair was stained and had a hole in the center of its seat, and inside the hole was a sleeping cat. George said, "He'll move when you start sitting down." As soon as I started sitting down, the cat hissed, then jumped out of the hole.

"Hi, Pig," I said because Pig was staring at me, but Pig didn't say anything.

"He doesn't like to talk," George said. "Never mind him." George turned toward the TV; the screen was full of static. "Who do you watch?" He picked up pliers and began twisting a plastic rod where there should have been a knob.

I was going to tell him which TV shows I liked, but I felt Raymond pressing on my bladder, trying to force out of me this morning's cup of hot chocolate. "I need to pee," I said.

"Up there," George said, pointing to a staircase.

I forced my butt out of the chair's hole. If my butt had been bigger, it might not have been a problem, but as it was, I feared getting sucked into the hole if I stayed there any longer.

The ceilings were lower upstairs than downstairs, making me feel taller, older. The rug had been worn down in places to the plywood underneath. Dust covered every imaginable surface so that the entire house looked furry. It was cold up there, too, as though all the windows were either open or broken. My teeth clacked together. A thin curtain inside one of the rooms blew around like a flag.

"Who are you?" someone asked, and Raymond released a squirt of pee into my pants. Inside the room with the flag was a woman too large to fit through the room's door. I'd never seen anyone that big before. She was four or five times the size of Dr. Stump. Krogerly wanted to say something, but I shushed him.

Propped up in bed, the woman fanned herself. She was wearing what my mother called a housedress, the same soft fabric of my pajamas with snaps all the way down the front. At first I thought her eyes had been blackened, but when I stepped closer I saw that she was wearing blue eye-shadow.

"I'm Hank," I said.

"You looking for something, Hank?"

"The bathroom."

She pointed to a room inside her room. I didn't want to get too close to her, though. I wasn't sure why. She hadn't yelled at me. She had even smiled, unless it had been a grimace from the effort it took to lift her sagging arm and point.

"Thank you," I said and waddled toward the room. I walked by her slowly, as if to show her that I wasn't afraid of her. The bathroom, I realized, didn't have a door. In fact, the space where the door had been was now twice as wide as a regular door. Instead of a door, there were two shower curtains you had to part to enter. I couldn't use a bathroom that didn't have a door—it wasn't a choice, I just *couldn't*—but I couldn't turn around and leave, either, so I parted the curtains and stepped inside. I stood by the window and stared for a good long time at the husks of old bugs on the sill. There were tweezers on the sink, so I used them to pick up the shell of a June bug. I held it up to the light, turning it one way and then the other. I wasn't sure why, but I felt like crying. Would this be me one day, the crisp and see-through shell of my former self being picked up by a giant, held to the light, and stared at? And would the giant himself want to cry?

I put down the bug, but I held onto the tweezers.

Take the tweezers, Raymond whispered. *Take them.*

No, I thought.

I flushed the toilet. Next to the tub sat an enema kit. My heart started pounding. The sight of the red rubber pillow with its long tail-like hose made me realize for the first time the possible danger I had put myself in.

When I returned to the bedroom, the woman said, "You didn't wash your hands, Hank."

"I'm okay," I said.

I wondered how long she had been trapped inside her room. When my mother and father weren't threatening me or Kelly with enemas, they threatened to ground us. Kelly explained to me once that if you were grounded you could never leave your room again, that you were under "lock and key," as she put it. Had the large woman been grounded? Was she under lock and key? And if so, who had grounded her? George? Pig?

I forced a smile and waved goodbye. I was certain I would never see this woman again. Ever. I had never seen her before, after all.

Downstairs, I saw that the cat had crawled back inside the

hole in the chair. Its eyes glowed at me from the dark cave.

"Just sit down," George said, "and the cat'll move." He said this as if he hadn't already told me the exact same thing a few minutes ago.

"You ever get an enema?" I asked.

George took a long drag off his cigarette and flicked the ashes into a Coca-Cola can. Without moving his eyes from the TV, he said, "Yeah. And it ain't pretty."

"I need to go," I said.

I must have expected some kind of goodbye because I was hurt when no one even looked my way.

"See ya!" I yelled.

George finally moved his eyes ever so slightly toward me, but just as fast they went back to the TV, where actors looked green and their voices were crunchy. Pig didn't move at all. But it was Raymond and Krogerly who, hanging back and not looking at me, surprised me. Why were they staying?

I zipped up my snowsuit and waddled away. Outside, I looked over my shoulder, but no one was following. I left the door wide open and waddled back across the street. When I turned around for one final look, I saw Kogerly sitting on the arm of the big padded chair that I had sat in while Raymond sat on the other arm. Raymond was staring down inside the hole at the cat. Normally I would have known what Raymond was thinking, but I couldn't for the life of me tell what he was thinking now or what he was going to do next, and when Krogerly looked up and said something to George, I couldn't hear what he'd said.

I walked into my house, where sunlight streamed through the windows and heat poured out of every vent.

Mom said, "Hank." She was staring at my hands.

"What?"

"Where did you get those tweezers?"

"Hunh?" I looked down. "I don't know," I said. "I guess I took them?"

I handed them over to Mom, who examined them closely. She sniffed them. "These aren't ours," she said. "They probably have some kind of disease on them. There's rust on the end. You could get tetanus, you know."

"What's tetanus?" I asked.

"It's something you don't want," she said. She carried the tweezers over to the trash can, lifted the lid, and dropped them inside.

I was so happy to be home, I started laughing. But there was something wrong, too, something I couldn't put my finger on, and my stomach felt empty and weird, like someone was tugging on it from below.

My father looked up from clipping his toenails. "Krogerly tell you a joke?"

"No," I said, because he hadn't. I still had to pee, so I said, "I gotta use the bathroom."

"Well, you know where we keep the can," my father said. He winked at me as I walked by and then he continued clipping his toenails. I heard him yelp, the way he always yelped whenever he cut a nail too short, and I heard my mother say, "For Pete's sake, be careful."

I opened the bathroom door, and Kelly, who was brushing her teeth, screamed.

"They're gone," I said.

Kelly's mouth was rimmed with foamy paste, like a rabid dog's. She tried asking "Who?" but sputtered and coughed instead.

"My friends," I said.

Kelly spit a blob of toothpaste and blood into the sink and said, "What friends? You don't have any friends!"

I teetered over in my snowsuit and hugged Kelly. Kelly stood stiffly at first but then relaxed. After a while, she even patted my shuddering shoulders. "There, there, little brother," she whispered when she realized I wasn't ever going to let go. "There, there."

11

Ralph wanted me to meet him at Ford City Shopping Center. "The entrance to Peacock Alley," he added. "Do you think you can you do that? Can you handle it?"

"Sure," I said. "Why couldn't I handle it?"

We were waiting for the crossing guard, a kid nobody liked, to blow his whistle and wave us across. Snow was packed hard on the ground, as slick as ice, and the crossing guard looked fearful of moving, afraid he'd fall in front of everyone.

"Just making sure," Ralph said. "Don't get all bent out of shape."

For Ralph, who was older and taller, the walk to Ford City was a cinch. It wasn't so easy for me, who would be easy prey, but I wasn't going to tell this to Ralph.

Unexpectedly, before the crossing guard gave us the go-ahead, Ralph stepped into the street, grabbed hold of the rear bumper of a slowly moving car, and, knees bent, began to skeech home. Everyone, including the crossing guard, turned to watch. Ralph made it three whole blocks, longer than anyone we'd ever seen, before the driver slammed on the brakes, jumped out, and yelled at him. After regaining his balance, Ralph waved at the man, then took off running down a side-street. I had meant to ask him a few more details about the trip to Ford City, but it was too late. Ralph, in a mere matter of seconds, was already long gone.

Even when it wasn't skull-numbingly cold outside, walking to Ford City was dicey. Part of the way you followed a fence that separated you from several factories. Attack dogs—Dobermans and Rottweilers—bared their teeth and trailed you from their side of the fence, growling the whole way. Eventually, you'd cross over into another grade school's territory, where kids would crouch between hedges for the sole purpose of jumping those who weren't from around there. To make matters worse, high school boys and girls were always walking to and from Ford City, and sometimes this meant having to cross all four busy lanes of State Street to avoid running into a group of infamous bullies who hadn't had their day's fill of pummeling. If all of this wasn't enough, you still had to cross Cicero Avenue, an eight-lane road that separated Ford City from my neighborhood, and you had to dodge traffic to get from one side to the other. Sometimes the traffic was so bad you'd end up stranded on the ridged island, fearful that two semis heading in opposite directions might crush you. There were dozens of factories up and down Cicero, and semis sped by all day long. I'd like to think that arriving at Ford City was like stepping into Oz or some other promised land, but in truth it presented a whole new batch of problems, namely that the teenagers here were even tougher and that the landscape of concrete and asphalt was more brutal.

My father liked telling the history of Ford City because, for him, a person who'd spent his entire life in Chicago, it was hard to imagine what Ford City had become. We lived only a few miles south of Midway Airport, and during the start of World War II, Ford City had been a government building, where Chrysler made B-29s, something called "The Superfortress," and engines for bombers.

After the war, sometime in the late '40s, a man named Tucker made automobiles there, the Tucker Torpedo, but that didn't last very long. A few years later, during the Korean War, the Ford Motor Company moved in and manufactured jet engines. Not until the early 1960s did a man named Harry Chaddick buy the property and turn it into what it was today: Ford City Shopping Center. It opened on August 12, 1965, a week before I was born, and my father took my mother, who was full-to-bursting with me inside, and my sister, only two years old at the time, to join hundreds of other people who had gone there to watch the Grand Opening Ribbon Cutting Ceremony and, more importantly, to catch a glimpse of Mayor Richard J. Daley, a man as famous in Chicago as the Pope.

My father didn't see Daley that day, and he took it personally, holding his grudge against Ford City Shopping Center itself. Each time we drove by, he'd say, "If you ask me—and, mind you, nobody has—the damned place still looks like a factory," or "Talk about your eyesores," or "One big red pimple on the ass of our fine city!"

He was right: it *did* still look like a factory. Even though names like Wieboldt's and Montgomery Ward adorned the building's various entrances, you could easily imagine those names gone, and instead of shoppers there would be streams of women with goggles pushed up onto their heads and lunch pails tapping against their thighs, all filing inside for a day of work on the assembly line, probably already waiting for the shrill whistle when they could finally take a lunch break.

The parking lot, with its long jagged cracks and poked-up dandelions, reminded me of an abandoned airport runway, and if a plane happened to be overhead while I was crossing the lot, I pretended that it was a Japanese fighter jet with blazing red suns painted on either side, and that a kamikaze pilot was inside spinning the plane toward the mall, spinning it like a gyroscope, prepared to take out the entire bomber assembly line. Sometimes, when I was alone, I would even yell, "Bonsai!" and then whistle the plane's dark descent, ending with a muffled explosion: *"Kuh-pkkkkkkkkkkk."*

Ford City Shopping Center was divided into two sections: the main building, with its dozens of stores inside, and then another strip of buildings, all the way across the parking lot, with several more businesses, each of which you could enter only from outside: the General Cinema movie theater, the bowling alley and pool hall, a fabric store that only old ladies went into, and a few other stores that no one could ever remember because they looked so dull.

I headed for the main building today, the *indoor* part of Ford City.

Certain stores fascinated me. The store that sold Wurlitzer organs, for instance. I always peeked inside because there were never any customers and because the salesman, bored, could be found playing "When the Saints Go Marching In" with a Rumba backbeat. Late at night, with the hope of luring in some of the younger kids, he'd play Yes's "Roundabout" or the Doors' "Light My Fire." It never worked, though. Instead, he was greeted by confused looks and the occasional insult. The organist, tall and bony, wore a white short-sleeved shirt, black slacks, and a long, skinny black tie that made him look like a preacher from one of the fuzzy UHF stations I'd flip past on Sunday mornings while desperately searching for cartoons. I was fascinated with this place because I'd never seen a single customer pushing an organ out to their pick-up truck, and so I couldn't imagine how they stayed in business.

Woolworth's was another place. It had an oval-shaped diner that took up a good part of the corridor just outside the store itself. It was an old diner with old people working there and old people eating there, and it wouldn't have seemed any more foreign to me if a spaceship had landed inside the mall. I'd never eaten at a diner, *ever*, but I was spellbound by this one—the long steaming grill, the dozen hamburgers sizzling at once, the outrageous mountain of hash browns. Old men with fedoras sat at the counter and read the newspaper. Since none of my friends' fathers wore fedoras,

I wondered where these men came from and why they read the newspaper here rather than at home. I asked my father once about the newspapers, and he said, "Don't get me wrong, I love your mother, but let's just say it's nice to go somewhere where no one's riding you all day long," and then he winked at me. Each time I walked by the old men at Woolworth's, I imagined old women at their homes chasing them around with brooms, sweeping them from room to room, accusing them of this or that, until they couldn't take it anymore and rode the city bus down to Woolworth's. Since these were their few precious moments of peace, I always tiptoed by and tried not to stare too long.

Today, I walked over to the entrance for Peacock Alley. Peacock Alley was an underground mall that you entered from a dank stairwell in the main mall. Painted on the stairwell's walls were the names of various businesses that were supposed to be in Peacock Alley, but I recognized only a few of them. The rest, like Chuck's Fine Photos or Betty's Boutique, were long gone. Since Ford City had been a factory before it was a mall, it was hard to say what Peacock Alley used to be. It was dimly lit, the hallway was narrow, and it twisted all the way beneath the long parking lot to the other buildings, where the movie theater and the bowling alley were. The rumor was that a tunnel ran from Ford City to Midway Airport, several miles north, and that this was how the engineers and mechanics transported important parts for their bombers during wartime. I always looked for secret entrances or walled-up corridors but couldn't find any. At a certain point inside Peacock Alley, there was a long tunnel where there were no stores, and if a large enough family was walking toward you, you'd have to suck in your gut and turn sideways to let them pass.

It was in one of the tunnels that I once saw a high school boy kicking another boy in the stomach with his steel-toed boot. This was two years ago; I was in sixth grade. My parents and my sister were shopping upstairs. It was almost closing time, so not many people were left in Peacock Alley. I needed to walk through the tunnel in order to get back to the entrance that led into the mall itself, but I didn't want to walk by the boy with the steel-toed boots, so I turned around and took the other way out of the Peacock Alley, the exit that led outside. The only thing more dangerous than one of the Peacock Alley tunnels was the Ford City Shopping Center parking lot at night, but I didn't have a choice: I needed to get back to the mall. I never knew what happened to the high school boy with the boots or the boy getting kicked, but I made it safely across the dark parking lot, entered Montgomery Ward from outside, and found my parents in the large home appliance section where my father was arguing with the salesman about the prices being jacked up and about how he was getting screwed over. "When it comes to my hard-earned money," he said, "I hate getting screwed over." My mother was tugging his elbow, trying to get him to drop it. I was dripping sweat, but no one noticed, not even my sister, Kelly, who had stuck her entire head inside one of the ovens, and who, when she saw me out of the corner of her eye, said, "A twelve-year-old girl with her head in a gas oven and nobody cares." She reached out of the oven and turned one of the knobs higher. I peeked behind the oven. "It's electric," I said, "and it's not plugged in." Kelly emerged, her face red as though she'd been holding her breath, and said, "That's not the point," and walked over to a deep-freeze, into which I imagined she might crawl and then shut herself.

I waited a good twenty minutes today for Ralph before heading down into Peacock Alley to look for him. The deeper down you went into Peacock Alley, the dizzier you got from the incense that burned in about a third of the stores. The incense had names like Jasmine, Funky Cherry, and the Sea of Tranquility. Some stores used strobe lights to lure customers inside. Down here, teenage girls still wore leather vests with long leather fringe circling their soft bellies. If you looked closely, you might even see a belly button, and although I tried not to give away that I was looking, I always checked to see if it was an innie or an outie. For reasons I couldn't quite put into words, my favorites were the outies, though maybe this was because mine was an innie. On no fewer than five nights I had fallen asleep to the thought of a girl pressing her outie into my innie.

The first store at the bottom of the stairs sold nothing but wicker furniture. I looked but couldn't see Ralph in there. The next store was what my mother called a "head shop." Teenagers hung out there, slumped at the counter, sometimes smoking cigarettes or looking, as my mother liked to put it, "doped up." Dad told me that if he ever caught me in there, he'd skin me alive. My father had never hit me—not really—but the punishments that he threatened me with varied in their degree of severity depending upon the offense. *I'll whup your butt so hard, you won't be able to sit down for a week* was the least serious, probably because of the words "whup" and "butt," but also because my dad usually said this without any emotion whatsoever, sometimes not even looking up from whatever he was doing. Next in seriousness was *How'd you like the belt?* Only once did he go so far as to unbuckle it, jerk it from his pants, and double it up, but that was enough to send me running and screaming, as if it were an ax he'd revealed and not the belt I'd bought for him at Kmart for Father's Day. Finally, there was the threat of being skinned alive, which scared me for three reasons. Number one: he'd threatened me with it only four times in my life, and *less* carried more power than *more*. Number two: he always looked me in the eye when he said it, and since he almost never looked me in the eye, this scared the wits out of me. Number three: I'd read a Scholastics book about Indians skinning their enemies, and so I knew how much pain my father was talking about. I imagined him going so far as to bury me up to my neck in the dirt on a hot day and then pouring honey over my skinned head, letting ants and wasps have a field day with me. The result of the threat was that I wouldn't even look at the head shop today, let alone step inside. The first place of business that I would step inside, however, was the record store, which was blocked off from the hallway not by walls but by a wrought-iron gate that was as high as my hip.

In the record store, where they burned incense not by the stick so much as by the pound, I looked at the Roxy Music album covers because there were naked women on them. I also looked at the Rolling Stones *Sticky Fingers* album because it had a real zipper on the front of it. In addition to being one of the strangest things I'd ever seen, it was the first time I saw how two things that weren't alike at all could come together to surprise everyone who came into contact with it. An album cover with a zipper! Who'd have thought it was possible? I looked at Linda Ronstadt and Olivia Newton-John albums because I had crushes on both of them, and then I looked at Styx albums because they were from the South Side of Chicago. I loved flipping through the record store's display of posters, too. One of my favorites was of W. C. Fields wearing a stovepipe hat and peeking up from a handful of fanned cards. I also liked the one from *Easy Rider* with some guy riding a chopper. I liked how choppers looked and wanted to turn my three-speed bicycle into a chopper, but when I asked my father if I could use his blowtorch, he asked me how I'd like his belt. The poster that I saved for last was Farrah Fawcett-Majors in a red swimsuit, her white teeth practically glowing, her loopy signature in the bottom right hand corner. I never bought anything from the record store because I never had any money, but looking at the stuff was good enough. Sometimes looking seemed like getting something for free.

After the record store came Nickelodeon Pizza, where high school boys sat at the counter and flirted with the waitresses. It was like a different planet, a different solar system, from the Woolworth's diner upstairs, and I wondered if the customers of one place even knew about the existence of the other. I doubted it. Beyond Nickelodeon Pizza was a gag shop that sold rubber masks of Richard Nixon, Gerald Ford, and Jimmy Carter. My father once suggested that the four of us go as presidents for Halloween one year.

"But I see only three presidents," I'd said.

My father shrugged. "One of us could go as the Wolfman, I suppose."

The masks were expensive and I knew that my father would never fork over that kind of money for four rubber masks, but it bothered me for days on end that he couldn't see how wrong it would be for only three of us to be presidents while one of us went as a monster. Why couldn't he see the problem with that?

I sauntered through the tunnel, still hoping to bump into Ralph, but the longer I went without seeing him, the less likely it was that we were going to meet up. Maybe I had misunderstood. Maybe we were supposed to have met tomorrow.

The end of the tunnel meant that the smell of incense would be replaced by the rich stench of perm solution. Ford City Beauty School was where my mother took me for haircuts. They charged half of what other places charged so that the girls, who weren't yet licensed to cut hair, could experiment on a bunch of different cheapskates' heads. Sometimes it looked pretty good when they were done, but more often than not one of my ears looked higher than it should have, or I appeared to be in the first stages of going bald, or, thanks to crooked bangs, one eye seemed an inch lower than my other eye. I didn't mind because the girls, who weren't much older than me, only four or five years older, would press into me while they snipped away.

I loved the beauty school. I'd never been to a funhouse, but I suspected that getting my hair cut wasn't so different: strapped in a chair, raised and lowered, tilted back, and so many mirrors that I could look nearly anywhere and see myself disappearing into infinity. I always left the beauty school knock-kneed—the lights had been so bright, the perm solution dizzying, the beautician's body so warm that my own temperature raised a few notches—and the whole time I wouldn't say a word. I'd just sit there, breathing heavier and heavier, until the girl I had fallen in love with, whichever girl happened to be cutting my hair, untied the drop-cloth and set me free.

Ford City Beauty School was the end of the road, the last main attraction of Peacock Alley, and then came the stairwell going up into the parking lot, into the first shaft of light. Climbing the stairs, I imagined that I was a coal miner who'd spent the better part of my day underground, eager to see all my loved ones again. I took the steps two at a time, sometimes three, straining, making a bigger production than necessary, until I reached the top, where, blinking and shivering, I had to shade my eyes from the blinding piles of snow and wait for everything to come back into focus.

"Where the hell have you been?" a voice asked. I heard him before I saw him, but when I turned around, there he stood. Ralph! Arms crossed, eyes narrowed, he was waiting for an answer.

"Where've I been?" I said. "I was looking for you."

"Me? I've been here the whole time."

"Here?" I said. "You told me to meet you at the entrance."

"This is the entrance," he said, and we both looked toward it for an answer, as if a sign might be posted, proving one of us right, but there was no sign. "Ah, forget it," he said. "It's not worth arguing about." He unfolded his arms and walked toward me. "I just don't know about you, Hank."

"Me?" I said. "What about you?"

Ralph, ignoring my question, started down the stairs. I was about to tell him that I'd already seen everything that I needed to see, but then the smell of perm solution hit me again, and I suddenly didn't mind working my way backward. I knew that every minute I lived was one less minute I'd be alive, but returning to Peacock Alley was different: it was like stealing time, getting back what I'd lost. It was quite a feeling, really, being thirteen years old and cheating death.

12

It was only a few months away from graduation, but in the ice-encased world that is February in Chicago, June shimmered like a mirage—within sight but unattainable. I knew that even if it warmed up, even if all of this melted, there would be more snow, more sludge, and more ice before we could say goodbye, once and for all, to Jacqueline Bouvier Kennedy Grade School.

On a Sunday when the sun came out, the temperature rose, and the sound of ice melting gave half the people in Chicago false hope that winter would soon be behind us, Ralph took me to the Scottsdale Shopping Center parking lot, where we met his cousin, Norm. The three of us stood by Norm's trunk looking like a chart you'd see in a doctor's office about age and height, but when Ralph started jumping up and down to keep warm and Norm sat on his haunches, I remembered drawings I'd seen of men evolving from monkeys. We were, I thought, finally returning to our former monkey selves.

Norm motioned for all us to crouch down to his level. He looked around to make sure no one was watching us, then he pulled an envelope from his back pocket.

"I've got these tickets to scalp, see?" he said.

Ralph nodded. When it came to Norm's hare-brained plans,

Ralph always became all-business, but I knew better, so I stifled a yawn. However, when Norm opened the envelope and showed the tickets to us, my whole body started to convulse. He was holding eight tickets for a taping of the TV show *Bozo's Circus*.

"You okay there?" Norm asked. "Don't tell me you're having a seizure." He looked at Ralph. "Is your friend having a seizure?"

Ralph, ignoring my violent shivering, said, "*Bozo's Circus*? Never seen it. Is it any good?"

"What do you *mean* you've never seen it?" I said. "Are you *crazy*? *Everyone's* seen it."

Bozo's Circus was one of the top-rated shows in all of Chicago—so popular, in fact, that there was a ten year wait for tickets. I hadn't met a kid who didn't run straight home for lunch to watch the show's ringleader announce, "*Bozo's Circus* is on the air!" The ringleader would then blow his whistle, prompting the band to start playing the show's theme song. Bozo's own famous catch-phrase, before cutting to a cartoon, was to put his face close to the camera and ask, "Who's your favorite clown?" to which a hundred kids would scream back, "Bozo!" Bozo would reply in his gravely voice, "Hey, that's me!" and start laughing like a crazy person.

I was shivering because I felt like that crazy person. There was no telling what I would have done to be able to see Bozo in person. My earliest memories were not of my mother, my father, or my sister. They were of Bozo. Bozo was a celebrity in Chicago, as big as they got. Bigger than Mayor J. Daley had been. Bigger than the Pope. The first word I ever spoke was Batman. The second? Bozo.

Ralph shook his head. "Nope. Never seen it."

"How much you selling those for?" I asked.

Norm fanned the tickets, staring down at them and frowning, then he looked up at me and said, "Two hundred dollars each."

I must have made a noise like a wild animal caught in a trap because a dog sitting in one of the cars in the parking lot started howling.

"Two hundred dollars?" Ralph asked. "Now, *what's* this show called again?"

"*Bozo's Circus*," I said impatiently. "*Bozo's! Circus!*"

"Okay," Ralph said. "You don't have to snap at me."

I wasn't a violent kid—in fact, I was a good kid, *too* good, as Ralph liked to tell me—but I had a sudden urge to punch Norm as hard as I could in his face, grab the tickets, and take off running with them.

Two hundred dollars? These tickets were sent to people for free! After a ten year wait! What if I threatened to turn him in? Maybe, I reasoned, Norm would simply give me a ticket in return for me keeping my trap shut.

I knew that this was only a fantasy. Ralph had told me dozens of stories about Norm, how he had gotten kicked out of grade school for stabbing a teacher in the thigh with a pencil; how, after getting in trouble with the police for breaking his neighbor's window with a baseball, he had set the family's dog house on fire (the dog, fortunately, was sleeping inside the real house); how he had flattened his parole officer's tires; how he had set a dozen paper bags full of dog crap outside the doors of St. Albert's one Sunday and then set them on fire mere moments before mass was over; how he had eaten a hundred thumb-tacks on a dare. The stories were Biblical. For Ralph, however, these were inspirational tales, a list of deeds Ralph himself aspired to do one day. From my perspective, the stories painted the portrait of a man who was the complete opposite of me, a man, in other words, who would do anything. I had a difficult time speaking up whenever a teacher called on me because my heart fluttered so hard and I would start to feel queasy. That was the kind of boy I was. Nervous. Afraid of not having the right answer. What was I going to do to Norm? Nothing.

"Two hundred dollars," Ralph said, staring at the tickets. "How'd you get them in the first place?"

"When I was in high school, I saw Gus Saviano scalping Peter

Frampton tickets, and I thought, dude, that's brilliant…"

"Didn't you beat him up once?" Ralph asked.

"Yeah. Anyway, I started thinking…what's the hottest ticket in town? I was home for lunch, sitting in front of the TV…"

"What were you eating?" Ralph asked.

"SpaghettiOs. Why?"

"Just trying to paint a picture here," Ralph said.

"So I'm home for lunch, eating SpaghettiOs, when *Bozo's Circus* comes back on from a commercial, and I thought, *bingo*. That's it. Nobody's selling Bozo tickets. So I spent the next week writing away for tickets. I used my mom's name, my dad's name, my aunt's name. I even used your name. You should be getting your tickets any day now."

Ralph looked at me and waggled his eyebrows.

"*My* tickets, I should say," Norm added. He stuck his tickets back inside the envelope and said, "You kids know of any takers, you know where to reach me."

Ralph and I started walking home. I tried explaining to Ralph the legend of Bob Bell, the actor who played Bozo—how he was a notoriously private man; how the fact that he refused to make public appearances beyond *Bozo's Circus* only added to his allure of the show; how, like the members of KISS, no one knew what the man looked like without his Bozo make-up on.

"I'm sure his wife knows," Ralph said.

"Besides his wife, I mean," I said.

Ralph said, "What? You think this guy goes to the A&P dressed like Bozo?"

"No," I said, "but since no one knows what he looks like without his make-up on, no one would know it's Bozo they're looking at."

"What kind of name is Bozo, anyway?" Ralph asked. "Sounds Polish to me."

"I'm sure it's made up," I said.

Ralph said, "All names are made up. But it's got to come from somewhere. Maybe it's Ukrainian."

"Maybe it's French!" I said, exasperated.

"French, huh?" Ralph said. "I think maybe you're right. They love their mimes, that's for sure. Anything having to do with guys wearing make-up, they eat it up. Does this Bozo character ever walk against the wind or pretend he's trapped inside of a box?"

"No!" I said. "He's a clown!"

"Okay, okay. Pipe down."

"No, you pipe down," I said.

Ralph stopped, glared at me. No one ever told Ralph to pipe down. "No, *you* pipe down," he said, stabbing my chest with his forefinger.

And that was that. For the rest of the walk home, we both piped down.

For days after Norm had shown us those tickets, I couldn't sleep and I could barely eat. At night, I fell asleep dreaming that I might get picked to play the Grand Prize Game on *Bozo's Circus*. The Grand Prize Game was comprised of a series of evenly spaced buckets, six of them, into which the contestant would toss a ping-pong ball. Each time the ball landed successfully in a bucket, the kid received a set of prizes. The further away the bucket, the better the prizes. The kid who made it all the way to bucket number six would win a brand-new Schwinn ten-speed, along with however much money had accumulated in the bucket, the total amount being a dollar for each day that someone hadn't gotten a ping-pong ball in bucket number six.

Sometimes they picked a kid who was too small and couldn't even make the first bucket. When this happened, I would scream at the TV and pull on my hair, frustrated that the game was being wasted on someone who probably had no idea where he or she even was, let alone the point of the game. "Come on," I would yell. "What were you *thinking?*" Other times, the kid was too old, and all he needed to do was lean forward and drop the ball into bucket number six. This, too, caused me to scream. Why couldn't they see, when the "magic arrows" landed on his pimply head, that he was too tall to play the game? "It's rigged!" I'd yell. "He's probably the band leader's son! What's going on here?" My mother would walk into the room and say, "Take it easy, Hank. It's just a TV show."

I practiced the game at home by lining up six make-shift buckets—a combination of empty tubs for margarine, my father's beer mugs, and an old grease-stained bucket from Kentucky Fried Chicken that I kept hidden in my closet. Since my buckets were of various sizes, my challenge was far greater than that of any kid on TV, and yet I still made all six buckets without a problem.

"What were you *thinking?*" I yelled, day after day. "What's your *problem?*"

"Hank," Mom would say, "Just settle down."

Since I couldn't sleep anymore, I started getting ready for school at 4:30 each morning, and then, with so much time on my hands, I would play with some of my old toys. One Thursday morning, I mindlessly placed my Dr. Zaius action figure on top of my Evel Knievel motorcycle. Dr. Zaius was the orangutan from *Planet of the Apes*, and though I normally would have had him giving a lecture about nasty, stupid human beings to the two chimps, Cornelius and Zira, today I wanted to see him attempt to jump all of my mother's new crockery on Knievel's motorcycle. Just as I was cranking the wheel that revved up the motorcycle, the phone rang. It was six in the morning. My parents were still asleep. When I let go of the crank to answer the phone, Dr. Zaius blasted off on his Harley, flying up the ramp and landing in the dog's bowl of Gravy Train.

"Hank," Ralph said. "Is that you?"

"What time is it?" I asked. "What're you doing up so early?"

"Listen," he said. "Meet me in front of White Hen. But hurry."

Without waking my mother or father to tell them where I was going, and forgetting to remove the orange-colored monkey from the dog bowl, I sneaked out of the house and ran all four blocks to White Hen Pantry. Norm was sitting in his car, revving the engine, while Ralph stood by the trunk, whistling a tune I didn't know.

"What is it?" I asked, out of breath. It was bone-chillingly cold again, and each time I opened my mouth, the air that escaped looked like smoke.

"You okay there?" Ralph asked. "You need CPR?"

"I'm fine," I gasped. "What do you want?"

And then Ralph explained it to me. Norm, unable to unload any the tickets for his asking price, wanted me and Ralph to hang around outside WGN and try to sell them for fifty bucks each. If we sold six of them, we could have the remaining two and go to the show. But if we didn't sell all six, he wouldn't give us the tickets. Norm had recently had a run-in with the Cook County police and didn't want to risk another one—otherwise, he'd have gone there himself.

"You're kidding," I said, laughing, and pushed Ralph so hard he slammed against the trunk.

"Ow!" Ralph said. "Take it easy."

"What about school?" I asked.

"Forget about school. This is more important."

I laughed again. I couldn't believe my good fortune. "I just need to tell my mom where I'm going," I said, but Ralph shook his head.

"No time for that," he said. "We need to go now or this ain't gonna happen."

The very idea of not telling my mom where I was going gave me an instant stomach ache, as if someone had poked a newly sharpened pencil into my belly button and then broke it off, but my desire to see Bozo in person, along with the possibility of getting to play the Grand Prize Game, snuffed out my worries. It was possible that Mom might turn on the TV at half past noon and see me, her beloved son, beaming between a set of Magic Arrows. And what mother wouldn't have been proud of her son in that moment?

"All right," I said. "Let's go."

I had no idea where WGN studio even was, but the drive took forever. We passed a dozen banquet halls, two dozen beef sandwich joints, a couple of psychics. Every time we passed a White Castle, Norm told us a story about eating too many of their sliders and how long he had to sit on the toilet the next day.

"Those things'll kill you," Norm said. "One time I spent a total of eighteen hours in the can. I'm not kidding you. I kept track. Eighteen hours! I actually fell asleep in there once with my pants down around my ankles. All I kept thinking was, *Why?* Why did I eat twenty-two cheeseburgers? Oh, sure, they're small and square and full of holes, but don't let that fool you." Norm squinted at the car in front of us, as if suddenly realizing we were at a stand-still, and honked his horn. "Move your crapmobile!" he yelled. "Move it! Move it! Move it!"

We stopped for a while at a Dunkin' Donuts, but Norm only bought donuts and coffee for himself.

"Aren't there union rules that workers need to be fed?" I asked Ralph.

Norm sat in the front seat, shoving an entire jelly donut into his mouth. He wheeled around and, with his mouth full, said, "Do I look like a Rockefeller? Is my first name Nelson?" He swallowed and said, "I've got overhead. Gas, for instance. Time. You think my time is cheap? And what if I get a flat tire driving there? Ever think about that?" He turned back around and jerked the gear shift in reverse.

We reached the television studio at 10:30, an hour and a half before the show was to start, but only a half-hour before people were supposed to start getting in line, according to the tickets. Norm circled back to Addison, where there was more traffic, and dropped us off on a corner, but not before popping the trunk.

"I made a few signs for you clowns," he said. "I'll be back at 1:00, okay? If you even *think* about going to that show without selling all six tickets, I'll skin you two alive."

"He bought a new knife last week," Ralph said calmly to me. "A Barlow. Right, Norm?"

Norm nodded.

"Will do!" I said, taking the envelope from Norm and getting out of the car. As soon as Ralph removed the signs and shut the trunk, Norm peeled out in front of a city bus, almost killing everyone on board.

A steady stream of cars flew by, but no one stopped. A couple of homeless guys and a woman wearing a babushka wandered past. I couldn't help thinking that not far away, only a short walk from where I now stood, were Bozo, Cookie the Cook, Mr. Bob the bandleader, maybe even Wizzo the Wizard. I was starting to hyperventilate a little.

"You're panting like a dog," Ralph said. "Hey, you didn't eat any White Castles last night, did you? You gonna puke?"

"I'm fine," I said.

Ralph held up the tickets, fanned like playing cards.

Each time someone drove past or walked near us, Ralph would say, "Getcha Bozo tickets right ch'ere." Into the window of a car that had slowed down, Ralph yelled, "NEED A TICKET?" The driver, a young woman who hadn't seen us standing on the sidewalk, screamed and sped off. Ralph looked at me, shrugged, and said, "Getcha Bozo tickets right ch'ere."

"Why are you talking like that?" I asked.

"Norm gave me a script to memorize," Ralph said. "He used

to work in a carnival." When two men wearing matching blue suits approached us, Ralph said, "Just a few minutes left, gents, don't miss a moment of the big top. A mere fifty bucks buys you one of these six tickets. Follow your neighbors, they know a good show when they see one. You'll see clowns of all denominations, clowns of all stripes, clowns of all orientations and affiliations, yes sir, they're just waiting for you to go inside to get things rolling. The best value on the midway is right ch'ere. Don't go off to your local tavern thinking you can come back here later and talk me down. No, sir, the show's gonna start any minute now. The timer is ticking. Once I'm gone, you can kiss this special price goodbye. Kiss it like you would your ex-wife. Kiss it like you would your dead grandmother. They're not gonna let you in once they shut their doors. That's a fact, Jack. That's the honest to God's truth."

One man grabbed Ralph's arm, and the other grabbed mine.

"This way," the one holding Ralph barked.

"Our posters," Ralph said.

"Leave them," the guy holding me answered.

They walked us all the way to the WGN building. At first I thought maybe they recognized me for what I was—the world's biggest Bozo fan—and that they were going to take us backstage to meet the great clown himself, but then the guy holding onto Ralph said, "You didn't think someone working here would drive by and see what you were doing?"

The guy holding me said, "Where do you think you are? A Shaun Cassidy concert?"

"No, sir," I said. "We hate Shaun Cassidy."

Inside WGN was a long hall packed full of parents and kids standing in line, and a little further down were two extra-wide, extra-tall doors: the entrance to the studio itself. Instead of heading into the studio, Ralph and I were yanked down another hallway, where nothing much was going on, and into a room, where an old man wearing a white shirt with a badge and dark pants sat staring at a bank of tiny TV sets, on which appeared not a single clown.

"Let me see those tickets," the seated man said.

"Fifty bucks apiece," said Ralph. "No pay, no play."

The man reached out and snatched them out of Ralph's hand before Ralph could do anything about it. "Well, now, this is a first, isn't it?" the man said to guys in the blue suits. He shook his head and said, "Scalping Bozo."

"Kind of ingenious, actually," the guy holding me said. "Which one of you two is the mastermind?"

Ralph said, "Sorry. Can't tell you," but then he cut his eyes toward me and tilted his head a little my way.

Everyone looked over at me.

"It wasn't *my* idea," I said.

The guy with the white shirt, who was clearly the boss, stared at both of us for a good long while before opening his desk drawer and placing the tickets inside. The sound of the drawer shutting was like someone pulling the plug on my life support machine. I knew right then that I would never get to go to a taping of *Bozo's Circus*. Even if I were to wait ten years for tickets, my name would be on a list, followed by four words: "DON'T LET HIM IN!"

The guys in blue suits separated us, the way I'd seen murderers separated on television shows, to ask us questions. Was Ralph telling them that it was all my idea, or was he keeping his mouth shut? As for me, I gave up Norm as soon as I was asked whose idea it had been. I also explained to them Norm's scheme of having tickets mailed to a bunch of other people he knew, including Ralph. I was not a loyal kid. I would have ratted out my own parents to save myself.

"Norm told me I could have one of the tickets if we sold six of them," I said, sniffling. "That's all I wanted."

"What?"

"To see *Bozo's Circus*."

The man nodded. He told me his name was Mr. Roush, and

that he had known Bozo for years.

"Nice guy," Mr. Roush said. "Private, though. He can be a little, I don't know, aloof. You know how I know him? We bum cigarettes off each other."

"Bozo smokes?"

Mr. Roush's brow furrowed. He must have realized he'd told me something he shouldn't have. He cleared his throat then left me alone in the room for over an hour. When he finally returned, he said, "Your story checks out, son. Every name you gave me is on our mailing list. *Was* on the list, I should say."

"Was?"

"Yeah, we cancelled all of them."

I was hoping he was going to offer a set of tickets to me as a reward for providing invaluable information, but Mr. Roush only opened the door and said, "Okay. You're free to go."

"Can I use your phone?" I asked.

"Local call?"

I nodded. Mr. Roush picked up the receiver and handed it to me.

"Dial '9' first," he said.

I was frozen in place, afraid of what my mother was going to say to me. I could hear a band nearby playing the opening song to *Bozo's Circus*. The show had begun. Mr. Roush leaned forward and dialed the number 9.

"You'll have to dial the rest yourself," he said.

I stood on the sidewalk outside WGN and waited for my mother to come get me. I worried that Norm would come roaring up, jump out, and skin me alive with his new Barlow knife, as promised.

I stood there for what seemed like several hours, kicking the same rock back and forth. Eventually, the studio audience came pouring out the doors. Everyone was smiling and laughing. A boy about my age held several toys against his chest while his parents carried what he couldn't hold.

Damn you! I thought, but at least he didn't have a new Schwinn bike and a bag full of silver dollars.

At the tail-end of the line was Ralph, yukking it up with some kid's father. When Ralph saw me, he shook the man's hand and waved goodbye to the rest of the family.

Ralph, grinning, said, "You were right."

"About what?"

"It's a great show. I should start watching it."

"What the hell do you mean?" I asked.

"When they took me to the other room," Ralph said, "I excused myself to go to the bathroom. Instead of taking a leak, I sneaked into the studio and grabbed a seat."

"*You saw Bozo?*" I yelled.

Ralph nodded. "After *Bozo*, they were going to tape something called *Donahue* in the next studio over. I was thinking about sneaking in there to see what that was like, but I didn't see any clowns." He tapped his wrist-watch. "Plus Norm's probably going to murder us as it is."

I couldn't even look at Ralph. "I'm waiting for my mother," I said coldly, staring at my shoes.

"Wise move, Grasshopper." Ralph slapped me on the back and said, "If you never see me again, I've been killed. I want you to give the eulogy, okay?"

"Whatever," I said.

Ralph headed back to Addison Avenue. An hour or so after Ralph had left, Mr. Roush stepped out of the building. Walking alongside him was an older man dressed in a suit jacket and dress pants but no tie. He was also wearing a long wool winter coat that stopped around his ankles. He was taller than anyone else I'd met that day, wore wire-framed glasses, and had gray hair parted on his side. I worried that maybe this was the president of WGN who, having heard how I had tried to sell free tickets to one of his shows, wanted to rough me up, but the older man looked over at Mr. Roush and said, "Is this the li'l fella you told me about?"

"Yes, sir, he's the one."

"What's your name?" the man asked, smiling. His voice was gravelly. His eyes, watery and surrounded by wrinkled skin but bright and familiar, caused me to relax.

"Hank," I said.

The man reached out and shook my hand. "I'm Bob," he said. He buttoned up his coat and said, "It's cold out here, Hank. Someone coming to pick you up?"

"My mom," I said. My voice was starting to quake. Mr. Roush, grinning, kept looking from me to Bob and then back to me.

Bob nodded. My heart was pounding so hard, my eardrums hurt. "Well, it was good meeting you, Hank. You look like a fine young man. Stay out of trouble now, okay?" Bob reached out and ruffled my hair.

"Okay," I said.

Mr. Roush and Bob turned, walked a few steps, and stopped. Mr. Roush pulled out a pack of cigarettes and shook it until a few appeared. When Bob pulled one from the pack, Mr. Roush turned back to look at me. He raised his eyebrows, as if to say, *See?*

The two men had no sooner gotten into their own cars and driven away when Mom pulled up next to the curb. I slid into the car and shut the door. I wanted her to say something, but she wouldn't even look at me. I rubbed my palms on my thighs. I thought, *Say something. Anything.* At a stop-light, I asked, "Who's your favorite clown, Mom?"

Mom gave me a look that warned me to quit speaking. She shook her head and said, "Hank." And then: "Hank, Hank, Hank."

I couldn't help myself. I smiled.

Hey, that's me! I thought, and I started laughing like a crazy person, the way Bozo laughed like a crazy person when everyone yelled his name, but unlike Bozo I couldn't stop laughing. I laughed and laughed until Mom pulled the car over and made me breathe into a paper sack.

"You're hyperventilating," she said.

I puffed the bag out and sucked it in, over and over, until the dizziness went away, and then we sat there for another few minutes, as though we were taking a commercial break from our lives, before Mom pulled back onto the road and took us home.

13

I usually didn't have enough money to buy any, but I loved record albums. When South Side Records opened, a tiny store with narrow aisles, I visited it once a week to see the new arrivals. The albums, set in row after row of plywood bins, were a buck-fifty less than what you'd pay for them at the local Kmart or Zayre, but I still couldn't afford them. Each week, though, you could pick up a free list of Chicago's top-selling music. The top ten albums were listed on the left side, the top forty singles on the right. On the back was a photograph of a Chicago deejay, and it always scared me to see how different they looked than their voices had led me to believe. Whenever my father had a disagreement with someone who wasn't particularly attractive, he'd nudge me afterward and say, "Talk about a face that was meant for radio." I never knew what he meant until I saw those photos.

The man who owned South Side Records was an old hippie, except that he'd trimmed his wiry beard and cut his wiry hair, grooming habits that probably didn't sit well with other hippies, the ones who still wore moccasins and leather fringe vests, who bathed only once a year and called everyone and everything (man, woman, child, or animal) "man." When I went into South Side Records, I started calling everyone "man" so that the owner understood that I could have been a hippie, too, if circumstances were different.

"How's it going, man?" I'd ask as soon as I had stepped foot inside, and the owner, whose name was Larry, would say, "There he is!" as if everyone had been waiting for me. Larry hired only pretty high school girls, and since he seemed to have different employees every couple of weeks, I made it a point to show the new girls that Larry and I had this special bond. Sometimes, after asking how he was doing, I'd point at him, wink, and nod all at once, and Larry would call me something new and startling like "The South Side Messiah!" or "Little Big Man!" or "The Merchant of Venice!" I loved hearing what he called me. I imagined that these names came to him in the form of a flashback from his hippie years, funny words and combinations of words still sizzling inside his head, itching to get out.

One day, in the spring of my eighth grade year, Larry said, "If it isn't Mr. Clean himself! How goes things for the almighty bald one?"

I pointed at him, winked, nodded. The two high school girls giggled.

"Listen," Larry said, "I was thinking. You come in here all the time, but you never buy anything. Why is that?"

Hippies on TV shows called money *bread*, so I shook my head and said, "Bread, man. No bread."

Larry nodded. "No *moulah*? No *dinero*? That's no way to go through life, pal. Tell you what. How'd you like to trade a few hours a day for an album of your choice? You come in, do a little sweeping in the back room, maybe unload a few boxes, and I'll let you pick whatever album you want."

"Really?"

"Absolutely. But here's the catch." He leaned onto the counter so that his head was level with my head, and said, "You can't tell your folks."

"Not a problem!" I said. My father had recently quit his job at the 3M plant, and my mother was mad at him, so I pretty much went wherever I wanted without either of them noticing.

"I mean it," he said.

"No, really," I said. "They don't even know I'm here right now!"

At this revelation, Larry's eyes widened. "Good!" he said. "That's terrific."

On my first day, Larry led me to the back room. It looked as though someone had opened up the service door and thrown a couple of grenades inside. The floor was entirely blanketed with empty and half-empty boxes, soda cans, broken albums, Styrofoam peanuts, and crumpled posters of rock bands. Taped to the far wall was a poster of The Bee Gees wearing white sequined jumpsuits. Someone had written underneath them THESE THREE MUST DIE FOR THE GOOD OF EVOLUTION!!!

Larry saw me looking at the Bee Gees and said, "You realize I'm kidding, of course. I'd never kill anyone." He said, "You don't *like* them, though, do you?"

"Nuh-uh," I lied.

"Good man."

After explaining the various chores to me and showing me where he kept the broom, a mop, and cleaning solvents, he left me alone. It wasn't easy figuring out where to begin. I needed a strategy, so I began dividing up the junk—boxes in one corner, shattered albums and torn album covers in another, posters stuffed into the room's only garbage can. At the end of the day, I picked out Elton John's *Goodbye Yellow Brick Road*.

Larry frowned when I handed it over. He said, "That's a double album, my friend. Single albums only. Sorry." I returned it to the bin and brought up Kiss's *Dressed to Kill* instead. "Is *this* what you want?" Larry said. "*Really?*" I nodded. Larry said, "Hey, it's your hard-earned money, pal, not mine." He slipped the album into a sack and handed it over.

Before reaching home, I slid the album up under my shirt so that my parents wouldn't see it. I wasn't sure why, but I didn't think that they would have approved of me working. My mother might have wanted me to start paying for my own groceries; my father might have thought that I had taken a job just to make a point about him quitting his job. But when I stepped inside the house, I realized that no one would have noticed if I had come home wearing a leopard skin loincloth, holding a spear, and dragging a King Cobra behind me. My mother had locked herself in the bedroom—I could see the light on under the door—and my father was sitting at the dining room table reading *1001 Best Jokes of the Century*. Every once in a while he'd chuckle. Even when I couldn't see my mother, I knew that the sound of Dad's chuckling multiplied her anger. It wasn't enough that he'd quit his job, but now he was in a good mood, walking around and smiling! I knew my mother. I knew that each chuckle was like a hot iron tapping the back of her neck.

In my bedroom, I put the album onto my turntable and kicked back to listen, but the album skipped every few seconds, the record player's needle jumping and landing with an amplified thud each time it skipped. I wanted to exchange the album, but since I wasn't sure what kind of return policy Larry offered, especially given our arrangement, I decided not to say anything to him.

The next day at work, as I studied a vandalized promotional photo of John Travolta, whose eyes had been cut out, someone began pounding hard at the service entrance. I opened the door and was surprised to see not a person but instead a custom van with a person inside. Everything inside the van was carpeted, shaggy. A Middle Eastern man with a thick mustache was sitting inside the shaggy van, smoking a cigarette and tapping, with one finger, the fuzzy dice that hung from his rearview mirror. His window was rolled down, and he blew a cloud of thick smoke at me. It was the first time I'd ever seen anyone knock on a door while still in their car, so I wasn't entirely sure how to greet him. I expected him to have an accent, but he didn't. He said, "Tell your boss that Ghassan is here." Before I could turn around, though, Larry was yelling, "*As-sallaamu-alaykum*, my brother. *As-sallaamu-alaykum!*" but Ghassan wasn't having any of it. He flipped his cigarette half-a-block away. With the engine still running, he opened the van's door and slid out.

"Gotta lay low for a while," Ghassan said. "Feds are cracking down. I got a friend who pirates all that Disney crap, and they arrested him last Saturday at the Twin Drive-In."

The Twin Drive-In was a flea market that opened on the weekend. Nothing I'd ever bought there worked—sparklers, a transistor radio, a wind-up toy car—but I couldn't bring myself to throw any of it away. I stuffed all the broken junk into a dresser drawer that was full of old socks with gaping holes that I couldn't bear to throw away, either.

Larry turned to me. "Give our friend Ghassan a hand."

The back of his van was packed full of thousands of black concert T-shirts, and I helped carry hundreds of them inside. They were grouped first by musician, then by size. After Larry'd handed over a fist of cash to Ghassan, and after Ghassan had driven away, I held up a Nazareth T-shirt and said, "These are cool, man."

"They're bootleg," Larry said. "I get 'em for a buck, sell 'em for four. If I went through the promoters, I'd be lucky to make fifty cents. You can't live with a profit margin like that. You do what you got to do. Remember that, buddy."

Although it was supposedly new, the Boz Scaggs album that I took home that night had a long scratch that ran from the label to the outer edge. It was deep enough that the song popped on every rotation. I knew that I'd have a hard time convincing Larry that every album I took home, every *new* album, was damaged before I even opened it up, so I filed it under my bed with the other damaged album.

The next day brought more pounding at the service entrance.

By this time I had cleared a path to the door, but now there were concert T-shirts piled everywhere, narrowing the room's width. I expected to see Ghassan sitting in his van again, but it was a guy in his early twenties with long greasy hair and whiskers sprouting from his pimples. He was sitting on a girl's bicycle. Pink and white plastic tassels hung from each handlebar. He handed over a stack of rubberbanded tickets and said, "Tell Lare-O this was all I could score. Tell him I'll do better when Nugent comes to town." When he saw me looking at the girl's bike, which had a tiny license plate that said BECKY, he said, "Found this leaning against a Dumpster. I'm taking it to a pawn shop right now."

I nodded, shut the door, glad I didn't have to look at him any longer. I brought the tickets to Larry and relayed the message.

"Pink Frickin' Floyd, and this was all he could get me? Okay, tell me again. What *exactly* did he say?"

Both girls behind the counter—new girls—gasped. "You got Floyd tickets?" one asked, and the other one, who was wearing several long bird feathers clipped to her hair, said, "Far out! We're going to *Floyd!*"

"Whoa," Larry said. "Easy, girls, easy. I was expecting more tickets than *this*. I mean, c'mon now, I've got bills to pay."

After picking out my album for the night—the soundtrack to *Rocky*, good music for jogging in place and punching the air—I found Ralph and told him what I'd seen these past few days.

"Bootleg T-shirts and scalped tickets?" he said. "You better watch your back."

"You think?"

"Do I *think? Yes*, I *think*. That's heavy stuff. And if you ask me, I bet it's just the tip of the iceberg lettuce, so to speak. You think things got bad with those *Bozo Circus* tickets? Well, you're not dealing with a couple of security guards here. This is underground stuff, my friend."

At home, my father peeked up from his book and said, "*You're* not mad at me, are you?"

"No," I said.

"Good. Because I want to tell you a joke. Are you ready?"

I nodded.

"Okay," he said. "Here we go." I had a hard time following the joke, but it had something to do with a priest walking into a bar and complaining to the bartender about his boss. Once the bartender realizes that God is the priest's boss, he gets sort of disturbed by the conversation. The joke didn't end there, though. It went on and on. My father kept going back and telling some of it over. He paused a few times, trying to remember what happened next. When he finally finished, he opened his eyes wide, waiting for my reaction.

I said, "Is that from your joke book?"

"You don't think it's funny?" he asked, but before I could answer, he said, "Did I leave something out? Maybe I forgot part of it."

I excused myself, fearful that he'd start telling the joke to me again.

In my bedroom, I listened to *Rocky*. Amazingly, it was the first album that didn't have any problems when I played it, but it was missing the inside sleeve. You could tip the cover and watch the naked L.P. roll out. But at least it didn't skip or pop. I was happy about that.

On my fourth day at work, I walked into the back room and found Larry kissing a woman I'd never seen before. He was sitting in a metal folding chair and the woman, who was his age, was sitting on his lap. She was pudgy and wore thick eyeglasses, and when she looked up at me, her lenses were steamed over. "Who is it?" she asked Larry, and Larry said, "It's Hankenstein." "Oh," the woman said. "Hello, Hankenstein."

"I can come back later," I said, but Larry held his palm up toward me. A few minutes later, they were both gone and I was alone.

By the end of the week, I had quit greeting people when I walked into the store and they had quit greeting me. No more "Little Big Man!" from Larry. No more winking, pointing, or nodding from me. I'd simply walk past everyone and head for the back room. The sooner I could start working, the sooner it would be over. The way I saw it, I wasn't getting paid for the time it took to chat to everyone. In fact, I wasn't getting paid at all anymore. I'd lost interest in picking out albums for myself. Something was always wrong with the album, so it didn't seem worth the extra time that I spent in the store looking for one. More depressing than that, though, was the disappointment that swallowed me each time I played an album and heard its fatal flaw. I found myself holding my breath until the first angry pop, and then I'd feel as though I'd stepped off the side of cliff. My heart actually hurt from pounding so hard.

On my seventh day at work, I was dragging all of the trash outside, taking it to the Dumpster in the alley, when a milk delivery truck pulled up beside me.

"Go get Larry," the driver said.

I didn't like getting ordered around—especially now that I was working for free—but I wasn't good at talking back to someone older than me. Besides, the driver was one of those fat guys who was hairier than an ape and who looked as though he'd run you over with his truck for the fun of it, so I trudged to the front of the store and found Larry. He was behind the counter, smoking a Tiperillo, and a new girl was sitting next to him, blowing on a stick of incense, watching the red ember glow then dim.

"Someone wants you," I said.

"Who?"

"How should I know who?"

The girl blowing incense stopped blowing, peeked up, and cocked her head the way dogs do when they hear a high-pitched whistle. "Dude," she said. "Chill." She shut her eyes and resumed blowing.

My father used to come home from work and, after telling us a story about someone who annoyed him, say, "One of these days I'm going reach over and choke that numbskull." Whenever he said it, which was several times each week, I feared he'd eventually choke one of his co-workers and end up in jail. As a customer at South Side Records, it had never crossed my mind to hurt anyone who worked here, but as an employee I had an urge to reach over the counter and choke the girl with the incense. The urge passed as quickly as it came, but nothing during that split-second would have made me happier.

Cracking my knuckles, I followed Larry through the store and into the alley. "Ah ha!" Larry said when he saw the milk delivery truck. He turned to me and said, "We need your help, maestro."

I stood at the back of the truck while Larry and the driver handed milk crate after milk crate down to me. Each crate, crammed full of albums, was as heavy as a cinder block, so I could carry only one at a time. I lugged each one to another room in back, a room I hadn't even been inside before today, and I set all of the crates against a wall. Larry gave the driver a fat wad of money and then the man got back into his milk truck. He put the truck in gear and then rumbled down the alley, his axle creaking with every shallow hole, thick blasts of exhaust appearing each time the truck coughed.

Larry's eyes, following the truck, eventually landed on me. "Oh. There you are," he said. "C'mon, kiddo, let's see what Santa brought us, shall we?"

Inside, squatting, Larry pulled stacks of albums from milk crates, resting them on his thighs, and flipping through them. "Not bad. Hey, look. The new Van Halen."

"Getting into the used record business?" I asked.

Larry laughed. He explained to me how all of these albums were recent returns at other stores, how he had connections, and how his connections made more money by selling the returns to him than if they actually returned them. "And I've got this machine here," he said, pointing to a contraption in the corner of the room. "It'll shrink wrap these babies so they look like brand-new."

It took a moment for Larry's words to sink in. "So all your new albums are already old?" I asked.

"I wouldn't say they're *old*," he said. "People buy albums, and for one reason or another they sometimes decide they don't want them. Most stores have a thirty day return policy, so they're not *that* old. Thirty days tops! My return policy is twenty-four hours. I can't afford returns. Who would I return them to?" He started explaining to me how the shrink-wrap machine worked, but I told him that I needed to go. Larry said, "Hold on, big guy. I need these puppies on display by tomorrow morning. You can't stay a bit longer, help out your old friend? I could probably swing that double album you wanted."

"Nah. I don't think so."

"Go then," he said. "Scram." He was trying to make me feel guilty, but I wasn't falling for it. As the door shut behind me, he yelled, "Don't come back! And don't take an album today! You hear me?"

I didn't take an album. I grabbed three concert T-shirts instead, and when I reached the front counter, I walked around behind it for the first time. The girl at the cash register quit blowing on the stick of incense. She pointed the red-hot tip at me and said, "Did Larry say you can come back here?"

"Actually," I said, "Larry wanted me to tell you something."

When I didn't say anything, the girl said, "Well? Do I look like I have all day?"

"Larry told me to tell you that you're fired."

"What?"

"You're fired," I said.

The girl put down the stick of incense onto the glass countertop. The tip, still on fire and radiating a circle of heat, started to leave a black mark on the glass. The girl narrowed her eyes, as if unsure whether to believe me, but then she looked toward the back room, holding her gaze on the wall, as if the power to see though drywall might suddenly possess her.

"Who came to see him?" she asked.

"I don't know her name," I said, trying to remember one of the other girls who used to work for Larry. "She has pigtails. Marcy, I think. Yeah. Marcy!"

"Is she back there with him right now?"

"They're in that other room," I said. "The small room." For dramatic effect, I added, "The room with the *shrink-wrap* machine."

Her eyes, filling with tears, lost focus on the wall. She walked around the counter, shot one last glance at the back of the store, then walked outside, a tiny bell jingling cheerfully over her head. I stood on a stepladder, slid two Pink Floyd tickets from the grip of its rubberband, and tucked them into my back pocket. With my new T-shirts draped over my arm, I walked out of South Side Records for the last time.

I hadn't realized how bad work had been making me feel until this very moment. I was breathing easier now, grateful for all the free time ahead. I walked down the exact same streets I walked down every day, but the way that everything looked so new, so strange, I might as well have been walking on a different planet. Quitting the job was like being pulled from the tight confines of a deep and narrow well, but when I started to picture the scene— rescue workers huddled around the opening and pulling on the rope—I was surprised to see that it wasn't my own head emerging from the well, that it was my father's, and the poor guy, blinking at the sunlight and smiling, had never looked happier.

14

On the last day before spring break, Jesus showed up at Rice Park, next to our school. He kept his distance, slinking around the monkey bars, looking pretty much like every drawing I'd ever seen of him: dingy-white robe, long brown hair, well-kept beard with a neatly trimmed mustache. I was in eighth grade, and none of my classmates knew what to do about him, so we loped around the blacktop with our hands jammed inside our pockets, occasionally shooting him a look that said, *Yeah, okay, we see you, but we're not really that impressed.*

Ralph nudged me and said, "Check out his feet. He's wearing flip-flops. Who does he think he's fooling?"

Ralph's voice had recently dropped two octaves, and the speed at which hair appeared on him reminded me of scenes in *The Wolfman* when Lon Chaney, Jr. watched his own arms turn from man to beast.

By recess, Jesus had moved to the seesaw, and he started luring over some of the eighth grade girls. One by one, the girls sauntered over with their heads bowed, returning minutes later to relay his messages. "He says he's the son of God," Gina Morales said. "He says he died for us," Mary Polaski reported. Lucy Bruno, weeping, muttered under her breath, "He says it was time for him to come back to Earth because there's too much cruelty."

When Mr. Santoro, our principal, finally spotted Jesus, he quickly lifted his battery-powered bullhorn, pressed the mouthpiece to his lips, and clicked it on. "Stay away from that man!" Mr. Santoro yelled. "He could be dangerous!"

Terrified of the bullhorn, we fell silent as the word *dangerous* echoed across the blacktop. Jesus merely stood from his crouched position at the seesaw and waved at us, as though from the deck of a departing ship.

Mr. Santoro was naturally a nervous guy, but lately he'd had good reason. It was 1979, and four months ago, in December, police had removed twenty-seven bodies from the house of a man named John Wayne Gacy. Gacy's house was only twenty miles away in a northwest suburb of Chicago. Where I lived, on the South Side, it wasn't unusual for a kid to get jumped by a car-load of bullies from another neighborhood, but what we saw on TV each night about Gacy was something altogether new for us. Between Christmas and New Year's Day, from a house nicer than ours, men carried out body bag after body bag; and just when we were starting to think that they'd found all that they were going to find, winter gave way to spring, the rock-hard frozen ground softened, and police discovered even more bodies. At last count, they'd found the remains of thirty-three men and boys.

Mr. Santoro clicked on the bullhorn, reassuring us that everything would be okay if we simply followed his instructions. Then he ordered us to form a single-file line and start heading for the building. "Chop, chop!" he said.

"You know what I'd do if I was him?" Ralph said, nodding toward Jesus. "I'd show up here with a burning bush. I'd probably have some sort of speaker rigged up inside the bush, maybe bury the wire underground, and then I'd have you"—he jabbed me in the chest—"hidden somewhere talking into a microphone. You know, saying things the bush might say."

"What would a bush say?" I asked.

"I don't know," Ralph said. "Maybe, 'Hey, look, I'm on fire! What do all you peckerheads think of *that*?' You ask me, a burning bush would have some attitude. It wouldn't just stand around and say a bunch of cheeseball things like this bozo."

The word *bozo* made me cringe. It seemed a blasphemous thing to say until we had a little more information on the guy.

Ralph, shaking his head, finally turned away from Jesus. He said, "Listen. Kenny and Norm had to bail on a side-job. I told them we could do it." The idea of doing anything Ralph's cousins did made me queasy.

"I don't know," I said. "What kind of job is it?"

"It's an acting job," Ralph said.

"They're actors?" I said. "What about their job at the Tootsie Roll factory?"

Ralph said, "They're not professional actors."

I waited for Ralph to explain what "not professional" meant, but he didn't.

"What kind of acting job is it?" I asked.

"We'll find out tomorrow morning. Kenny'll pick us up."

"Why's Kenny picking us up?"

"Because," Ralph said, cocking his head and pausing after each word, speaking as if to an alien. "He's. The. One. Who's. Taking. Us. To. The. *Job!*"

"Oh," I said. "And where's that? The job?"

Ralph said, "Would you quit asking so many questions?"

I couldn't ever seem to get a handle on Ralph. For starters, I didn't understand how he could agree to do something without knowing what it was that he was agreeing to do.

"Okay," I said, meaning that I would quit asking questions, but Ralph took it to mean that I would do the job with him.

"Good!" he said, cracking me on the back. "I knew we could count on old Hank."

•

After recess, Mrs. Davis quizzed us on Stephen Crane's "The Bride Comes to Yellow Sky." I hadn't read it, but even the brains of the class, distracted by the arrival of a squad car, weren't participating today. The cops had come to haul Jesus's sorry butt away.

"This is *exactly* what happened to him the first time!" Gina Morales cried.

Lucy Bruno, the class weeper, began weeping. "It's starting all over again," she whined.

Mary Polaski, who was in my weekly CCD class at St. Fabian's Church, looked pleadingly at Mrs. Davis. "Can't you *do* something? Can't you *stop* them?"

Mrs. Davis ordered the girls away from the windows. She said, "The young man outside is nothing but a hippie." She spit the word "hippie" at us. I liked hippies. If he was a hippie, I'd have liked him.

I looked over at Mary Polaski to see how she was holding up. Earlier that month, I had fallen insanely in love with Mary Polaski. She had long blonde hair parted in the middle and feathered like Olivia Newton-John's. She was seeing a jug-eared high school boy named Chuck McDowell, and she spent the better part of her days in school drawing bulbous hearts with their names lewdly intertwined inside. Just a week ago I had sent Mary an anonymous love letter. Alluding to her evenings spent with Chuck, I quoted my favorite Journey song, "Lovin' Touchin' Squeezin'," the part about being all alone while she was out with somebody else.

In a careless moment, I had shown a copy of the letter to Ralph's cousin Kenny, who was twenty-six years old. Kenny read the letter, turned it over to see if I had redeemed myself on the opposite side, and then flipped it back again. He said, "You should have quoted Zeppelin, man. 'Whole Lotta Love.'" With his air guitar, he started playing the opening riff: "Nuh, nah, nuh, nah, NAH *nuh-nuh* NAH *nuh-nuh* NAH *nuh-nuh* NAH..."

Since sending the letter, I'd begun calling more attention to myself. For the past eight years I'd been a quiet kid, a solid B+

student, but now that my grade school career was careening to an end, I had become, to use my father's words, a Class-A wisenheimer. The problem was that no one ever laughed at my jokes, and today wasn't any different. Lucy Bruno sat in front of me, and after my sixth wisecrack in a row, her arm shot up.

"Mrs. Davis!" Lucy said. "I just wanted to let you know that if you're hearing any snide comments, it's not coming from me, it's coming from *him*!" She turned around and pointed at me. I turned around, too, as if searching for the real perpetrator, but since I was surrounded only by girls, it was clear that I was the *him* in question, the one making snide comments.

"Enough!" Mrs. Davis said. "All of you. You may think that because you're graduating in a few short weeks that you don't have to take these assignments seriously anymore, but let me assure you that nothing could be further from the truth. Keep in mind, if you don't pass this class, you will *not* be graduating with your fellow classmates. Have I made myself clear?"

A grim silence fell over the room. We knew that Mrs. Davis wasn't bluffing. All we had to do was look at Ralph. He served as our constant reminder of how bad things could get.

"Good," Mrs. Davis said. "Let us continue then."

Most of the houses in our neighborhood looked alike, but the house Ralph lived in with his mother was at least thirty years older than the others and covered on all four sides with roofing shingles. Long and narrow, it was what my father called a shotgun shack. Since I'd never stepped foot past the sagging fence, let alone inside the house itself, I waited by the gate tonight, hoping Ralph would look out a window and see me.

I never told my parents that I was going over to Ralph's because I knew that my mother would sigh loudly and say, "Just remember:

you're judged by the company you keep." To which my sister, Kelly, would add, "You are what you eat." The sad fact was that I constantly worried about being judged by the company I kept, and so I was always walking a razor-thin line—being Ralph's friend, on the one hand, but pretending to everyone else that that we weren't friends. My family would be disappointed in me if they knew that I was friends with Ralph, and Ralph would be disappointed in me if he knew that I told people that we weren't. My stomach ached just thinking about it.

Ralph finally opened the front door, bounded down the front stoop, and walked over to the gate, but he didn't invite me inside. He was wearing a too-tight T-shirt with a decal that read "Class of '73." It was 1979, and Ralph hadn't graduated from anything yet. The shirt was probably a hand-me-down from one of his cousins.

"I saw you stalking around out here. What do you want?"

"Have you talked to Kenny again?" I asked.

"Kenny? Why?"

"The job," I said. "I was wondering what kind of acting we need to do. Do you think we'll need to memorize any lines?"

"Memorize lines?" Ralph said. "What for?"

"For the parts we're going to play," I said.

"Go home and get some sleep. Tomorrow'll be here before you know it." He shook his head and said, "Sometimes I don't know what to make of you, Hank." He huffed, then turned and headed for his house, his T-shirt creeping further up his back with each step.

The very next morning, the first day of spring break, Kenny roared up in front of my house in a souped-up Nova that he'd been working on since I'd started grade school. Each time Kenny pressed down on the accelerator, toxic clouds exploded from the dual exhaust pipes. Coughing, eyes watering, I was reminded of the air pollution movie we were forced to watch in Science every year, a movie about the year 2000, and how the few remaining people on Earth would be wearing space suits with oxygen tanks, thanks to inconsiderate people like Kenny. I was going to tell Kenny about the movie, but when the Nova violently backfired and Kenny, clutching his stomach, said, "Excuse me, boys," as if the noise had come from him, I no longer saw the point in bringing it up.

Ralph was sitting in the passenger seat; I rode in back next to two overstuffed Hefty bags.

"What's in these?" I asked, poking one.

"Our costumes," Ralph said.

"Costumes?"

Kenny, peeking into the rearview mirror to look at me when he spoke, explained how Frank Wisiniewski, owner of Frank Wisiniewski Ford, had hired him and Norm to greet customers at the grand opening of their remodeled car lots, but Norm was temporarily incarcerated. Here was where Ralph and I stepped in. The job would last all day, and we'd get paid six dollars an hour.

"Six bucks an hour?" I yelled. "Just to greet people?" I'd never heard of anyone making six bucks an hour. Minimum wage was $2.90.

Kenny whispered to Ralph, "I told you he'd wet his pants, didn't I?"

I poked the bloated Hefty bag again. "So," I said. "What are the costumes?"

"You," Kenny said, pointing at me in the rearview mirror, "are going to be Big Bird. And Ralph here, he's that elephant from the show."

"Snuffleupagus?" I asked.

"Whatever," Kenny said.

"You're going to be Snuffy?" I asked Ralph.

Ralph said, "I know, I know. People like elephants better than they like birds, but since I landed us the job, I figured I could pick first. Don't worry, though. People like birds, too."

The way Ralph was talking, I wasn't sure he'd ever actually seen *Sesame Street*. On *Sesame Street*, it was clear who the star was, and it wasn't the elephant. Snuffleupagus was Big Bird's imaginary friend, a giant brown elephant that only Big Bird could see, and while Snuffy certainly enjoyed his own cult following, Big Bird was nobody's sidekick. I wanted to be Big Bird, but I was worried that I wasn't tall enough.

I was about to say something about my height when Kenny issued a warning: "I had to put a deposit down on those suits, so if either of you damage them, I'll come knocking at your door with a lead pipe." Then he pulled into Wisiniewski Ford and told us to beat it.

Ralph and I, abandoned at the dusty outer edge of the parking lot, each held a Hefty bag. Ralph said, "Let's find the john and suit up."

We lugged our bags through the showroom, to the restroom, where, locked inside, Ralph stripped out of all of his clothes, including a gray pair of Fruit of the Looms and mismatched tube socks. Buck-naked and hairy in a way that only wild animals were hairy, Ralph wiggled into his Snuffleupagus costume. I considered telling him that I didn't think people wore full-body costumes without any clothes on underneath, but then, holding Snuffy's head as if it were the prize trophy from an African hunting expedition, he asked me to zip him up.

"Okie doke," I said. Working as fast as I could, I snagged some of the hair on his back with the zipper's teeth.

"Ouch!" Ralph yelled. "Watch it!" He lifted Snuffy's head and placed it over his own head. Except for slight modifications—instead of four legs, he now had two legs and two arms—the Snuffleupagus in front of me looked like the Snuffleupagus from TV, and my feeling of revulsion melted into warmth. Here was this make-believe creature I had spent my early grade school years watching. I'd even had my own Snuffy hand-puppet, and I almost got teary-eyed at the thought of this part of my life coming to an end when Ralph, through the head of Snuffleupagus, said, "What are you screwing around for? Put the bird suit on."

As fast as possible, and with my underwear and socks still on, I slipped into the Big Bird costume. For my hands, I wore yellow gloves made of felt. Each hand had only three triangular fingers to give the illusion of claws. The most gratifying part of the transformation was placing Big Bird's head over mine. I wasn't sure how it was going to work—I had assumed that I'd be staring out of Big Bird's eyes—but in order to make Big Bird taller than the person inside, I was staring out of the beak from behind a sheet of wire-mesh painted black. It worked like a two-way mirror: I could see out, but no one could see in. The beak, however, remained permanently open, which didn't seem particularly authentic.

We unlocked the door and stepped out of the bathroom. A mechanic waiting his turn flinched at the sight of us. Ralph said, "Sorry for the wait, bud," and I nodded my beak at him.

The owner, who saw us before we saw him, called out from his office: "There you two are!" It was Frank Wisiniewski himself. I'd seen him on TV my entire life, a razor-thin, baldheaded man with bulging eyes who was always yelling about zero-percent finance charges and no money down. What I remembered most from those commercials were his hands. They never stopped moving, like a pair of battery-powered toys that wouldn't shut off.

Frank said, "Norm and Kenny, right?"

Ralph scratched his trunk and said, "At your service."

"Well, listen. I want this grand opening to be something special, okay? I want each family to leave here with a Ford automobile and memories to last them a freaking lifetime."

People passing by the glass-walled window of Frank's office slowed down at the sight of us, and I was starting to get a taste of celebrity. I sat down in one Frank's overstuffed recliners and casually crossed my feathered legs, but Ralph motioned with his elephant head for me to stand back up.

Frank rubbed his palms together, quickly, as if trying to warm up. Then he clapped a few times, snapped his fingers, and, dedicating one hand to each of us, pointed at both me and Ralph. He said, "Big Bird stays here at the new car lot. Snuffy goes across the street to the used lot. Wave at the passing cars. Later, we'll have one of you come inside so that folks can get their photos taken with you. We've got a professional photographer scheduled from noon to five. Any questions? None? Great! Let's go and sell some friggin' cars, then."

Back in the showroom, Ralph said, "What if someone wants to buy a new car from the elephant? It seems screwy to have me all the way across the street."

"I don't think we're actually going to be selling the cars," I said.

"All I'm saying," Ralph said, "is that it's not a savvy business move putting the more popular animal across the street."

I took my position at the curb next to the highway. Ralph attempted to cross over to the used cars, but a VW van quickly turned a corner and nearly took him out. Ralph, frozen in the middle of the road, lifted his shaggy brown arms over his head and swore at the van.

The rest of the morning wasn't much of an improvement. Adults driving by didn't notice me, while carloads of teenagers threw things at me. I peered across the street to see how Ralph was holding up, but Snuffleupagus was lying on a grassy strip next to the highway, taking a nap. I yelled across the traffic, trying to wake him up, but he wasn't budging. The elephant, it appeared, was out for the count.

•

No one ever came to relieve me for lunch. Meanwhile, the grand opening itself, fueled by free hot dogs and Canfield sodas, gained momentum. In less than an hour, I was surrounded by dozens of women and children. They touched me, poked me, hugged me, and prodded me. Everyone seemed to want a piece of Big Bird, and in the course of this frenzy, I worried loose several of my own feathers. Ralph was finally coming to, but other than a beefy salesman sitting in a lawnchair, no one else was over there with him.

Frank Wisiniewski came out to work the crowd. He raised his arms into the air, as if conducting an orchestra, and yelled, "Who wants their picture taken with Big Bird?"

A dozen hands rose. "Me!" the kids yelled back.

"All right," he said. Frank looked into my beak and said, "You're doing great, big guy." Then he glanced across the highway at Ralph, who was sitting with his shaggy legs over the curb and swatting flies with his trunk.

I was concerned about the authenticity of my costume, afraid some of the kids might decide to call me on it—the beak, after all, didn't move, and I couldn't speak because my voice didn't sound anything like Big Bird's—but to my surprise, the kids didn't want their picture taken with me so much as their mothers did. One by one, the kids' mothers sat on my lap, slung an arm around my neck, and cooed into my ear.

"He's so *cute*," one of the young mothers said, stroking the side of my head. "Look at those big eyes!"

Lucy Bruno, holding a helium-filled balloon in one hand and a hot dog with relish in the other, came waltzing in with her mother. Her mother had the sour look of someone who'd just realized she'd stepped in dog poop. Lucy, with the same sour look, sized up the situation before joining the line. When her turn to sit on my lap finally came, she gave me the once-over and said, "You're a little *short* to be Big Bird, aren't you?"

I shrugged. I was still steamed about her finger-pointing in

Mrs. Davis's class, a traitorous act, so when she sat on my lap, I took the quill of a feather that had come loose this morning and poked her butt with it. Hard. Lucy yelped and hopped off.

"He stuck me with a pin!" she yelled.

When I opened my arms to hug her, she screamed and ran to her mother.

Moments later, Frank Wisiniewski marched over. He offered his TV grin to the others in line, then crouched and whispered into my beak, "You drew blood on that kid. I don't want any lawsuits, you hear?"

By three o'clock, I was starving and hoping for somebody to give me a break, but now that people were getting off work at the mall, the line grew even longer. At one point, a fat man stepped up to me, narrowed his eyes, then plopped down onto my lap. My legs felt as though they were going to snap in half, but I kept quiet. The man claimed that he wanted to take a good look at my costume up close, and that he wanted a photo so that he could study it later at home. "Tell me, pal, what's the beak made out of, *plaster*?"

"I don't know," I said. "I'm only renting." These were the first words I'd spoken in hours, and my voice was hoarse.

The guy said, "I bet I could make one of these costumes myself. They sell the eyes in any half-decent arts and craft store. The feathers, hell, they would be a cinch to get. But the *beak*. I'd have to make that myself, I suppose. Papier-mâché, you think?"

"I really don't know," I said. The circulation in my legs had been cut off under the crush of weight, the initial pain dissolving into numbness with occasional bursts of tingling.

Before he heave-hoed himself up off my lap, he took one last look at me and said, "Yep, I think I could piece me together a costume as good as yours."

"Good luck," I said.

I watched him walk away. I wondered if he was a John Gacy type. John Gacy'd been a big, fat clown in his own killing-spree heyday—Pogo was Gacy's clown name—and seeing all those body bags night after night made me curious about grown men who wore make-up. What were they really up to? Here was some guy three times my age and six times my weight talking about making a bird suit for his own private use. *For what?*

By the end of the day, the bird suit stunk, and just as the stink was reaching new heights, Mary Polaski appeared in the showroom with a throng of other girls from our class. When she saw me, she squealed. "Oh-look-oh-look!" she said. "I *have* to get my picture taken with him."

Mary Polaski was the very last person in line. When her turn came, she hopped up onto my lap. Already overheated, my breathing growing heavier and heavier, I sounded more like Darth Vader than Big Bird.

While the photographer loaded a new roll of film into the camera, Mary turned her head and stared dreamily into my beak. Her eyelids were heavy, as if she had woken from a deep sleep, and I was starting to think that she could see through the perforated holes of the wire-mesh, and that she could tell it was me, Hank, but then she reached into my beak and, with the tip of her finger, tapped the screen twice. "Who's in there?" she whispered. "Who's the real Big Bird?"

I said nothing. I held my breath. I wanted to lean forward and kiss her, but I'd have engulfed her entire head with my beak if I'd tried.

"Talk to me," she said. "It must get lonely in there."

I knew that I had to say something—I couldn't let the moment slip by—so I said, "Break up with Chuck McDowell. You can do better than that."

She leaned back. "You know Chuck?" she asked.

Before I could answer, the photographer interrupted: "Let's give Big Bird a smooch!" he said. When Mary put her lips against the corner of my beak, the photographer squeezed the rubber bulb and a flash of light exploded.

Blinking, Mary put her finger back inside my beak, resting it on my petrified tongue. She was about to speak when a group of tiny kids rushed over, plucking my feathers. Then Ralph, still dressed as Snuffleupagus, stepped into the showroom, his trunk swaying like a pendulum. When he patted himself down, mushroom clouds of dust erupted from his costume. A few flies buzzed around his head. He looked over at the kids and said, "Beat it, you punks. The bird's ride is here."

Mary Polaski hugged me hard and said, "Thanks for the advice. You're absolutely right. I *can* do better." On her way out the door, she turned and said, "You're a sweetheart!" She winked, then bounded joyfully out the door and into the ever-gray Chicago spring.

After changing into my clothes and stuffing the costume into my Hefty bag, I found Ralph and told him that the restroom was all his.

"I'm fine," Ralph said. "Kenny's already here. Waiting."

"You're not going to take the Snuffleupagus costume off?" I asked.

Ralph wagged his head.

Kenny's Nova was parked where he'd dropped us off this morning. Ralph and I took our usual seats, though Ralph's fit was tighter now and he spilled over onto Kenny's seat.

"So?" Kenny said. "How'd it go, girls?"

I told Kenny what a great time I'd had, how I was surrounded all day by women who kept sitting on my lap, and how, at the end of the day, Mary Polaski had sat down on me and flirted.

"But she didn't realize it was you," Kenny said.

"Doesn't matter," I said.

"It does matter," Kenny said. "I know that kind of girl, the kind who'll flirt with a guy inside a bird suit. She didn't care who was inside. Could've been *me* in there. You can't trust a girl like that. Listen to your Uncle Kenny. I know. Believe me, I know."

Kenny wasn't my uncle, and I didn't want his advice. Ralph turned his elephant head toward Kenny and nodded, as if taking it all in, but he didn't say a word the whole way home. At one point, I thought I heard him snort, but since he was still wearing his costume, it was possible he'd fallen asleep and was snoring.

Kenny slammed on the brakes in front of my house and said, "You'll have to take the costume back yourself. Return the deposit to me in full and I'll pay you for the job. You got that? Good. I guess me and the elephant are outta here then."

Ralph turned to face me, but the pull of my instincts being stronger than my logic, I stared into his huge fake eyes, waiting for recognition, instead of looking into his mouth, where I knew his face was. The recognition never came, and then Kenny peeled away, wrapping me in a cocoon of exhaust.

I rubbed my eyes and saw dimly through the smoke my parents looking at me from the picture window. They must have wondered what was making all the noise, but what they found instead was their son materializing out of vapor, as if I'd returned home from another world. I started to wave, but my mother reached up and yanked the drapes shut, making me wonder if they'd even seen me at all.

The next day, at Waldo's Trick Shop and Costumes, Waldo pulled the costume from the Hefty bag and carefully inspected it. "You lost some feathers," he said and pointed at Big Bird's crotch. He opened the cash register and counted out half of the deposit money—fifty dollars. My entire pay check would be forty-two dollars, meaning that I would owe Kenny eight dollars for my day of work. I knew

Kenny would make me pay it, too. I wanted to argue with Waldo, but what could I say? I'd lost enough feathers that anyone could easily see the nylon body-suit beneath. It looked worse than I remembered, so I took what little money he offered.

That night, Mom waited until Dad came home before serving dinner, and when he did finally arrive, three hours late, it was clear he'd been at Lucky's Tavern for a few drinks. He was grinning at everyone and everything—clear sign that he'd lost a boat-load of money tonight playing poker. I already braced myself for the argument that I would hear later, muffled behind my parent's bedroom door.

"These are great green beans!" Dad said, nearly yelling. "Are they FRESH?"

"No," my mother said. "They're canned."

"Green GIANT?"

"No. Generic."

"Oh." Dad took another spoonful. I hated generic green beans. They were too green, still had the stems, and felt like tubes of rubber on my tongue. Dad looked up at me and Kelly, then waggled his eyebrows, trying to make us smile, but we weren't falling for it. His eyes widened and he said, "Oh, crap, I almost forgot. I saw the damnedest thing on the way home. Actually, I'm not sure *what* I saw, but it looked like an elephant walking down 79th street."

"You've been drinking," Mom said. "Don't scare the kids."

"No, listen," Dad said. "It wasn't a real elephant. It was sort of rust-colored and it was walking on its hind legs."

Mom stood up abruptly, gritting her teeth. She scooped her food into the trash and slammed her plate into the sink. Then she went to the bedroom, locking herself inside.

Dad helped himself to more green beans. He said, "An elephant on the prowl. Craziest thing I've ever seen. Honest to God."

School may have been out for the week of spring break, but CCD was still in session, meeting on Thursday night, as usual. As far as I knew, everyone in Chicago was Catholic. All of my classmates, except for Hani Abdallah, were Catholic, and so every parent in the neighborhood, except for Hani Abdallah's, sent their kids to CCD. No one knew why they had to go to CCD, though. "Why do I have to go?" I'd ask my mother. "I'm missing *The Bionic Woman*! How can I follow what's going on in *The Six Million Dollar Man* if I'm missing *The Bionic Woman*?" "Your job," my mother would say, "isn't to ask why. Your job is to do what I tell you to do." So far as I could tell, that's what everyone's parents were telling their kids. Meanwhile, it was Hani Abdallah's job to fill me in on *The Bionic Woman*.

The only good thing about CCD this year was that Mary Polaski was in my class. The bad thing was that this was where she had met Chuck McDowell, a latecomer to Catholicism. Tonight, though, they were sitting at opposite ends of the room, a sight that made my palms moist, my heart thump faster. She had taken my advice and broken up with him, and now she was on the lookout for someone better—possibly me.

My CCD teachers, mostly single women, were getting more than they had bargained for. They'd taken the job because they liked kids, but they had not anticipated that kids in theory were always more appealing than real kids, particularly when those kids would rather spend their Thursday nights doing nearly anything else—drilling holes in walls, for instance, or breaking boards over their own heads. I wasn't any better. I yawned too much, cracked lame jokes, barely listened.

Tonight, the teacher talked about Jesus baking loaves of bread and catching fish. Hoping to prove to Mary that I was a serious student of *The Bible*, I tried to concentrate, but all that I could picture was the Jesus who'd shown up at our school handing out loaves of Wonder Bread and cans of Starkist tuna. Before long, my brain clicked off, as if it were controlled by a thermostat, and I drifted away. My eyelids were starting to flutter when someone yelled, "Look!" and pointed out the window.

Crossing the church parking lot was Snuffleupagus, except that it was hard to tell that it was actually Snuffy. His fur was matted and his trunk seemed to be holding on by a long thread.

"What *is* that?" Chuck McDowell asked.

"It looks like an alien," another boy said.

Mary Polaski said, "I've seen it before, but I can't remember where."

I wanted to announce that it was just Ralph, but I wasn't sure that it *was* Ralph. Ralph might have returned the costume by now and someone else might have rented it. Or maybe the guy who'd sat on my lap, having lived up to his promise of making his own costume, now spent his nights haunting church parking lots. But it was really too dark to tell who it was.

The teacher, already irritated with us, told us to ignore him. "It's a bum," she said. "What he wants is your attention. If you ignore him, he'll go away."

The rest of spring break, I paced our house with nothing to do, feeling out of sorts inside my own body. I'd hoped Frank Wisiniewski would call Kenny and say he wanted us back for another day. I'd have done it for free, too. I was that bored.

Outside, I found half of a soggy newspaper next to a curb. It was a story about John Wayne Gacy. Gacy was in the news every day. Today's story included a long list of items investigators had found inside Gacy's house shortly before they arrested him. Among the suspicious items, according to the article, were an address book, a scale, a stained section of rug, and clothing that was much too small for Gacy. Inside my own house, I found an address book, a scale, a stained section of rug, and clothing that was much too small for me. There were other things on Gacy's list, like handcuffs. I looked around my bedroom, but the only suspicious items were a copy of *The Unauthorized Biography of Peter Frampton*, a poster of Elton John wearing a mink coat and eyeglasses that looked like two grand pianos, and three yellow feathers extracted from an extraordinarily large bird costume. What conclusions, I wondered, would investigators draw? Who exactly, they might ask, was this Hank character?

On Saturday, a letter arrived for me, a genuine letter with a local postmark, and I was hoping it was from Mary Polaski, but it was a bill from Kenny for the damaged costume. He wanted twenty bucks. Thanks to taxes, social security, and other deductions, my paycheck was less than I had calculated, resulting in me owing Kenny even more money.

I was eager to see how much he'd charged Ralph, so I biked over to Ralph's house. I waited by the gate, as usual, but apparently he didn't see me. It was possible that he was staying with Kenny, which he sometimes did, but I didn't have Kenny's number, and I wasn't sure I'd have called him even if I did.

When school resumed on Monday, Ralph wasn't there, either. It wasn't like Ralph not to be at school. He'd already failed two grades, and I knew he didn't want to fail a third time.

Lucy Bruno *was* there, however, limping dramatically into class and easing herself into her chair. Mary Polaski was there, too, honking into Kleenex and drawing fresh hearts, inside of which she wrote JESUS LOVES MARY. I wasn't sure if she meant the Jesus who'd shown up at our school or *Jesus* Jesus. I needed to clarify what I meant when I told Mary that she could do better than Chuck McDowell. What I meant was that she should dump Chuck for me, not for Jesus.

In art class, when Mrs. Richards gave each of us some chicken-wire, papier-mâché, and a small coffee can full of water for dipping,

I rolled up my sleeves and got to work, shaping chicken-wire until my fingers were raw. I stuffed newspaper inside the chicken-wire sculpture, and I started slapping down one strip of papier-mâché after another, trying to finish my project by the end of the hour. I was making Big Bird's beak, as the guy on my lap had suggested, and I was doing a pretty good job, too. It looked like a beak, except that it wasn't painted and it wasn't attached to the rest of Big Bird's head. Still, it was a beak, and when I finished making it, I tried getting Mary Polaski's attention.

"Psssst," I said. "Hey, Mary. Psssst."

Mary glanced up, her hands draped with strips of gooey newspaper. She looked like the Mummy starting to unravel.

"Mary," I whispered. "Does this look familiar?" I held up the beak, hoping she would make the connection and understand what I had meant.

Mary stared at it, but there were no burning signs of recognition in her eyes.

"Remember?" I asked. I held it up as an extension of my own mouth.

Mary smiled, but there was a faraway look in her eyes. Around her neck hung a gold cross I'd never seen before. The beak had been my last chance to win her over, but it was too late. Mary Polaski, for all practical purposes, was a goner.

I spent the better part of recess kicking a lumpy chunk of concrete from one end of the blacktop to the other until a crowd began gathering at the far corner. I figured Jesus, released from jail for loitering, had returned to Rice Park, so I wandered over to catch a peek, hoping to see what sort of stunts he was going to pull today, but it wasn't Jesus. It was Ralph.

Ralph was standing by the monkey bars, where Jesus

had stood, only no one knew that it was Ralph because he was wearing his Snuffleupagus costume. But no one recognized him as Snuffleupagus, either. The head was crushed on one side; his trunk appeared to have been severed, doing away altogether with the idea that he was an elephant; both eyes were gone; and patches of fur were missing, as though he had mange. To confuse matters further, this new, haunting Snuffleupagus had a cigarette dangling from its humongous mouth. Ralph had somehow rigged it so that the mouth now opened and closed, actually allowing him to smoke.

Mr. Santoro rushed over to see what was going on, and when he saw Ralph, he quickly lifted the bullhorn to his mouth. But then he squinted and cocked his head, as if unsure what he was looking at, and lowered the bullhorn, waiting along with the rest of us to see what would happen next.

I was about to yell out to Ralph when a wall of feedback hit us, causing everyone to jump back and clutch their ears. Next came a voice through a P.A. system, but the words sounded slow and warped, the way Ralph spoke to me when he was irritated, carefully pronouncing each syllable, as if I were an alien. The problem today, I decided, was with Ralph's portable cassette player and the size-D batteries inside that were quickly running out of juice. Even so, the effect was haunting. The voice, distorted and amplified, said, "You. Want. To. See. Something?"

We waited, looking around. When nothing happened, someone said, "See what?" Then the voice came back, louder this time, answering the question.

"Watch. *This.*"

With one mittened paw, Ralph removed the cigarette from his huge mouth and threw it into a nearby bush. The bush burst into flames. The amplified voice said, "Do. You. Know. Who. I. Am? Well. Do. You?"

No one knew, not even me. I knew that it was Ralph, sure, but beyond that I didn't know what Ralph was doing or who he was supposed to be. And there was no way to know, either, whether or not he was getting the reaction he wanted, but every last one of us stared at him in horror. No one doubted that what they were seeing was something otherworldly, and I suppose at first it could have gone either way—Ralph as angel of mercy or Ralph as messenger from Hell—but the longer we stood there watching Ralph squirt the burning bush with lighter fluid, flames so high that the tree branches over his head were catching fire, the clearer it became from which sad and unholy world this visitation had come.

15

Duke's was where my dad took me to pick up the best Italian beef and Italian sausage sandwiches on the southwest side of Chicago. The building wasn't much bigger than a hut, but the lines sometimes snaked out its two side doors. Once you were within reach of the counter, ordering food turned from a spectator sport into a competitive event. The men and women who worked the counter would yell out, "Hey, YOU. Whaddaya want?" or "Who's next? Are YOU next?" Sometimes they pointed randomly and yelled "YOU" over and over until someone claimed to be the YOU in question.

The closer my father and I got to the counter, the harder my heart pounded. I hated being pointed at or yelled at, but at Duke's the chances were pretty good that both of these would happen to you, possibly several times, even after you'd ordered. And once you were picked, you'd better know what you wanted, and you'd better know how to order it. Ordering had its own language, and it took years of listening to my dad to understand what all of it meant.

"Gimme two beefs extra juicy, a sausage, make it bloody. Gimme two dogs."

"What'll it be on the dogs?"

"The works."

"You want the beefs dipped?"

"Yeah, soak 'em."

"You want peppers on those beefs?"

"Yeah, gimme peppers."

"Hot, mild, or both?"

"Both. Extra cukes on those dogs."

"You got it."

One time, a really fat guy in line ordered about half the menu. By the time he left, he was sweating like mad, three bags in each hand, forcing everyone to smoosh together so that he could reach the door. As soon as he was safely out of earshot, everyone looked at each other and sort of snickered and shook their heads, partly because he was so fat and partly because he'd ordered so much food, but mostly out of admiration for a guy who could eat that much.

"Must have an appetite, that guy," someone said, and someone else said, "I wonder how much he spends on groceries, huh? How much you think a guy like that spends?" and then a few people whistled and one guy added, "I wouldn't even want to guess." This was how conversations unraveled in Chicago: one minute you'd be standing in line with a few dozen people you didn't know; the next, everyone would be laughing and talking. All they needed was a topic, but once that topic revealed itself, there would be no stopping them.

My father never pitched in. He never added anything. He wouldn't even smile or look at the people talking.

On our way home, I said, "Man, that guy was *fat*."

My father said, "*You*," and poked me in the shoulder with his forefinger. "*You* know better."

"Whaddaya mean?" I said, but my father didn't have to say anything. I could hear the answer in the tone of my voice, the way I'd shot back my reply, and it scared me.

The next time we went to Duke's, the fat guy was there again.

We went to Duke's the same time every week, so our schedules must have started overlapping. I watched the fat guy order. I watched him dig through his pants pockets for money, then pay for his food. I watched him make his way out the door, mumbling "Excuse me," as people pressed into one another to make room.

I always wondered who would be the first person to speak up, who would get the ball rolling, and so when no one stepped forward, I decided to give it a try. I cleared my throat. Louder than I meant to, I said, "Man, that guy was F-A-T *fat!*" I looked around. When no one responded, I said, "Did everyone see that fat guy? *Whew!*"

I had expected someone to echo what I had said, to add to it, to spin off of it and start their own riff, but no one said a word. They exchanged looks, or they glanced from me to my dad and then back again. Beads of sweat appeared on my dad's forehead. I tried picturing the man from last week who had called the fat guy *fat*, but then I couldn't remember anyone actually calling him fat. What they'd said was that the guy had an appetite. But what was the difference? Wasn't saying that a guy had an appetite and then laughing about it the same as calling someone fat?

Outside, my father and I each carried a sack of food. I could hear distant birds, the low squawks of their approach, but when I looked up the sky was clear, not a bird in sight. I turned and saw that the noise was coming from Duke's, from the men and women inside, and I knew that fat wasn't the topic. *I* was the topic. I wanted to go back inside and protest, I wanted to make my case, but I knew it wouldn't help. Everyone's turn eventually came. Yesterday it was the fat guy's. Today it was mine. The next day it might have been my sister's or my mother's or my father's. It could have been anybody's, really. It could have been yours.

16

Rumor had it that Styx, the greatest band of all time, was going to perform a surprise concert in our city's reservoir. The reservoir was bone dry, used these days only for drainage, the perfect spot for a full-blown rock concert. Members of Styx had grown up on Chicago's South Side, and the word on the street was that they wanted to pay back a little something to their hometown fans. The only mystery now was the concert's date.

Every night a procession of cars crept slowly around the reservoir, watching for the arrival of Styx's road crew. Our classmate Wes Papadakis had vowed to camp out until Styx arrived, and some nights you could hear the faint reverberations of "Come Sail Away" or "Lady" floating up from the very bottom of the reservoir's concrete basin where Wes, clutching his boombox, lay like a castaway atop his bicentennial inflatable mattress, waiting. It was a foregone conclusion that Wes was going to fail eighth grade.

I went over to Ralph's house to see what he knew about all of this, but when I got there, he was on top of his mother's garage, peering through a magnifying glass. I made my way around to the alley, found the ladder, then climbed to the top of the garage. "Ralph," I said, tiptoeing across the lumpy tar, afraid of falling through. "What are you doing?"

He pointed at Mr. Gonzales, his next door neighbor, and said, "I'm trying to set him on fire." Mr. Gonzales was sitting in a chaise lounge and drinking a beer, naked except for a pair of Bermuda shorts. He was unemployed that year and was almost always outside, as naked as you could get without actually being naked. Crushed beer cans decorated his lawn, glinting in the sunlight, while a tiny speck of light from Ralph's magnifying glass seared into the man's bare shoulder blade.

"Why?"

"Shhhhh," Ralph said. "Watch this. Here it comes."

Mr. Gonzales twitched a few times, then reached up over his shoulder and swatted the dagger of light, a phantom mosquito.

"Wow," I said. "How long have you been doing this?"

"Two weeks," Ralph said. "I put in at least an hour a day. Some days, two. Every once in a while I think I see smoke."

"But *why?*"

"Why what?"

"Why do you want to set him on fire?"

Ralph reached into a grocery sack and pulled out three Big Chief notepads, a thick rubber band holding the batch together.

"What's this?" I asked.

"It's my revenge list," he said. "It's a list of everyone I'm going to get even with."

"Really!" I said. I removed the rubber band, eager to read the list, expecting to find our teachers' names sprinkled among Ralph's school work and doodles, but what I found was a much more frightening and detailed accounting. On each page were twenty names—I saw Lucy Bruno's, Gina Morales not far from Lucy—and each notepad, according to its cover, contained a hundred pages.

"Ralph," I said. "There must be six hundred names here."

Ralph jammed his magnifying glass into his back pocket. He said, "Look. I've met a lot of people since I was born, okay?"

The pages were filled with everyone I knew, including my parents—everyone, as far as I could tell, except for me and my sister Kelly.

"Geez, Ralph. Who's not on this list?"

Ralph shrugged. "Are you done reading that yet?" he asked. He snatched the notebooks away and stuffed them deep inside his grocery sack.

I liked Ralph, but danger always lurked close behind him. Sooner or later he was bound to drag me along with him into the swamp of low-life crime, and I'd been meaning all year to break off my friendship with him, only I couldn't figure out how to do it without repercussion. His revenge list now confirmed what I'd feared all along, that Ralph wasn't going to make it easy for me.

"Styx," he said after we had climbed down from the roof and I had told him why I'd stopped by. "You want front-row tickets to the reservoir concert? I'll talk to my cousins, see what I can scare up."

"Great," I said. "I appreciate it."

My sister, Kelly, had her first real boyfriend that spring, a skinny buck-toothed kid named Unger. Unger was not at all the sort of future in-law I had ever imagined. I suppose I made my feelings clear to him by pulling out my Mortimer Snerd ventriloquist doll each time he came over, settling the doll onto my right knee, and yanking the string that opened his mouth, out of which came, "Hi, my name's Unger," or "Boy, my girlfriend, Kelly, is one hot babe. I can't imagine what she sees in me," or "What's an orthodontist?!"

For her part, Kelly quit speaking to me, except to insult me. "*Your* problem," she liked to say, "is that your only friend is a hoodlum."

Sadly, she was more or less right. Ralph was a hoodlum. Sort of. I was still determined to break things off with him, but the next day he called to say that he had a surprise for me, and when I showed up at his house, he appeared on his front stoop, grinning, a giant tie dangling from his neck. He met me at the gate and said, "Here," pressing into my hands another necktie, equally as large. "Put it on."

"What?"

"Put it on. I know where Dennis DeYoung is having dinner tonight."

Dennis DeYoung was Styx's lead singer. "You're kidding," I said. "*The* Dennis DeYoung?"

"No," Ralph said. "Dennis DeYoung the dog catcher."

"How do you know he'll be there?" I asked.

"Sources," Ralph said. Ralph's sources were his cousins, no doubt. In addition to working the assembly line at the Tootsie Roll Factory, they apparently doubled as music insiders, privy to the secrets of the world's most successful rock stars. Robert Plant, for instance, couldn't hold a note if not for the electronic vocal augmenter installed in each of his microphones and controlled by a man working a soundboard. Gene Simmons had had a cow tongue surgically attached to his own tongue. After *Frampton Comes Alive* became the best-selling album of all time, Peter Frampton ballooned up to four hundred pounds and moved to Iceland, too fat to play his guitar anymore; his new albums, all flops, were written and performed by his identical twin brother, Larry Frampton.

Though I was wearing a yellow T-shirt with an iron-on decal of a gargantuan falcon, our school's mascot, I slipped the tie over my head and tightened the knot. We walked nearly two miles to Ford City Shopping Center, the area's first indoor shopping mall, then over to Ford City Bowling and Billiards, home to a few dozen pool-hustling hooligans who liked to pick fights with adults and flick lit cigarettes at kids. Next door was a Mexican restaurant: El Matador.

"You sure this is where Dennis DeYoung's supposed to be?" I asked. "It's sort of rough around here."

Ralph adjusted his tie's knot. "This is the place. From what I hear, he loves tacos."

We stepped into the crushed-velvet dining room decorated with sombreros and strings of dried red peppers. A fancy acoustic guitar hung on the wall next to our table.

"You think he'll play a song while he's here?" I asked, pointing to the guitar.

"Maybe," Ralph said. "I wouldn't mind hearing a little 'Grand Illusion' tonight. Acappella," he added.

"No kidding," I said. I started humming "Lorelei" when I noticed that Ralph's thoughts were elsewhere. He looked as though he were staring beyond El Matador's walls and into some blurry vision of his own past. Years ago, Ralph had admitted to me that he wanted to do something that would make our classmates remember him, and for a fleeting moment, while playing the bongos in Mr. Mudjra's music class, hammering out his own solo to Led Zeppelin's "Moby Dick," Ralph had succeeded in winning the hearts of twenty-one seventh graders, one of whom was me. We watched, awestruck, as one of our own moved his hands in expert chaos, keeping up with the music in such a way that we weren't quite sure what we were watching. Veronica Slomski and Isabel Messina, sitting in the front row, wept after Ralph had finished.

I had a feeling Ralph was rolling those ten minutes over in his head right now, and so I asked him if he was okay, but he just cut his eyes toward me and said, "Of course I'm okay. What's your problem?"

"Nothing," I said.

When the waitress arrived, we ordered drinks and several appetizers, along with our main courses and dessert—everything at once. I had never ordered my own food at a restaurant (my mom or dad always took care of it) and so I was unprepared when the food began arriving in droves, plate after plate, way too much for a single table. Even so, Ralph and I scarfed it all down, until our bellies poked out and we could no longer sit up straight in our booth.

I groaned and then Ralph did the same, only louder. I spotted Lucy Bruno and her parents on the other side of the restaurant. All three were staring at us, so I lifted my glass of pop, a toast, while

Ralph carefully peeled back his eyelids and stuck his tongue out at them. Lucy shrieked and looked away.

"When do you think Dennis DeYoung's gonna get here?" I asked. "I'm not feeling too good."

"Maybe he's not coming tonight," Ralph said. "Maybe he ate Chinese tonight. I hear he likes chop suey, too."

When the check came, Ralph said, "It's on me." He pulled a bent pen from his back pocket, flipped the check over, and wrote, *I.O.U. a lot of money. Thanks!*

"Good one," I said. "We can hide the money under an ashtray. Give her a heart attack until she finds it."

Ralph stood from the table, stretched, then started walking away. I had to grip the edge of the table and brace myself to stand.

"Hey, Ralph," I said. "Don't forget to leave the money."

Ralph turned quickly and shot me a look that said, *Shut up.*

I didn't have any money, so I had no choice but to follow. My heart felt swollen, pounding so hard it hurt: food and fear, a lethal combo. Outside, beyond the Ford City parking lot, I asked Ralph what exactly had just happened.

"We didn't pay for our food," he said.

"Why not?" I asked, my stomach starting to gurgle more dangerously.

"Listen," he said. "Restaurants work on the good faith system. They give you a check, and you're supposed to leave money. You wave to the waitress on the way out, and she waves back. 'Have a nice day,' she says, and you say, 'Will do.' Well, they got stiffed this time. The way I see it, I'm teaching the whole industry a lesson."

"What lesson's that?"

"Not everyone's honest," he said.

"Oh. I see," I said, but I didn't. Not really.

•

After the restaurant incident, I avoided Ralph, afraid he was going to land me in jail, where I would grow old and rot. A few days later, while concocting hair-raising scenarios in which the cops came roaring up to my parents' front door looking for me, I walked into my bedroom and found Unger holding my Mortimer Snerd ventriloquist doll.

"What the hell are you doing in here?" I asked.

He pulled the string at the back of Mortimer Snerd's head, and Snerd's mouth opened. Unger messed with the string some more until Snerd's teeth chattered. Then, in a high-pitched voice and without moving his lips, Unger repeated what I had said: "*What the hell are YOU doing here?*"

"Hey," I said. "That's pretty good. You can throw your voice."

Mortimer Snerd turned his head first left, then right. "*Hey,*" Snerd said. "*That's pretty good. You can throw your voice.*"

I felt silly now for all those times I'd used Snerd to insult Unger, not so much because I'd insulted him, but because I had made no bones that it was me doing all the talking. I had never bothered to change my voice, and I had always moved my lips. Unger, on the other hand, reacted to everything the dummy said. He asked it questions, treating it as a creature beyond his control, which is what drew me into his show. For their finale, Unger drank a tall glass of water while Snerd sang "You Light Up My Life."

When he finished, setting Snerd aside, I stood up and applauded. "You should go on *The Gong Show*," I said.

"I've thought about it," Unger said.

"Seriously," I said. "You've got talent."

Unger blushed. I don't think I'd ever actually seen another boy blush before, so I quit complimenting him. "What are you doing here, anyway?" I asked. "Where's Kelly?"

"Oh, she's still at pompom practice," he said.

"Pompom practice?" I said. "What the hell's that? I didn't know Kelly did anything at school."

Unger smiled and said, "There's a lot you don't know about Kelly." He tried to look mischievous when he said it, but then he blushed again, and I had to look away. It embarrassed me too much to watch.

"Listen," I said. "I don't want to hear about you and Kelly. If I want to watch a horror movie, I'll stay up and watch *Creature Features*, okay?"

Two days later, I found Unger in my bedroom again. "What the hell?" I said.

Unger blushed, but Mortimer Snerd said, "*I hope you don't mind. We were just practicing.*" And then Snerd laughed: "*Uh-huck, uh-huck.*"

"Hey," I said. "That sounds just like him, Unger. Seriously."

Unger set Snerd aside. "I found some of my dad's old Charlie McCarthy records. I worked on it all weekend."

I stared at Unger; I didn't know what to say. I didn't know anyone my age who spent all weekend working on anything.

Unger said, "I came over to tell you about this great idea," and then he told me about how he and a few of his friends were going to start a band, an *air* band, and how they needed a drummer.

"I can't play the drums," I said.

"It's an air band," Unger said. "All you do is pretend to play. We'll put together a tape with a bunch of songs, and we'll play those at parties."

"Whose parties?" I asked.

"Anybody's parties," he said. "This is the best idea we ever thought of. People will pay us to come over and play. They'll think we're a hoot."

Hoot was a word only my grandparents used, but I tried to ignore it. Maybe he'd picked it up over the weekend, listening to Charlie McCarthy. "People will actually pay us?" I asked. "Are you out of your mind?"

"There's nothing out there like this," he said, "and that's what you need these days, a gimmick."

He seemed so sure of our success, I couldn't help getting a little excited myself. "What'll we play? You think we could play some Styx?"

Unger frowned. "Maybe," he said. "I don't know, though. I'd have to talk to the other guys. We were thinking about some cutting edge stuff, like Roxy Music or Elvis Costello or The Knack." He looked at his shoes and said, "The thing is, we need a place to practice. Do you think we can use your basement?"

I laughed. "Are you kidding? My parents would never let a band practice in their basement." Unger stared at me patiently, waiting for my brain to catch up to the conversation. "So what you're saying," I said slowly, "is that no one would actually be playing any instruments?"

"Right."

"Would I need a drum set?"

"Nothing," Unger said. "All we need is a boombox, and Jimmy Cook has that."

"And you want me to be the drummer?"

"You'd be perfect," he said. "You've got the muscles for it." He squeezed my bicep.

I wasn't very muscular, and I didn't like Unger squeezing my arm, but I didn't say anything about it. "Okay," I said. "Sure. I'll do it. Why not?"

After I joined the air band, Kelly quit talking to me for good. She thought the whole thing had been my idea, a ploy to keep her and Unger from seeing each other. The rehearsals, as it turned out, were pretty grueling—two hours each night, five nights a week.

"We have to practice," Unger told her, a whine creeping into his voice. "How are we going to get any good if we don't practice?"

I felt totally ridiculous at first, the five of us pretending to play instruments that weren't even in the room: Joe Matecki tickling the ivory, Howlin' Jimmy Cook belting out the lead vocals, Bob Jesinowski sawing away on the electric guitar, Unger dutifully plucking the bass, while I went nuts on the drums. But after a few weeks, an odd thing happened. I started getting into it. The more I picked up on the quirks of different drummers, the more I would lose myself to the music. And when I shut my eyes, an amphitheater would roll out before me with thousands of crazed girls screaming, crying, throwing themselves against the stage, their arms in the air, stretching and arching toward me. It was as if I were holding a gigantic magnet, and the girls—weighted down with silver bracelets, pewter rings, and stainless steel watches—couldn't help but to be pulled into my circle of energy.

Once, in the midst of such a vision, my arms flailing wildly to The Who's "Won't Get Fooled Again," I opened my eyes and saw Ralph standing at the foot of the basement stairs. My mother must have let him in and told him to go on downstairs. The other four guys in the band were lost in their own private worlds, twitching or swaying or, as with Unger, bouncing up and down, eyes squeezed shut.

"Ralph!" I yelled over the music. My voice startled the other band members. They looked up, saw Ralph, and stopped playing. Someone reached over and turned down the boombox. No one knew quite what to do with their hands now that their instruments had vanished. Jimmy violently scratched his head, using the tips of all his fingers. Joe rubbed his palms so hard against his jeans, I thought he was going to spontaneously combust in front of us.

"Hey," I said to Ralph. "The porkchop sideburns are looking good. They're really coming in." I pointed at his head. Ralph didn't say anything. He looked from one musician to the next, squinting, sizing us up. "Ralph plays the bongos," I said, hoping to snap Ralph out of whatever trance he appeared to be falling into. "I've never seen anyone play the bongos like him, either," I added. "You should've seen him last year in Mr. Mudjra's class. *Man!* You guys would've dropped dead." I smiled at Ralph, shook my head. "Hey, listen. I got an idea. Why don't you play the bongos in our band? That'd be okay, wouldn't it guys?"

Unger said, "I don't know. We'd have to talk about it. I mean, we've been rehearsing and everything. Our first gig's next week."

"Well," I said, "he can sit in with us today, though, can't he?"

"Sure," Unger said. "You want to sit in with us, Ralph?"

"C'mon, Ralph. Sit in with us."

Ralph's focus seemed to widen now to include all of us at once. Then, without so much as a word, he placed a business card of some kind onto my dad's toolbox, turned, and walked back upstairs, disappearing into the light above.

"Okay," Unger said. "Back to work."

After everyone had left, I walked over to my father's toolbox. What Ralph had left behind was not a business card. It was a ticket for the Styx concert. The ticket was made of blue construction paper with black ink that had bled until each letter looked sort of hairy. It said, STYX: LIVE AT THE RESERVOIR. NO CAMERAS. NO RECORDING DEVICES. RAIN OR SHINE. There was no date on the ticket. No time, either. No seat number, no address. I kept it with me, though, tucked inside my back pocket, ready at a moment's notice to be there, to be a part of history.

Bored, I went upstairs to my room and made a few dozen crank phone calls to Lucy Bruno. A few hours into doing this, her parents picked up another phone and announced that the line was tapped, and that the police would be at my house in short order. I didn't believe them, of course. After all, I had deepened my voice and put a couple of tube-socks over the mouthpiece, but their threats caused me to question what I was doing. Why was I making prank phone calls in the first place? What sort of person was I turning into?

On the night of our first gig, the five of us showed up early. We were to play in the rec room of a new condo on the far edge of town, and from the looks of it, everyone at the party was at least five years older than Unger, who was sixteen.

"Who set this gig up?" I asked.

"Jimmy did. These are his brother's friends."

A man wearing a powder-blue tuxedo came over and introduced himself as Chad. "Bad Chad," he said and laughed. "What do you guys call yourselves? The Air Band? Is that what your brother told me, Jimmy?"

"Yeah, that's right."

"What sort of tunes do you play?"

"Anything," Unger said. "You name it."

"Disco?" Chad asked.

"You bet," Unger said. "We play disco all the time."

Chad was one of those white guys who tried to pull off an afro, but from a distance it appeared that a small toxic cloud—a vapor— had attached itself to the top of his head. He'd also jammed a jumbo pitchfork of a comb into his hair to give it that final touch, but each time Chad nodded, the comb wiggled wildly.

Chad said, "You can set your equipment up over there."

"Cool," Unger said.

While Joe set up the boombox, the rest of us took our positions. We had made several specialty tapes: Hard Rock, Disco, Punk, even Country. I knew from all our weeks of practice what to do and when to do it, so I shut my eyes for dramatic effect. "Play That Funky Music" was the first song on our disco tape, opening with the electric guitar and followed by vocals. Then came the drums, a simple but seductive beat.

Moving my head in and out, finding the groove, I played well over a minute before looking up and into the audience. No one was dancing. No one was singing along. They stood in groups of two or three, watching us. The only people getting into the song were the other guys in the band, who were clearly as lost in the music as I had been. Bad Chad ran the tips of his fingers along his suit's lapels. Our eyes met, and I stopped playing.

Somewhere along the way there had been a misunderstanding, and the very thought now of the gap between their expectations and what we were actually doing made me instantly queasy. They had expected a real band; we hadn't even brought instruments. The gap couldn't have been any wider.

Chad motioned with his head, so I reached over and turned off the boombox. I might as well have been a hypnotist clapping my hands: Joe, Jimmy, Bob, and Unger suddenly came to, shaking their heads and looking around, bewildered. As simple as that, I had snapped them back to the here and now.

Chad took two steps forward and opened his mouth, as if to scold us, but nothing came out. He shut his eyes and shook his head, then stopped and looked at us again—crazed, this time—before throwing his arms into the air, turning around, and stomping toward the keg at the back of the room.

The school year was winding down, and I hadn't hung out with Ralph in over a month. Kelly and Unger had broken up, but Unger still came over to practice throwing his voice. Meanwhile, our air band was put indefinitely on hold.

One night in the middle of May, with a tornado watch in progress, Unger and I sat in my room, and I watched him put on a show with my Mortimer Snerd doll. I had to admit, his new act was pure genius. Using his boombox, he played Rolling Stones songs, and while Mortimer Snerd lip-synched the lead vocals, Unger actually sang back-up. It was dizzying to watch. I couldn't even begin to imagine how much time he'd spent at home figuring out the logistics of it all.

Every few minutes my father would bang on my bedroom door to upgrade us on the status of the approaching storm. "The watch is on until ten o'clock," he said the first time. "That's for *all* of Cook County." Then an hour later: "It's been upgraded to a warning now, guys. Eighty mile an hour winds. Hold on to your hats."

At first all we heard was the soft patter of rain, though not much later our lights started flickering while fists of hail pounded the house. Somewhere, a window shattered.

"Wow," I said.

"Sympathy For the Devil" was playing now, and Unger kept singing the "Oooooo Oooooooh" parts until an explosion nearby caused us both to jump.

"One of those giant transformers must have blown up," I said, though before I finished saying it, our lights shut off for good. "Great," I said. Unger didn't say anything. His battery-operated boombox chugged on, and Mick Jagger continued singing. It was my favorite part of the song, the part where Mick asks who killed the Kennedys, and so I closed my eyes. While Mick's words rumbled through me, I felt a hand touch my knee, then Unger's breath against my face, then his mouth against my mouth.

I screamed.

When Unger put his hand against my mouth to quiet me, I bit down, sinking my teeth into his knuckles, and then he screamed. My father bolted into the room with a high-powered flashlight, yelling, "What's wrong? You guys all right? What happened?"

"We're all right," I said. "Nothing happened."

My father swung the flashlight toward Unger. "Cut your hand?" he asked.

"Nah," he said. "I'm okay."

Dad said, "The two of you'd better quit screwing around then. This house is under siege. The basement's flooding and a tree's down out back. I sure as hell don't need the two of you testing my patience tonight."

"No problem," I said.

Much to my horror, my mother insisted that Unger spend the night. She put him up in my bedroom, so I took the couch in the living room and wrapped myself in a quilt. I don't know what time it was when I finally fell asleep, but I woke up the next morning to my father nudging me with his foot.

"Don't you know this kid?" he asked. He pointed his big toe at the TV.

I was so tired I could barely make sense of where I was or what was going on, but when I finally did, I saw my father in his LA-Z-BOY, holding a bowl of cereal, still nudging me with his foot; my mother and sister, side-by-side, staring at the TV screen; and Unger, who blushed when I looked over at him.

"I remember him from back when you were in Cub Scouts," Dad said. "Isn't that the same kid?"

On TV was Wes Papadakis, and he was being interviewed by Walter Jacobson of Channel 2 news. The interview had been conducted late last night, and it was the hottest story on all the stations. Later I would hear the whole thing, how Wes had been sound asleep at the bottom of the reservoir when the storm hit, and how he had been there—as he had been there every night—waiting for the arrival of Styx. Apparently, he'd fallen asleep listening to *Pieces of Eight* when the first ball of hail cracked him on the head. Not much later, he noticed water pouring over the sides, filling the reservoir. The sides proved too muddy for climbing out, leaving him, as he saw it, with only one option: to ride the storm out. And that's exactly what he did. Clutching his bicentennial inflatable mattress, and with all the city's flooded streets draining toward him, Wes floated twenty, thirty, forty feet, until he reached the upper lip of the reservoir and, swept along by a heavy current, rode his raft down Rutherford Avenue, all the way home.

"It's a miracle," my mother said, "that he's alive."

Kelly, tears in her eyes, turned and asked if I had his phone number.

"*No*, I don't have his phone number," I said. Until last night, Wes had been a mere shadow on the playground, a bit player at recess. Could his life really have changed that quickly?

"They should give that kid a medal," my father said.

"A medal?" I asked.

My father cocked his ear and turned his head slowly, pointing his chin at me. *And what have you done lately?* was what this look meant. Disgusted, my father finally turned away. "Hell," he said. "They should at least give him a key to the city."

My mother agreed. "That's the *least* they could do," she said.

I didn't see Unger anymore that school year. For those last few weeks of May, I couldn't shake the thought of Unger's mouth against my mouth. Panicked, I called Lucy Bruno three times in three days, finally convincing her to go to Haunted Trails Miniature Golf Range with me, where, much to my own amazement, I chipped a fluorescent green golf ball off Frankenstein's head. The manager promptly asked us to leave, I walked Lucy home, and we never spoke again. Whatever Lucy Bruno had thought of me before our date was now confirmed in spades by my recklessness with a golf club, by the threat I posed to society, and by the fact that I was far more amused by what I had done than anyone else at the golf range.

On the last day of May, I stuck my Mortimer Snerd ventriloquist doll and a hacksaw into a grocery sack with the general plan of sawing off Mortimer's head, and I walked to the reservoir where I intended to perform this act. Carefully, I made my way down the slope. I had never been down there before, but now, after everything that had happened with Wes, I wanted to see it.

Styx, of course, had never shown up, and now that I was down here, I couldn't imagine how it was going to happen anyway. There were no electrical outlets, the sides were too steep for people to sit, and the acoustics were awful. What had Wes been thinking? What had any of us been thinking?

"HELLO," I yelled for fun. "HOW ARE YOU?" I listened to my voice hit the wall and come back toward me. It bounced off another wall, then came back again. This continued for a while, my voice bouncing and creeping up behind me, to the side of me, or head-on, fainter and fainter, until it became a bunch of half-words and grunts, then nothing at all.

"HELLO," I yelled again. Someone from above yelled back, "HELLO," and together our voices surrounded me, one voice answering the other, overlapping, mocking one another. I looked up. A cop was peering down at me. With his billy club, he motioned for me to climb out of the reservoir. After struggling up the incline to reach him, he said, "What's in the bag?"

"A ventriloquist doll and a hacksaw," I said.

He nodded. "You see this sign?" He tapped it with his club. NO TRESPASSING, it said.

"No," I said. "I've never seen it before."

"It's there for a reason," he said. "Kid almost drowned a few weeks ago."

"Wes Papadakis," I said.

The cop looked at me, as if what I'd said made absolutely no sense to him. He said, "Got to start teaching you kids the meaning of laws. Got to start somewhere."

I guess I thought he was simply talking out loud because I was smiling when he read my rights to me, then pulled out his handcuffs. He asked me to set my bag down, and then he cuffed my hands behind my back. I was still smiling, but I was starting to shiver now, too.

"What's so funny?" the cop asked.

"Nothing," I said.

"Well," the cop said, "I wouldn't be smiling if I were you."

"I'm cold."

"It's not cold out," he said.

"I'm freezing."

With his hand on top of my head, the cop guided me into the backseat of his cruiser. "You know what? All you kids are nuts." He shut the door. After settling himself into the driver's seat, he set my bag down beside him and said, "That kid who almost drowned? He was nuts, too. Kept saying he was down there waiting for *sticks*, whatever the hell that's supposed to mean. Now look at him. A hero. You ask me, this whole city's nuts."

At the police station, the cop uncuffed me and returned my bag before handing me off to a woman cop who sat at a desk, smoking a long, thin cigarette. "Identification?" she said.

"I don't have any."

"How old are you, honey?"

"Thirteen."

"Boy," she said, "they get younger every day." She stood up and said, "Hold your horses, okay?"

I passed the time looking over some mug shots, until another cop, a bald one, lugged Ralph in, shoving him hard into a chair. Like me, Ralph was holding a grocery sack. The cop said, "Don't do anything that would require us to shoot you. You got that?"

Ralph shrugged.

"I wouldn't hesitate to use force," the cop said, leaving the two of us alone.

"Hey, Ralph," I said. Ralph looked over, and I smiled at him. "They got me, too," I said. I expected him to get up and come over, but he didn't. Instead, he narrowed his eyes at me, as if I were a witness who'd been called in to point him out in a line-up.

"I'm under arrest," I said and laughed. "Do you believe that?" I shook my head, unable to believe it myself. "Hey! You shaved off your porkchop sideburns," I said. "Why'd you do that?"

Ralph touched his face, where one of the sideburns had been, as if he no longer remembered what had been there. "What's in the bag?" he finally asked.

"A ventriloquist doll and a hacksaw," I said. "What's in yours?"

"My revenge list."

"Oh yeah," I said. "That's right. I forgot about that." I knew, of course, that my name had been added to Ralph's revenge list—how could it not have been?—and the very thought of its being there gave me goosebumps. "So," I said, changing subjects. "What'd they get you for?"

"Skipped out on a restaurant without paying the bill."

My heart sped up. "El Matador?" I asked.

"Nuh-uh. They never caught us for that one." He grinned, pleased that we'd gotten away with it, and I relaxed. "Last week," he said, "they nailed my cousins for selling fake Styx tickets. Styx's management heard about what they were doing and they set up a sting operation." He shook his head and said, "Norm and Kenny. They're screwed."

Had Ralph forgotten he'd given one of the tickets to me? Had he known all along that it was a fake? I didn't tell Ralph, but I still had the ticket; I kept it on display in my bedroom, sealed under the glass top of my dresser, between a stub for the only White Sox game I ever attended and a stolen ticket for a Pink Floyd concert that my parents wouldn't drive me to.

"What they nail you for?" Ralph asked.

"Trespassing," I said.

Ralph snorted.

"They caught me in the reservoir," I said, "you know, where Wes Papadakis almost drowned."

Ralph nodded, then turned away. He crumpled shut the top of

his grocery sack and waited for his officer to return. We both seemed to know that our friendship was winding down, and Ralph must have seen no point in prolonging the end of it. I feared deep down that in a few years our classmates would not only not remember the day Ralph had played his bongos in Mr. Mudjra's class but that they would have a hard time remembering Ralph at all. He was old enough to drop out of school now, which I'm sure he was planning to do. I worried, too, that it would be only a matter of time before he moved through the town like a ghost, invisible even to those who had once known him.

It was possible, though, that I was worried about my own self and not Ralph. Whatever any of us had done before, whatever accomplishments we'd achieved, it all paled by comparison to Wes Papadakis. Wes had become the South Side's very own Noah. His journey out of the reservoir would be passed along to children for generations, as powerful as any Bible story—*more* powerful, since he was one of our own. No one would ever forget the morning they first saw Wes on TV, his raft blown up to look like the American flag. Rain pelting the umbrella above his head, lightning snapping in the distance, Wes looked directly into the cameras and into our homes, and he told us his story.

The bald cop returned and said, "Looks like we'll have to put the two of you in a holding cell until we get your parents on the horn. Come along now. Both of you."

Ralph and I walked side by side down the police corridor, trailing the cop. Our grocery sacks rubbed together, and when we passed the police station exit, Ralph looked out the glass door and into the sunlight, as if considering making a break for it. And I had decided in that instant that if Ralph bolted for the door, I would bolt with him. I was hoping he'd do it, too. Nothing before had ever seemed so real to me than that moment, waiting for Ralph's decision. But Ralph suddenly faced ahead, setting his jaw in grim defeat, and I followed his lead. As always, I remained by Ralph's side.

17

Ralph and I had always called it Red's, but its real name was R & D's. We started calling it Red's, I guess, because neither of us had bothered to look closely at the sign. Not that it made a difference, really. It was one of those places nobody knew by name, anyway. If they called it anything at all, they'd have called it "that ice cream joint on the corner of 79th and Narragansett" and left it at that.

At least once a week during the spring of our eighth grade year, Ralph and I would agree to meet at Red's. A husband and wife ran the place. The husband was there by himself all morning and for a good part of the afternoon, and then the wife came by later to help out with the nighttime rush. She brought her poodle and kept it in their car, a Ford LTD, with the windows rolled down part way. The dog usually stood on an armrest and watched everything going on. If it started to bark, the wife would poke her head out the service window and tell it to shush.

The husband and wife were older than my parents, probably in their fifties. They never smiled; they never talked to each other. If I said "hello," the husband would say, "What can I get you?" The wife didn't help with anything but the ice cream. The husband took all of the orders, he fixed all of the hamburgers and hot dogs, and he dealt with all of the customer complaints. He always wore a white T-shirt tucked into dress pants; she wore a pink polyester dress that could have been a waitress's uniform she'd taken from another business years ago. An old electric fan, spray-painted black, ran all the time, turning creakily one way and then back the other.

Ralph and I went there only after it had gotten dark out. By then, the owner would have flipped on the yellow bulb where bugs of every kind met and hung out. That's how it was there at night: swarms of customers in the parking lot, swarms of bugs in the air. There were always bugs I'd never seen before with extraordinarily long legs and flimsy, almost see-through bodies, or some kind of metallic-looking beetle, twice the size of any other beetle, with pincers that looked capable of chopping off a small child's finger. The poodle in the car watched me watch the bugs, and whenever I'd look over at the poodle, it would let out a little whimper. Its breath steamed the glass, and tiny paw prints dotted the window's bottom edge.

One time, Ralph asked, "Why do you like this place?"

"I don't know. Don't you like it?"

Ralph didn't answer.

The counter outside, the one where I rested my money while peering through the sliding screen door to watch the man inside make my hot fudge sundae, had been painted so many times that you could sink your thumbnail into it and watch it bubble up somewhere else. It reminded me of blisters I'd had, still full of goo. If my mother had been with me, she'd have ordered me not to touch it and then told me how many thousands of other people had touched it, and how many of those thousands were filthy. But since I always came alone or with Ralph, I couldn't help it: I touched it. I pushed my thumbnail in and watched it bubble up. It was revolting, but I didn't have a choice in the matter. Sometimes I'd tell myself that I wasn't going to touch it and I'd try holding out as long as possible, but then, at the last second, as the husband finished up my sundae or turned to get my change, I'd dig my thumbnail all the way in, trying to pop through the paint, but leaving only a deep quarter-moon gouge instead.

One particularly busy night, the husband was there working all by himself. The wife wasn't back there with him. The car and the poodle weren't in the parking lot, either. The husband was sweating, working like a madman in a laboratory, and when he did something that required only one hand, like making change, he'd dial the phone at the same time. You could tell by looking at him that whoever he had called wasn't answering, that the other phone kept ringing and ringing. Twice he gave teenagers the wrong change, too little each time.

"Where do you think she is?" I asked Ralph.

"Who?"

"His wife."

"His wife? What, you know these people personally? They're family friends?"

"What do you mean?"

Ralph sighed. He said, "How do you know they're married?"

I thought about it a minute; I didn't know. I finally said, "They have a poodle."

"What poodle?"

"The poodle they keep in the car."

"What car?"

"The LTD," I said. I pointed at the empty spot, but the fact that the spot was empty confirmed for Ralph that he was right.

As the teenagers in front of us finished up, getting their last orders, the husband kept the phone cradled on his shoulder, pinned by his ear and chin. Ralph and I stepped up to order, but the moment I brought my thumbnail to the counter, the husband flipped the OPEN sign to CLOSED, and then pulled down the shade.

"What the hell?" Ralph said. Behind us came mutters, curses.

Ralph said, "Anyone got the time?" No one gave Ralph the time. It was a question that didn't need an answer. Someone answered Ralph by saying, "No kidding."

I biked to R & D's the next day, but it was closed. I biked there every day for a week, but each day was the same. Then one day a realtor's sign appeared on the corner. Six weeks later, a new business moved in, an insurance company, and they bricked up the hole where we used to order ice cream. It looked odd, though, because the bricks were a slightly different color. The counter with the hundreds of layers of paint was gone, too.

In June, on the first hot day of the year, one week before eighth grade graduation, I walked inside the insurance company, and a blast of ice-cold air-conditioned air hit me. It felt so good that I wanted to sit down and stay there, but I couldn't: the two girls who worked in the office were looking at me, eyes narrowed, as if I were a raccoon who'd wandered in looking for food. They were both young and pretty, and one of them was snapping a wad of gum. They were probably only a few years out of high school, not that much older than me, really. The shorter of the two, the one who wasn't chewing gum, smiled and walked over to the counter where I stood.

"Can I help you?"

I'd never done anything like this before, walk into a place where I didn't belong, and I suddenly felt that I'd made a mistake, but it was too late now. I said, "I was wondering if you know what happened to the ice cream place that was here."

The short girl turned to look at the gum snapper. They both shrugged and shook their heads, then the short one turned back to me. "No, I'm sorry. We don't." The one with the gum blew a huge bubble just then. It popped, then wilted, hanging out of her mouth like a shriveled tongue.

"Thanks for your time," I said.

"Maybe," the short one said, "we can interest you in some life insurance?" The other girl started to giggle but caught herself.

"Nah," I said. "I don't think so." But before I could turn to go, she had come around the counter to stop me. To my surprise, she wasn't any taller than me. She took my arm and led me to the desks where she and her friend did their work.

"Here," she said and handed over a brochure. "Now, sit down."

The one with the gum said, "*Tracy*," and then laughed, covering her mouth with the back of her hand.

I looked through the brochure. It didn't make a lot of sense. The best I could tell, I would have to pay a little bit of money each month while I was still alive, but when I died, someone else would hit the jackpot. I kept thinking that I was missing something, that maybe I was misreading it. I felt something touch my ankle, and when I reached down to brush it away, I saw the tip of the short girl's shoe rubbing against me.

"Well?" she said. "Can we offer you some insurance? Shall we write up a policy?"

"I don't know," I said. "I guess I don't get it. Why do I need insurance?"

The girl chewing gum pulled up a chair and sat next to me. She leaned into me, whispering into my ear, "Because life is full of surprises." The shorter girl leaned toward me, her palms resting on my knees, and said, "Because you never know what's going to happen from one minute to the next."

18

It was the last week of May with only five days of eighth grade to go when I saw Ralph at the opposite corner of the blacktop talking to a group of boys he normally never spoke to. Some of them, like Joey Rizzo and Pete Jones, were also in eighth grade, but others looked like they were in only third or fourth. One kid might even have been a first-grader.

Ralph had always been able to command attention and fear from any of our classmates, especially those he usually ignored, so I wasn't surprised to see a platoon of kids gathering around to hear what he had to say. But Ralph and I were friends, so why wasn't I there with him? Why hadn't he called me over?

Ralph's meetings weren't the only odd thing happening. Our teachers had quit teaching us. It was as though they'd given up. And if that wasn't enough, our principal smiled at us now instead of yelling while the janitor, an old man who normally *did* smile at us, had begun to glare and nod slowly whenever he passed us, as though silently letting us know, now that it was all coming to an end, that he was going to beat us up. Strangest of all, however, was that girls had started wearing tube-tops to school.

The tube-tops were the most disturbing change, not because I didn't like them—I did—but because now I walked around all day thinking about nothing else. These thoughts lasted from seven-thirty in the morning, when I first arrived on the blacktop and saw Lisa Sadowski smooshed into her yellow tube-top, until the three o'clock bell rang, when I stood behind Gina Roush, whose ever-so-slight pudge bunched up where the tube-top squeezed the hardest. The tube-tops presented the girls I knew—girls I had known for eight years now—in an entirely new light. I saw how soon, very soon, they would be dating guys much older than me, guys with cars and jobs, guys with beards and gold chains.

On Monday of that last week of classes, Mr. Lawrence—our Algebra teacher—kept shuffling off to the bathroom to smoke. Our class was held in one of the three mobile units outside, and there was one bathroom in each unit. He, too, had quit teaching, so when he wasn't borrowing one of my issues of *Mad* magazine to read, he would lock himself inside the john for a cigarette break. Smoke would roll out from the vents, as though the mobile unit were on fire, and then the toilet would flush and Mr. Lawrence would appear, coughing and spraying the classroom with Lysol.

Ralph wasn't in my Algebra class. His status was such that he spent all day with a teacher none of us even knew. What sorts of things did Ralph do with his special teacher? Nobody dared to ask him.

Lisa Sadowski, however, was in my Algebra class—she sat in front of me—and during those last few weeks, she wore her yellow tube-top every day, like a uniform.

"Psssssst," I said to Lisa that final Monday of eighth grade, after smoke started pouring through the bathroom vent. "Hey. What're your plans for the summer?"

Lisa turned to face me, looked me up and down, and said, "Do I know you?"

"Ha-ha," I said flatly.

"No, really," Lisa said. "Who are you?"

For a moment, I was thinking that maybe she didn't remember

me, even though we had been in at least one class together every year since first grade, but then she poked me in the chest and said, "I'm going to spend it with *you*, Hank."

I smiled.

"So you *do* remember me," I said.

Lisa leaned toward me. "I'll always remember you, Hank," she said dramatically and then laughed. "Always!"

I tried not to look at her tube-top, but I couldn't help it. It was like being told not to look at a solar eclipse, that it would burn holes through your retinas and cause you to go blind, but how could you not? I looked. Just a fast look down, but Lisa caught me, cocked an eyebrow, and then spun back around.

Ralph scratched the few wispy whiskers on his chin when I approached him after school, and then his minions scattered like flies, as though scratching were a signal. Ralph yawned and said, "Hey, Hank."

"What's new?" I asked.

Ralph frowned and shook his head. "Same ol', same ol'."

I was weak in my knees, knowing that Ralph was planning something without me, but I kept quiet. The harder I pressed Ralph, the more he'd pretend nothing out of the ordinary was happening.

We started walking home now, just the two of us, like old times.

"The teachers quit teaching," I said. "What do you think about that?"

"Probably taught us everything they know," Ralph said. "If we learn one more thing, we'd be smarter than them. They don't want that to happen."

"I bet you're right."

"I know I'm right," Ralph said and punched my arm, hard.

"But I've got a different arrangement than you do, so I don't have that problem."

This was the first time Ralph had ever mentioned his own unique situation, so I decided to inch ahead.

"Your teacher hasn't stopped teaching yet?" I asked.

"Nuh-uh," Ralph said. "In fact, we passed the rest of you up three years ago."

"Really?" My impression was that Ralph had been assigned a special teacher because he'd failed two grades. The possibility that he was a genius who'd flunked those two years out of boredom had never crossed my mind. "Hey, have you noticed how many girls are wearing tube-tops?" I asked.

"Tube socks?"

"*Tops.* Tube-*tops!*"

"What's a tube-top?"

"What's a *tube-top?*" I repeated. "Are you kidding me? What's a *tube-top?*"

"Oh, hey," Ralph said. "I've been meaning to tell you. I'm starting a club. You're welcome to join, but I didn't think you'd be interested."

So, this was it. A club!

"How would I know if I'm interested or not," I said, "if I don't know anything about it?"

"Good point," Ralph said. I waited for him to tell me more, but he didn't. He knew he had me on the hook. He could toy with me now, reeling me closer or flinging me out to sea. "Tube-tops," he said. "You mean those things the girls are wearing?"

"Exactly," I said.

"Wasn't someone in your class wearing a yellow one?" he asked. "What's her name?"

"Lisa," I said, nodding enthusiastically. "Yup."

"And the teachers aren't teaching anymore?"

"Mr. Lawrence goes to the bathroom and smokes every couple

of minutes," I said.

"It's anarchy," Ralph said. "Just as I predicted to the boys."

"I guess," I said. I shrugged. I didn't know what anarchy was.

Ralph said, "You've heard of Skylab, right?"

I collected postage stamps and was in possession of a mint condition Skylab stamp from 1974. For a while, stamp collecting took over my life. I owned a dozen stockbooks, thousands of stamp hinges for stamps I hadn't yet found, four different magnifying glasses, and a pair of stamp tongs that were actually my sister Kelly's tweezers for plucking her eyebrows. Of all the stamps I owned, from countries all around the world, the ten-cent Skylab postage stamp was my favorite.

I told none of this to Ralph, though. I merely grunted and nodded.

"Well, it's coming back to earth," Ralph said, "and it ain't gonna be pretty."

And then he told me how Skylab might hit a major city and set the entire place on fire, burning it the way Chicago had burned a hundred years earlier, or how it might just kill a family after they'd sat down to eat macaroni and cheese, or how it might hit the earth so hard it would knock us off our axis, causing dramatic changes to the weather. The polar caps might even melt, he told me.

"And then you know what would happen?" Ralph asked.

I shook my head. I had no idea.

Ralph leaned in close. "The end of life as we know it."

"So, this group," I said. "Are you protesters?"

"Nuh-uh," Ralph said. "Scavengers. I heard about this newspaper—I can't tell you which one—that'll offer ten thousand big ones for a piece of Skylab when it crashes to earth. I'll pay five hundred bucks to whoever finds it."

"And you keep the rest?"

Ralph shrugged. "I know which newspaper has the dough, and I've got the means to get the piece there." He smiled and said,

"I knew you wouldn't be interested."

"You're right," I said. "Count me out."

"I'm also teaching them survival skills," he said. "You ever read *Lord of the Flies*?"

I shook my head.

"Oh yeah, I forgot," Ralph said. "Your teachers quit teaching. Anyway, I had to read it. It's got some great survival tips in there."

"Survival tips?" I said. "*Lord of the Flies*? Really?"

We had reached Ralph's street. Ralph, walking backwards but still talking, said, "Don't come to me when a solar panel smashes through your parents' roof. Insurance won't pay for it. I already checked."

"You've got all the angles covered, don't you?"

"All of them!" Ralph said, tipping an imaginary hat to me and then turning around just in time to step over a child on a Big Wheel.

When I got home, I looked up "anarchy." *A state of lawlessness or political disorder due to the absence of governmental authority.* I looked at other words on the page, like "anamnesis." *A remembering, especially of a supposed life before this life.* Or "anan." *Eh? What? What is it?* The longer I studied the dictionary, the more I realized that my teachers hadn't taught me anything. I hadn't even seen most of the words in there, let alone known how to pronounce them or what they meant.

As the week wound down, I had a harder and harder time imagining my years of grade school coming to an end. It must have been how prisoners felt when they were about to be set free. Even though I hadn't even graduated yet from eighth grade, I bought a T-shirt with an iron-on decal. "Class of 1983," it read, optimistically. I wanted everyone to know that I was already thinking about my release from high school. I wanted people to see me and think,

Now, that's a kid with his eye on the future!

Meanwhile, Ralph's group tripled in size. There were even girls in the group now, including a pudgy-kneed first-grader whose eyes, like a kitten's, barely focused on whatever she stared at. The entire time Ralph talked, he made wild hand gestures, and more than once I saw him reprimand a child for not paying close enough attention.

Normally, a recess monitor would have broken up the meeting and escorted Ralph to our principal's office to explain his suspicious behavior, but even the recess monitor didn't care what we did anymore. She sat on the hood of her Gran Torino and ate Ding Dongs from a box while one kid pulled another kid's hair.

Ralph was right. Everything was up for grabs now. I was looking directly in the face of anarchy, and it was as ugly as Ralph predicted.

I escorted a small boy who'd wet his pants into the school. I delivered him to the front desk of the main office, where Mrs. Lurch, who normally smiled at me and asked about my mother, was busy filing her nails and reading a copy of *Man, Myth, & Magic*. On the cover was some kind of man-beast. "The most unusual magazine ever published," it proclaimed at the bottom of the cover.

I took the boy back outside and told him to go home.

"Go on," I said. When he hesitated, I said, "Come back when you've got clean clothes on. You're not going to get in trouble. Nobody cares anymore," I said.

The boy ran away, and I never saw him again.

I wasn't sure how to spend my school days anymore. By Tuesday, we could go to whatever classes we wanted, so long as we were still in school. The brightest and most promising students were now sitting in the same room with delinquents who farted at will and, using one finger and a nostril, played Boston's entire album on the nose harp. Some students spent the whole day in gym class throwing a medicine ball at each other while the teacher slept on an exercise mat on the gymnasium stage.

My science teacher, Mr. Gerke, showed the John Wayne movie *The Quiet Man* in his class. I wasn't sure why he chose that particular movie—maybe it was the only feature length sixteen-millimeter movie the school owned—but he put a sign on the door announcing that the movie would begin at one p.m. As it turned out, I was one of only two students who showed up. Lisa Sadowski was the other.

At first we sat at desks, the way we normally would have, but then we moved to the floor at the back of the room, up against the cabinet that held the beakers and test tubes. Lisa kept scooting closer and closer to me. Light from the projector's lamp shot out from the seams, intermittently illuminating Lisa and her tube-top. There were goosepimples all along the skin that her tube-top didn't cover up, and I wanted to run my finger across them, every one of them, but I was afraid to touch her.

"I'm sleepy," Lisa said when she finally slid right up next to me. She lay down, resting her head in my lap. "Do you mind?" she asked, looking up at me.

"No," I said. "No, no."

She smiled and then turned her head, facing the movie again. When John Wayne kissed Maureen O'Hara in a rainy, windblown cemetery, Lisa nuzzled closer, and I couldn't resist: I rested my hand on the soft, prickly flesh below her tube-top and left it there until Mr. Gerke flipped on the lights and, wiping tears from his eyes, said, "Damn fine movie, kids. Damn fine."

•

On my way home, I noticed how many people littered. Scattered along the ground were crumpled bags and straws and Kayo cans and rubber gloves. Two cars had apparently crashed into each other, because in the middle of the intersection was a mound of broken glass. But why didn't anyone pick it up?

Anarchy had arrived, and not just at school. It was spreading across the entire city like a rash.

On Wednesday, students I didn't recognize at all sat in our classrooms and played cards. Were these kids from other schools? Were they someone's cousins from Tennessee or Mississippi?

On Thursday, very few students showed up and those that did were reprimanded by Mr. Gerke.

"I don't want to have to babysit you," he said. "Why don't you go home, like the rest of your friends?"

One kid, Jimmy Gonzalez, gathered his belongings and left the room without saying a word. The remaining four of us, unable to do something wrong even when we were told it was okay, sat with our eyes averted, afraid Mr. Gerke would yell at us if we looked at him.

Mrs. Davis, my Reading teacher, flipped off the lights once we were all seated. I had brought along a paperback book titled *Beyond Belief: Eight Strange Tales of Otherworlds* with the hope that reading something, anything, would be encouraged, but it was too dark to see the teacher at the head of the room, let alone words on a page. I wondered if maybe we were all part of an experiment and if one day I would appear in a medical book as "The Boy Who Wouldn't Stop Going to School."

"Mrs. Davis?" I called out in the dark. "Mrs. Davis?"

Lisa Sadowski walked over to the exit and turned on the lights. Mrs. Davis wasn't even in the room. At some point she had slipped out, perhaps through the door that joined the library, which also remained dark.

During recess, I watched Ralph and his troop perform a

battery of synchronized activities, many of which involved slowly approaching an invisible person and choking them. "Now *again!*" Ralph shouted, and they did it once more.

From behind, someone grabbed my neck and started choking me. I managed to break away, only to discover that it was Lisa Sadowski. She laughed and said, "You didn't think I was really going to choke you, did you?"

"How should I know?" I said. "Nothing else is making any sense."

Lisa shrugged. "I think I'd have liked school if it was always this way."

"What way?" I asked. "*This* way? With no rules?"

"I guess," she said.

Until then, I'd admired the fact that Lisa had continued coming to classes, same as me, but I realized now that she was as crazy as everyone else.

"I kissed a girl last night," I lied, hoping to hurt her. "We were in a closet, and when her father found us, he threatened to shoot me." When Lisa didn't say anything, I said, "He had a gun."

Lisa stepped up close to me and kissed me on the lips.

"You have a wild imagination," she said. "That's why I like you." She kissed me again, longer this time.

"It was at an Amway party," I whispered, although I had never been to an Amway party.

Lisa said, "You don't stop, do you?"

"It's true," I said, still in Lisa's grip, our mouths almost touching. "Amway is short for the American Way, and the girl I kissed was named Wycherley."

"Wycherly? Now I *know* you're not telling the truth," Lisa said.

"Wycherly Wozniak," I breathed.

Out of the corner of my eye, I saw Ralph watching us. Lisa kissed me once more and then backed up. Ralph yelled, "Now *again!*" and everyone took three creeping steps, reached out, and choked the air in front of them.

On our way home, I asked Ralph how his Skylab project was coming along, but Ralph wasn't interested in talking about it. He said he was more interested these days in teaching survival skills to Ralph's Raiders.

"Ralph's Raiders?" I asked. "What the hell's that?"

"You've seen them," he said. "We train on the blacktop." Ralph stopped walking and said, "Actually, you were looking right at us today when you were with…now, tell me her name again?"

"Anan?" I said, trying out my new vocabulary word.

"What?" Ralph asked.

"Eh?"

Ralph glared at me.

"What is it?" I said.

Ralph shook his head.

I started walking and said, "I used to take karate lessons with my dad."

Walking beside me, Ralph snorted. "Karate's a good way to pass an afternoon, I suppose, but I put my trust in the *U.S. Army Combat Skills Handbook*. Did you know that a nuclear blast will crush sealed objects like food cans and fuel tanks? Nuclear radiation hits, and there goes all your food and water. Tell me how a karate chop to the left shoulder blade is going to get you out of any of those pickles."

"I don't know," I said. "I guess I would just die then."

"Not an option," Ralph said. I couldn't tell if he was the one crossing the line between mentally stable and mentally unstable, or if it was me. He must have noticed my expression because he smiled and said, "Don't worry. I've got your back, buddy."

"Good," I said. "I appreciate it."

"Oh, and don't think I've given up on Skylab," he said. "We're going to find us a piece of that baby if it's the last thing we do on this sad, doomed planet."

On Friday, the final day of classes, I put on my "Class of 1983" T-shirt and my favorite pair of Toughskins. I probably looked like someone from the future, already privy to what the next several years held for me. I wanted my teachers to say something about what a good student I had been and how I would no doubt excel in high school. I wanted girls to see me and ask to touch the iron-on, which sparkled from some kind of glitter in the decal itself. Most of all, I wanted Lisa Sadowski to tell me how much fun we were going to have together in high school, the two of us. I was determined to make the first move today. I would hug her, the way John Wayne had hugged Maureen O'Hara in *The Quiet Man*, and I would pull her close to me and press my lips against hers. I wouldn't care who saw us, either. I was a man from the future, already sure of the moment that would mark the end of my shy years, ready to embark upon four glorious years of reckless abandon.

When I showed up at school, no one was there except for a few teachers, and they hung out in the hallway and gossiped with each other, or they wandered off to the teacher's lounge for hours at a time. The only other kid at school was Roark Pile, whose hair never looked washed and who always smelled vaguely like meat on the brink of going bad.

Roark saw my shirt, pointed at the year, and laughed. "Good one," he said.

"It's not a joke," I said.

Roark squinted at my shirt, then looked up at me, and said, "Yeah, but…" He seemed hesitant to break the news to me. "We're class of 1979, Hank."

"I *know*," I said. I felt like weeping, but I didn't.

I left Roark alone in the art classroom, where he was considering putting his schoolbooks in the kiln and turning it on. I wandered the halls until I found Mrs. Dunphy, the school's nurse. She was a short, almost entirely round woman whose gums were black instead of pink.

"Excuse me," I said, "but do you know why Lisa Sadowski isn't in school today?"

I realized that my question was a preposterous one, since practically no one was in school today, but Mrs. Dunphy looked up to the ceiling, as though maybe Lisa Sadowski had passed on. "Lisa," she said finally, thinking. "Lisa Sadowski. She's got mono, I think."

"Mono?"

"The kissing disease," she said. She smiled, exposing her black gums.

My heart pounded.

"*You* didn't kiss her, did you?" Mrs. Dunphy asked, raising her eyebrows expectantly.

"Me? No. Why?"

"Because it's contagious," she said. "If you kissed that girl, you should probably go home."

"Is that why no one's here?" I asked. "Did everyone kiss her?"

"It's entirely possible," Mrs. Dunphy said. "A lot of your classmates have mono."

"Thank you," I said.

Mrs. Dunphy placed her hand on my forehead, as if checking for a child's fever were an instinct, and said, "My pleasure."

I waited until two o'clock—one hour before the end of my grade school career—before calling it quits and heading home. I couldn't tell if my throat hurt or not, so I poked at my lymph nodes until they started growing, and then my throat started pulsing.

Outside, walking past all my old classrooms, I saw Roark Pile in the room where I had left him. Using a giant pair of tongs, he was pulling something burnt and flaking from the kiln. When he saw me, he opened a window and yelled, "Loser!"

I tried yelling something back, but a coughing fit overtook me, and I had to keep walking, half bent over, my hand over my mouth.

The next day, I stayed in bed. Twice, my sister looked in on me and said, "Yep, you're dying." She looked pleased. Long ago, Kelly had vowed to outlive me. "You've got a week," she said. "Two weeks, tops." But the next day, I was up and about. Whatever I'd had, it was gone. I would live, after all, much to my sister's disappointment.

Graduation came and went in a blur of relatives, cake, and too-stiff shoes. I saw nearly everyone at the ceremony, including Ralph, despite his claim that graduation would be for him a private affair held in the principal's office, but most of the girls I saw, including Lisa Sadowski, were too busy getting their photos taken or squealing with their best friends to say hello to me.

It wasn't until July that I saw Lisa Sadowski again. On that particular day, Thursday the twelfth, I was so bored I biked to Rice Park to watch a Little League game. For the past month, no matter where I went, I would hear "My Sharona" by The Knack playing on somebody's radio, and every time it came on, people stopped what they were doing to snarl and bob their heads super hard. And that's what Lisa was doing now, snarling and bobbing her head to "My Sharona" playing on her transistor radio. She was wearing her yellow tube-top and blue jeans that had been made into shorts with a pair of scissors. A thousand white threads circled her tanned legs. She was wearing flip-flops and eating a corndog.

"Lisa!" I called out. "Over here!"

Lisa looked right at me, still snarling, head bobbing, but it was as though she had no idea who I was.

"It's me!" I yelled. "Hank!"

She squinted, but the sun must have made it difficult for her to see me, or maybe her eyesight had weakened since graduation. Maybe she was blind now. I was about to yell her name again when a man with a mustache and a gold chain around his neck walked up beside her. He was holding two cans of Coke. She raised up on her tiptoes and kissed him, and then she tried to force-feed him the corndog. He laughed and backed up. His shirt was unbuttoned almost to his brass belt buckle, and he wore a pair of aviator sunglasses on top of his head, as if there were a second set of eyes peeking up through the hair on his scalp.

"Here, take this," I imagined him saying, handing her the Coke. "You're one crazy chick, you know that?"

That's when I noticed that all the other girls from eighth grade were with much older guys—guys smoking cigarettes, shirtless guys, guys with incredibly bad acne. Who were these guys, and where had they come from?

I said hello to some of the other girls as I biked away, girls who used to be happy to see me, but either they didn't recognize me or they were ignoring me. I wanted just then to get the hell away, so I stood up on my pedals, but before I pushed down to leave, I saw what appeared to be a small army approaching Rice Park from the dirt hills.

The hills were where tough kids went to race mini-bikes and make out with girls, a place my parents had warned me to stay away from. As the army approached, I saw Ralph at the front leading his soldiers toward the ballpark. Here were Ralph's Raiders, and they were carrying something long and shiny.

"We found it!" Ralph yelled, and all the girls who had ignored me, girls who were now hooked up with older men, rushed over to see what wonderful and glorious thing Ralph had found.

Ralph was happy, truly and undeniably happy, for the first time since I had known him. The Raiders marched in unison behind him, exhausted from their mission but clearly exhilarated. A few of the boys whose fathers worked construction wore hardhats.

The closer they came, the clearer I saw what they were holding. It was a severely mangled bumper from a car and not a piece of the famous space station, which I'd heard had crashed into Australia the day before. At Ralph's command, his army raised the bumper triumphantly over their heads, as though it were an enormous trophy and they were the victors.

"Behold!" Ralph said to the approaching mob. "Skylab!" As more people rushed over, Ralph yelled, "Don't touch it! Back up! Don't crowd us!" but he was trying not to grin, and I figured he was imagining how to spend all the money he thought would be coming his way.

I wanted to tell everyone that it was just an old bumper, but who was I to take away their fleeting moment of joy? Who was I, of all people, to tell anyone what truth and happiness really were?

I walked over to Ralph to shake his hand, but he wrapped both arms around me instead. He whispered, "What a year, Hank. What a strange and wonderful year."

When Ralph let go, I saw in his eyes that he already knew the truth about the bumper but that it didn't matter. The only thing that mattered was what people *thought* it was. And so I lifted my arms into the air to touch this shiny thing that had brought us all together. I stretched and stretched, hoping to feel the magnetic power of something ordinary while Ralph, raising his arms beside mine, yelled, "Hallelujah! Hallelujah!"

19

It was early morning, a few weeks before the start of high school, but I was back at my old grade school with a can of spray-paint. There was still dew on the grass, and the sky was shot through with pink. I shook the can and then, crouching, got to work. When I was done, I stood and backed up.

Over the place where someone had sandblasted away Ralph's drawing, I drew the same man standing behind the counter of a wig store.

"Wigs in stock!" the man was saying out one side of his mouth. Out the other side: "All the hair you want!"

I snickered and stuffed the can of spray-paint in my back pocket, but then I shivered. I couldn't help it. I had a feeling that someone was standing behind me, that someone had been standing behind me the entire time I was out there, and I expected to turn and find Ralph there watching me, but when I spun around, no one was there except for an old, bald guy across the street walking his toy poodle, and even they didn't see me.

Acknowledgments

I'd like to thank Victoria Barrett, publisher of Engine Books, for starting the conversation about this book, and Andrew Scott, editor of Lacewing Books, for carrying it forward.

Several chapters in this book first appeared, in somewhat different form, in the following publications: the *Sun*, *G. W. Review*, *Punk Planet*, *Sleepwalk*, the *Florida Review*, *Third Coast*, *Sun Dog: The Southeast Review*, *bandit-lit: The Journal of Empirical Literature*, the *Idaho Review*, *Crab Orchard Review*, *Natural Bridge*, *Chelsea*, *Annalemma*, *Whiskey Island*, *Knee-Jerk*, *Booth*, *Long Story Short: Flash Fiction by Sixty-Five of North Carolina's Finest Writers* edited by Marianne Gingher (Chapel Hill: University of North Carolina Press, 2009), and *New Sudden Fiction: Short-Short Stories From America and Beyond*, edited by Robert Shapard and James Thomas. (New York: W.W. Norton, 2007). A significant portion of this book comprised my novel *The Book of Ralph*, originally published by Free Press/Simon & Schuster in 2004. I'd like to thank all of the editors with whom I worked over the years on this book. There are many.

About the Author

John McNally is the author of three novels, two short story collections, and two books about writing. He has edited, co-edited, or guest edited seven anthologies. His stories, essays, and book reviews have appeared in over a hundred publications, including the *Washington Post*, *One Teen Story*, and the *Sun*. He grew up in Burbank, Illinois, a southwest suburb of Chicago, and now lives in Lafayette, Louisiana, where he is Professor and Writer-in-Residence at the University of Louisiana at Lafayette.